MW00438192

Publishing the Fine and Applied Arts
1500–2000

PUBLISHING PATHWAYS
PREVIOUS TITLES IN THE SERIES

EDITED BY ROBIN MYERS & MICHAEL HARRIS

EDITED BY ROBIN MYERS, MICHAEL HARRIS & GILES MANDELBROTE

Publishing the Fine and Applied Arts
1500–2000

Edited by
Robin Myers, Michael Harris
and Giles Mandelbrote

THE BRITISH LIBRARY
&
OAK KNOLL PRESS
2012

© 2012 The Contributors

First published 2012 by
The British Library
96 Euston Road
London NW1 2DB
and
Oak Knoll Press
310 Delaware Street
New Castle, DE 19720

Cataloguing in Publication Data
A CIP record for this book is available
from both The British Library
and the Library of Congress

ISBN 978-0-7123-5847-7 (BL)
ISBN 978-1-58456-299-3 (Oak Knoll)

Typeset by Norman Tilley Graphics Ltd, Northampton
Printed in the United States of America
by Sheridan Books, Ann Arbor, Michigan

Contents

Introduction

AMONG THE PUBLICATIONS ISSUED by the early modern European book trade, one strand of material, which developed over time into a distinct category, comprised practical advice and technical guidance on a range of social, cultural and economic activities. Through print the reader was offered an educational experience in which a direct transfer of skills and information could take place. Publication of the 'how-to' book mirrored the development of the trade itself, as its clientele broadened out into the middling and artisanal communities. The substance of the earliest works on architecture, art, gardening, husbandry, music, and such leisure activities as fishing, gaming and chess, was increasingly made available in the towns and cities of western Europe. This process was closely connected with the expansion of trade, commerce and urbanization. On one hand, it can be tracked through the production of the increasingly pragmatic and cheaply priced books themselves. In London, for instance, by the late seventeenth century, booksellers working from shops in the Royal Exchange were publishing a wide range of cut-price titles in small formats, which could be slipped into the capacious new style of pockets and referred to at opportune moments. Information about business and commerce figured largely in these works. Crammed with tables of all sorts to be used in the calculations of everyday business, the printed texts increasingly provided a structure for the working lives of anyone in trade.

Among the many themes of these didactic how-to books were architecture, design and the decorative arts. These subjects retained their high-culture associations, often through massive folios in which classical principles were applied to the development of country houses and estates. Across Europe, however, the built environment was also being transformed. As the intricate lines of streets, houses and squares were thrown up at speed by tradesmen with limited theoretical knowledge of the building process, the demand was created for practical, small-scale works explaining how to conduct and organize building and its associated trades at street level. Embodying the classical elements of form and style, they helped to create one of the bridges between different sectors of the market which were implicit in the process of modernization.

The contributors to this collection of essays are concerned with the role of the book trades in the process of cultural diffusion, at several different levels of the market and crossing some of the frontiers, both geographical and chronological, within the early modern and modern period. The overarching theme is the transmission of architectural and artistic ideas, practice, and techniques.

Is bookbinding a form of art? Mirjam Foot's essay investigates the relationship between art and craft using the various definitions of 'art' proposed by dictionaries from the sixteenth to the twentieth century. She comes to the conclusion that bookbinding, however beautiful or artistic it might be, has never been seen as a branch of fine art. There are exceptions – the designer bookbinders of the nineteenth and twentieth centuries consciously aspired to make their bindings works of art – but in general, and in earlier times, commercial bookbinding was regarded as a skill or craft. Art was called for only in the same sense that the 'art and mystery of a stationer' is mentioned in the full title of the Stationers' Company, all of whose members participated in the book or allied trades. Mirjam Foot concludes that bookbinders worked independently from the world of fine art, and were mostly oblivious to it.

In 'Metal-cut border ornaments in Parisian-printed Books of Hours as design sources for sixteenth-century English works of art', Malcolm Jones examines the process of the transmission of ornament designs from print into a radically different medium, from two dimensions into three, and from one country to another. He shows, in a series of images, how the figures and patterns in metal-cut borders decorating sixteenth-century French books of hours were copied by the craftsmen who carved misericords and other woodwork in English churches, transforming designs created for relatively expensive printed books into popular or folk art.

Palladio's *I Quattro Libri dell'Architettura* was first published in Venice in 1570, originally for a relatively wealthy and culturally sophisticated audience. In his account of its reception and publishing history in England, Charles Hind shows how this work combined the theoretical analysis of classical building with practical advice on such topics as the choice of materials. He suggests that one reason for Palladio's popularity and influence in England was that Palladio 'democratised architecture, proclaiming the value of domestic structures, believing that farmhouses, barns and bridges were works of as much value as churches and palaces and that any building could be beautiful without the use of costly materials'. During the eighteenth century, some astute publishers saw the commercial potential of this and issued versions of his work in cheaper formats. It was through these manuals and pattern-books that Palladio's ideas reached practising architects and craftsmen in England.

More explicitly didactic was *A Book of Drawing, Limning, Washing or Colouring of Mapps and Prints, or A Young-Mans Time Well Spent*, first published in 1647, a drawing manual which was repeatedly reprinted and adapted up to the middle of the eighteenth century. Drawing is presented here as a useful skill to be acquired as part of the educational process, leading into the scientific study of perspective and anatomy, rather than as a leisure pastime. In her study of a single anonymous work, Meghan Doherty is able to demonstrate how a notional association with Albrecht Dürer's pioneering *Four Books on Human Proportion* (1528) could promote a routine educational work, through a series of editions, into a bestseller in a highly competitive market.

Turning to the users and consumers of these new genres of artistic and architectural works, Susan Palmer provides a case study of the working library of the architect Sir John Soane (1753–1837). She focuses on the trade in art and architectural books in the late eighteenth and early nineteenth century and makes good use of the vast accumulation of booksellers' and bookbinders' bills in Soane's archive. Soane's correspondence documents his relationship with the book trade throughout his career, from the time of his apprenticeship until his death. From this emerges a clear picture of his book-buying habits and of the selling methods of contemporary dealers, both in this country and in Paris.

Abraham Thomas examines a very different kind of architectural book from Palladio – Owen Jones's *The Grammar of Ornament* (1856). He shows how a practising architect's attempt at popularising oriental forms of architecture had some immediate influence on contemporary structures and their decoration, but its lasting aesthetic impact was on book design itself, especially in the innovative use of chromolithography for colour printing. Jones's architectural work, by which he himself set such store, is now mostly forgotten, while he remains justly celebrated as a designer and a pioneer of the technologies of book illustration.

Colour printing is also one of the themes of Rowan Watson's essay on 'Art publishing and the leisure market, from the 1840s to the 1870s'. He shows how the use of colour printing raised awareness of fine art and opened up a mass market of people who could not afford original works of art. These new techniques of book illustration were deployed not only in educational guides to some of the recently opened public collections, but also in genres such as handbooks for amateur artists, aimed particularly at a female audience. Using the resources of the National Art Library, Rowan Watson brings together a substantial body of material, such as coloured catalogues and flyers, which was cheaply produced and did much to facilitate the transmission of visual culture from an elite to a popular audience.

Following in the tradition of the collectors whom he has studied, Charles Sebag-Montefiore's essay on the printed catalogues of art collections, from the early 1600s to the early 2000s, draws its examples from his own library. 'A study of such catalogues,' he maintains, 'is in effect a study of the history of collecting.' While these records of sale-room coups and trophies are very different from the cheap guidebooks described by Rowan Watson, the publication of private art collection catalogues also contributed to the spread of knowledge about works of art and to a process of diffusion of taste and aesthetic fashions. They stimulated not only competition and emulation, but also offered the vicarious pleasures of country-house visiting and collecting by proxy. Charles Sebag-Montefiore shows how these catalogues map the evolution of English connoisseurship, providing important provenance information for the art historian, and he concludes his essay with a look at the transfer of private collections into public ownership.

Acknowledgements

All but one of the essays in this collection are based on papers given at the 31st annual conference on book trade history, held at the Foundling Museum in Brunswick Square, Bloomsbury, on 29 and 30 November 2009. We are very grateful to Mirjam Foot for offering an essay for this volume to take the place of Nick Savage's conference paper on 'The Formation and Growth of the Library of the Royal Academy of Arts, 1769–1901', which was unfortunately unavailable for publication here. We must also thank the Benevolent Fund of the Antiquarian Book-sellers' Association for their financial support, and the staff of the ABA office for generous practical help with the organization of the conference.

The publishers and editors are extremely grateful to the Marc Fitch Fund for a grant towards the cost of publication of this volume.

Robin Myers
Michael Harris
Giles Mandelbrote

London
January 2012

Contributors

MEGHAN DOHERTY is the Director and Curator of the Doris Ulmann Galleries and Assistant Professor of Art History at Berea College in Berea, Kentucky. Her research focuses on the connections between art and science as seen in the visual culture of the early Royal Society of London, and her current book project, 'Carving Knowledge', features studies of primary visual and written materials relating to Hooke's *Micrographia*, Francis Willughby's *Ornithology* and the *Philosophical Transactions* of the Royal Society.

MIRJAM FOOT is Professor Emeritus of Library and Archive Studies at UCL; she was formerly Director of Collections and Preservation at the British Library. Her publications include: *The Henry Davis Gift*, volumes I, II and III (1978–2010), *Studies in the History of Bookbinding* (1993) and *Bookbinders at Work, their Roles and Methods* (2006).

CHARLES HIND is Associate Director of the RIBA Library and has been H. J. Heinz Curator of Drawings there since 1996. An architectural historian specializing in British history of the seventeenth to nineteenth centuries, he is a Fellow of the Society of Antiquaries of London and a Visiting Fellow of the Centro Internazionale di Studi di Andrea Palladio, Vicenza.

MALCOLM JONES retired from Sheffield University's School of English in 2009. His book, *The Print in Early Modern England: An Historical Oversight*, was published in 2010. He now lives in the Cairngorms where he busies himself, researching and trying to keep warm.

SUSAN PALMER has been Archivist to Sir John Soane's Museum since 1989, and Archivist and Head of Library Services since May 2010. Her publications include *The Soanes at Home: Daily Life at Lincoln's Inn Fields* (Soane Museum, 1998) and a number of articles on aspects of Soane's life and career. She is a Fellow of the Society of Antiquaries.

CHARLES SEBAG-MONTEFIORE is a director of a corporate advisory house in the City and Hon. Treasurer of various bookish charities, including the Friends of the National Libraries and the National Manuscripts Conservation Trust. Over the past 40 years he has formed a library devoted to the study of the British as collectors. His book on *John*

Smith & Sons and the art trade in early 19th-century London is expected to be published in 2012.

ABRAHAM THOMAS is Curator of Designs, and lead curator for architecture, at the Victoria and Albert Museum. He was the curator of the V&A's Owen Jones bicentenary retrospective exhibition, 'A Higher Ambition' (2009), which toured internationally. He also curated 'Paper Movies: Graphic Design and Photography at *Harper's Bazaar and Vogue*, 1934 to 1963' (2007) and '1:1 – Architects Build Small Spaces' (2010). He is currently writing a book on the V&A's collection of fashion drawings and photographs (for publication in 2013).

ROWAN WATSON is a Senior Curator in the National Art Library. He contributed a chapter on 'Some non-textual uses of books', to the *Companion to the History of the Book*, ed. Simon Eliot and Jonathan Rose (Oxford: Blackwell Publishing, 2007). Recently published was his *Western Illuminated Manuscripts. A catalogue of works in the National Art Library from the eleventh to the early twentieth century, with a complete account of the George Reid Collection*, photography by Paul Gardner, 3 vols (V&A Publishing, 2011). He teaches on the MA in the History of the Book at the Institute of English Studies, University of London.

List of those attending the Conference

Alice Abi
Artist

Rossitza Atanassova
The British Library

Alexandra Ault
Assistant Curator, National Portrait Gallery

Susanna Avery-Quash
Research Curator, History of Collecting, The National Gallery, London

Vernon Barnes
PhD Student, Institute of English Studies, London University

Hugh Brigstocke
Art historian

Ruth Brimacombe
Postdoctoral Fellow, Paul Mellon Centre for Studies in British Art

Gillis Burgess
Bibliophile

Andrea Cameron
Hon. Librarian, The Stationers' Company

Stephen Cape
Cataloguer of Rare Books, Lilly Library, Indiana University

Helen Cole
Chawton House Library & Southampton University

Alan Crookham
Archivist, The National Gallery

Siobhan Dundee

Rosemary Firman
Assistant Librarian, Longleat House

Erica Foden-Lenahan
Special Collections Librarian, The Courtauld Institute of Art

Alice Ford-Smith
Dr Williams's Library

Joan M. Friedman
Urbana, Illinois

Claire Gapper
Architectural historian

Roger Gaskell
Roger Gaskell Rare Books

Caroline Good
York University & Tate Britain

Jacqui Grainger
Librarian, Chawton House Library

Julie Gregory
Retired conservator

Paul Grinke
Antiquarian bookseller

David Hall
*Retired librarian, Cambridge
University Library*

Helen Hardy
Travis & Emery

Daisy Hawker
Henry Sotheran Ltd

Emily Hayes
Henry Sotheran Ltd

Jolyon Hudson
*Pickering & Chatto, Marlborough
Rare Books*

A. W. Huish
Retired librarian

Nancy Ives
*Researcher, Low Countries Research
Group*

Judy Crosby Ivy
Art Historian

Elizabeth James
*National Art Library, Victoria &
Albert Museum*

Dr Elizabeth James
The British Library

Suzanne Johnston
Teacher

Christopher Lee
Independent scholar

Colin Lee
Book collector

David Lee
Bibliographer

Yvonne Lewis
The National Trust

Karen Limper-Herz
The British Library

Christina Mackwell
Lambeth Palace Library

Keith A. Manley
Institute of Historical Research

John Martin
Mayfly Ephemera

Hope Mayo
*Houghton Library, Harvard
University*

Fiona Melhuish
*Rare Books Librarian, University
of Reading*

Chris Michaelides
The British Library

Peter Miller
Ken Spelman Booksellers

Miriam Miller
Retired librarian

Sheila O'Connell
Department of Prints and Drawings, British Museum

Hugh Pagan
Antiquarian bookseller

Stephen Parkin
The British Library

Michael Perkin
Retired Special Collections librarian

Nicholas Poole-Wilson
Bernard Quaritch Ltd

Nan Ridehalgh
Independent researcher, Ephemera Society

Rose Sanguinetti
Book cataloguer, Lawrence Fine Art, Crewkerne

Susanne Schulz-Falster
Bookseller

Dr Rebecca Scragg
Leverhulme Early Career Fellow, University of Warwick

Julianne Simpson
Wellcome Library, London

Dr Margaret Smith
Independent scholar

Kay Staniland FSA
Independent scholar

Chris Stork
Maggs Bros Ltd

Christine Thomson
Freelance library cataloguer

Jean Tsushima
Archivist Emeritus, Honourable Artillery Company

Jos van Heel
Museum Meermanno-Westreenianum, The Hague

Susie West
Department of Art History, The Open University

Priscilla Wrightson
Collector/researcher of drawing manuals

Plate I. A Paris binding by the *Atelier du relieur du roi, c.*1555. L. B. Alberti, *L'Architecture et art de bien bastir* (Paris, 1553). A Greek-style binding of brown calf over wooden boards, tooled in gold. 352 (358) × 225 × 43 mm. British Library, Davis 396. (See p. 4 below.)

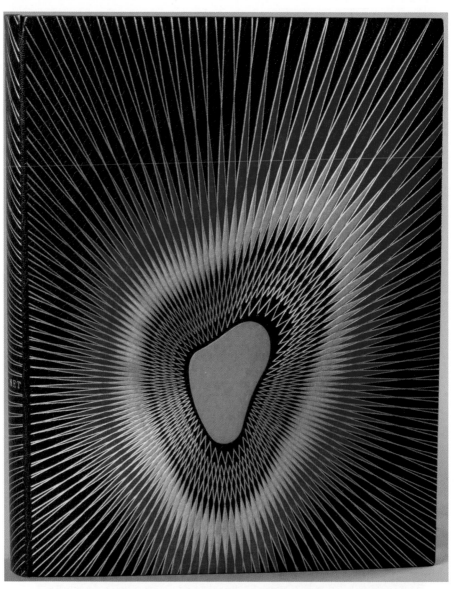

Plate II. A Paris binding by Paul Bonet, 1962. Paul Valéry et al., *Paul Bonet* (Paris, 1945). Green goatskin over paste boards, onlaid in orange, red and pale blue-green calf and tooled in gold to a sunburst design. 331 × 254 × 43 mm. British Library, Davis 415. (See p. 12 below.)

Plate III. Frontispiece portrait of Albrecht Dürer, from *A Book of Drawing* (London, 1660). (See p. 53 below.)

Plate IV. The exterior of Dulau and Co.'s bookshop in Soho Square, *c.*1809. Watercolour drawn by a pupil in Soane's office as an illustration to one of his lectures as Professor of Architecture at the Royal Academy. By courtesy of the Trustees of Sir John Soane's Museum. (See p. 85 below.)

Plate V. Drawings of tilework at the Alhambra Palace, by Owen Jones and Jules Goury, 1834 (9156N). © V&A Images. (See p. 104 below.)

Plate VI.   Drawing for *Architecture Arabe ou Monuments du Kaire*, by Pascal Coste, *c.*1820
(SD.272:32). ©V&A Images. (See p. 106 below.)

Plate VII.   Plate 9 from *Designs for Mosaic and Tessellated Pavements*, by Owen Jones,
published by J. M. Blashfield, 1842 (NAL: 89.G.8). ©V&A Images. (See p. 113
below.)

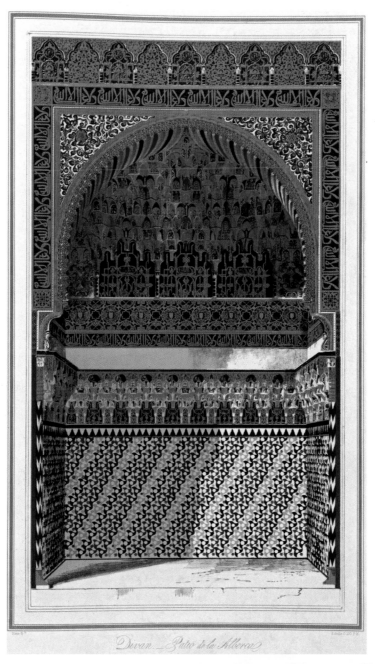

Plate VIII. Plate from *Plans, Elevations, Sections and Details of the Alhambra*, by Owen Jones, 1845 (NAL: 110.P.36). © V&A Images. (See p. 108 below.)

Plate IX. Original design for Great Exhibition interior decoration scheme, by Owen Jones, 1850 (546-1897). © V&A Images. (See p. 119 below.)

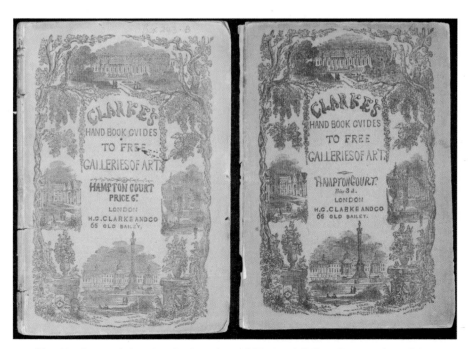

Plate X. Covers of the 6*d.* and 3*d.* versions of *The Royal Gallery, Hampton Court Palace* (London: H. G. Clarke & Co., 1843). (See p. 138 below.)

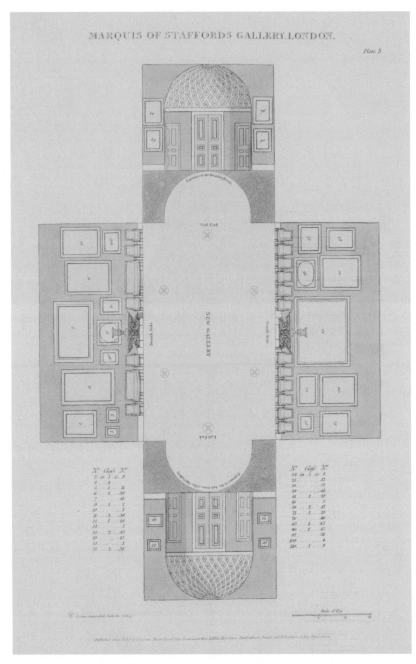

Plate XI. 'The New Gallery of Cleveland House', by Ottley and Tomkins, 1818, showing the hanging arrangement of the pictures. (See p. 175 below.)

'It's pretty, but is it Art?'

MIRJAM FOOT

'the Devil whispered behind the leaves, "It's pretty, but is it Art?"' [1]

ALL MY PROFESSIONAL LIFE I have striven to avoid calling book-binding an art. Bookbinding is a craft or a trade and the study of its history is the province of historical bibliography, not of art history. This dogmatic position was somewhat shaken by my study of a variety of descriptions of bookbinding practice by binders and interested observers, dating mainly from the sixteenth, seventeenth, eighteenth and early nineteenth centuries,[2] where this craft is almost invariably called an art, sometimes, but by no means always, with the qualifying adjectives 'useful', 'mechanical', 'decorative', and in the early twentieth century even: 'fine'.

This led me to investigate the earlier meanings of the word art, from which it was clear that 'art' in the sense of 'fine art' is a comparatively late usage, with recorded examples dating from 1668 onwards. The earlier meaning, with examples recorded from *c.*1225 onwards, is a 'skill in doing anything as the result of knowledge and practice', or, for our purpose more apt: a 'skill in applying the principles of a special science; technical or professional skill', recorded from *c.*1300 onwards.[3] The word craft, meaning 'skill, skillfulness', or 'a branch of skilled work. An art, trade, or profession requiring special skill and knowledge, esp[ecially] a manual art, a handicraft', is considerably older and its first usage has been attributed to King Alfred.[4]

From the examples quoted in the complete *Oxford English Dictionary* it is clear that the words art and craft were used synonymously. However, it is interesting to see what earlier English dictionaries and encyclo-paedias made of these words. With one exception, those eighteenth- and early nineteenth-century dictionaries and encyclopaedias that I have consulted,[5] either do not list the word craft at all or have it only as meaning: fishing tackle, and small boat. Art is altogether a different story. Many of the eighteenth-century dictionaries repeat each other and several copy the definition of previous 'authorities' more or less verbatim. Therefore a few examples will suffice.

Chambers' *Cyclopaedia* (1728) is the first and probably the most useful source. It is also a work much copied or paraphrased in later dictionaries and encyclopaedias. Art is defined as 'a Habit of the Mind prescribing Rules for the due Production of certain Effects.' Arts can be divided into 'active', those that leave no product, and 'factive', those that leave something tangible. Quoting Bacon's definition of art as 'a proper Disposal of the Things of Nature by human Thought and Experience, so as to make them answer the Design and Uses of Mankind', Chambers opposes art and nature and sees art as 'a certain System or Collection of Rules, Precepts and Inventions or Experiments, which being duly observ'd, make the Things a Man undertakes succeed, and render them advantageous and agreeable'. A further division leads to divine and human art, the latter further subdivided into civil, military, physical, metaphysical, philological and mercantile; to the last named of which belong the mechanical arts and manufactures. Another division of art proposes liberal and mechanical arts, the former being 'noble and ingenious, worthy of being cultivated without any regard to Lucre arising from them' [our fine arts], and the latter are 'those wherein the Hand, and Body are more concern'd than the Mind; and which are chiefly cultivated for the sake of the Profit they bring with them . . . [they] are popularly known by the Name of *Trades*'. In the preface to his *Cyclopaedia*, Chambers further expands on the concepts of art and science, where they differ and where they may be touching, stressing the personal and moral aspects of art.

J. Barrow, *A new and universal dictionary* (1751),[6] defines art as 'a system of rules, which, being carefully observed, render undertakings successful, advantageous and agreeable', not that far from Chambers, but more succinct. His division into liberal and mechanical arts and their description are very close to those in the 1728 *Cyclopaedia*. Johnson's *Dictionary* (1755) defines art as '1. The power of doing something not taught by nature and instinct . . . an habitual knowledge of certain rules and maxims, by which a man is governed and directed in his actions. 2. A science; as, the liberal *arts*. 3. A trade. 4. Artfulness; skill; dexterity.' Owen's *New and complete dictionary* (1754) introduces in its preface a new aspect: 'ARTS, in general, might be referred to the imagination, but we choose . . . to class them according to the various uses they are intended to serve.' This work also quotes Bacon, but here as observing that 'the arts which relate to the eye and ear, are accounted most liberal: the others being held in less repute, as approaching nearer to sensuality than magnificence'. The word art is simply defined as 'a system of rules serving to facilitate the performing of certain actions; in which sense it stands opposed to science, or a system of speculative principles', a nice compact definition with shades of Chambers and Johnson, which is copied in T. H. Croker's *Complete dictionary* (1764). The latter, however, introduces two new concepts. In his preface Croker calls what we would now understand under fine arts, 'arts of imitation', and states of 'the mechanic arts' that they, 'depending upon manual operation, and confined to a certain beaten track, are assigned over to those persons whom prejudice place in a lower class', adding an element of snobbery about which the binders themselves in their manuals frequently complain.

The *Encyclopaedia Britannica* (1771), J. Cooke (1771, 2) and E. Middleton (1778) define art in the same way as Owen and Croker. G. S. Howard, *The new royal cyclopaedia* (1788) relies heavily on Chambers, but adds: 'the *arts* which relate to the eye and the ear are accounted as most liberal, and usually called the *fine arts* . . . at their heights, the liberal *arts*; and when on the decline, the *arts* of luxury'. Here we see the modern, narrower usage of art as fine art in a dictionary all but a hundred years earlier than *OED* led us to believe.[7] All these Dictionaries or Encyclopaedias also have entries under bookbinding,[8] which vary from 'the Art of *binding*, or covering *Books*' (Chambers) to 'the Art of gathering, and sewing together the Sheets of a Book, and covering it with a Back' (from D. De Coetlogon, *An universal history of arts and sciences* (London, 1745) onwards), although Rees's *Cyclopaedia* (1819) follows *The book of trades, or library of the useful arts* (London, 1804–5, pt III (1806)) in expanding this somewhat unsatisfactory definition to: 'the art of sewing together the sheets of a book, and securing them with a back, and strong pasteboard sides, covered with leather &c.' All refer to bookbinding as an art.

So much for the definition of art – and to a much lesser extent of bookbinding – in the dictionaries and encyclopaedias of the eighteenth and early nineteenth centuries. But how do the binders describe their own trade? The bookbinders' manuals that I have consulted date from before 1840, as by then the development of bookbinding machinery was rapidly transforming a hand craft into a mechanised industry. However, as mechanization proceeded, a reaction, in England best epitomised in William Morris's and T. J. Cobden-Sanderson's Arts and Crafts movement, revived binding as a craft and, by the next century, some of the Designer Bookbinders again judged their craft also an art.[9]

English binders and amateurs of bookbinding were not as keen to produce written descriptions of their chosen subject as those in Germany and in France.[10] The earliest surviving useful English description of bookbinding fills a section in G. Smith, *The laboratory or school of*

Fig. 1.   A Paris binding by the *Atelier du relieur du roi*, *c.*1555. L. B. Alberti, *L'Architecture et art de bien bastir* (Paris, 1553). A Greek-style binding of brown calf over wooden boards, tooled in gold. 352 (358) × 225 × 43 mm. British Library, Davis 396. (See Plate I.)

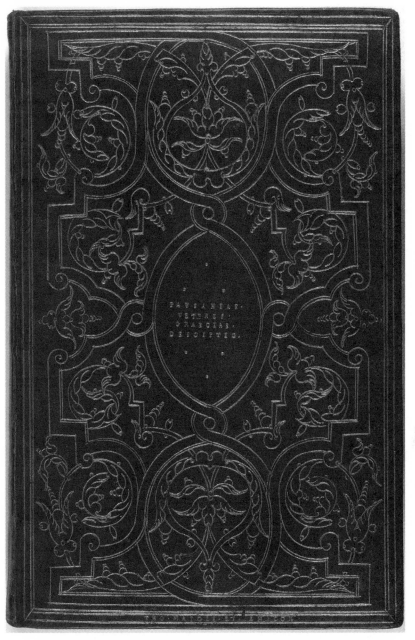

Fig. 2. A Paris binding for Thomas Mahieu, *c.*1560. Pausanias, *Veteris Graeciae descriptio* (Florence, 1551). Red-brown goatskin over paste boards, tooled in gold with the ownership inscription and (on the lower cover) the motto of Thomas Mahieu. 354 × 229 × 53 mm. British Library, Davis 403

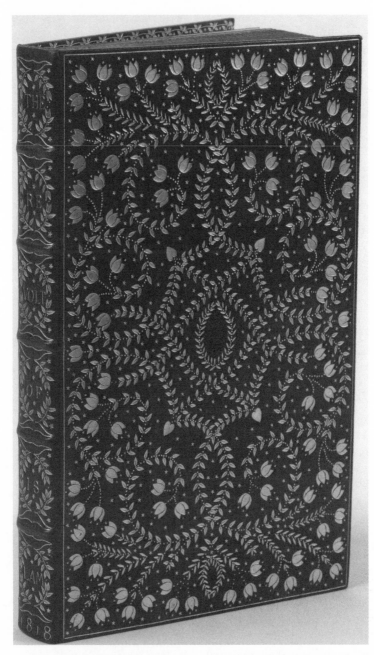

Fig. 3. A binding by T. J. Cobden-Sanderson, 1888. P. B. Shelley, *The Revolt of Islam* (London, 1818). Red goatskin over mill boards, tooled in gold to an all-over arabesque design. 216 × 137 × 25 mm. British Library, C.68.i.10

arts (London, 1738),[11] which itself was translated from the German. Smith mentions in his preface 'lovers of Art' and 'Artists and Craftsmen'. The chapter 'Choice Secrets for Book-Binders' gives a number of recipes which, though interesting, do not reveal his concept or classification of binding as an art or craft. De Coetlogon's definition of bookbinding we saw above, but he also mentions 'The Art of *Binding Books*' and in his preface talks about the division between 'liberal' and 'mechanical' arts, bookbinding clearly belonging to the latter.

R. Dossie's *Handmaid to the arts* (London, 1758), dedicated to 'The Members of the Society for the Encouragement of Arts, Manufactures, and Commerce', talks about 'useful arts', 'polite arts' and the 'application of arts [as] the perfection of manufacture'; he also mentions 'secondary or auxiliary arts that are requisite to the practising design; or the execution of works dependent on it'. It is tempting to see this as applying to the various forwarding and finishing techniques used by the binder to produce a bound book, but Dossie is not specific in his designation. J. Baxter, *The sister arts, or a concise and interesting view of nature and history of paper-making, printing and bookbinding* (Lewes, 1809), refers to his subjects as 'Arts which are intimately connected with the cause of literature'. The anonymous author of *The whole art of bookbinding* (Oswestry, 1811), calls his own work a 'treatise in the art of bookbinding', giving 'instructions in the art of bookbinding'. He sets out the various steps of forwarding and finishing, devoting most space to the latter, with various helpful recipes for colours. Thomas Martin (pseudonym of John Farey), *The circle of the mechanical arts* (London, 1813), calls bookbinding an art, but in his preface he talks about arts, manual arts and trades as all but interchangeable, calling bookbinding one of the 'trades, on which the literature of the country depends'.

The first chapter of H. Parry, *The art of bookbinding* (London, 1817), is headed 'Whole art of bookbinding' and deals with a step-by-step description of the techniques involved in binding a book, 'Gilding and Finishing' being dealt with in the next chapter. G. Martin's *The bookbinder's complete instructor in all the branches of binding* (Peterhead, 1823) is a reprint of the chapter on bookbinding in T. Martin (J. Farey)'s *Circle*. G. Cowie's *Bookbinder's manual* (London [1828]) talks about 'the art of Binding' and boasts that 'Modern binding . . . has considerably improved: beautiful specimens may be seen in the shops of the various respectable booksellers in London.' John Andrews Arnett (pseudonym of John Hannett, who in later editions uses his real name), *Bibliopegia; or, the art of bookbinding in all its branches* (London, 1835), borrowing for his title a word probably coined by Thomas Dibdin,[12] refers several times to

Fig. 4. A Paris binding by Nicolas-Denis Derome *le jeune*, after 1761. P. Ovidius Naso, *Le Metamorfosi di Ovidio* (Venice, 1584). Dark blue goatskin over paste boards, tooled in gold to a dentelle design. 242 × 175 × 34 mm. British Library, Davis 545

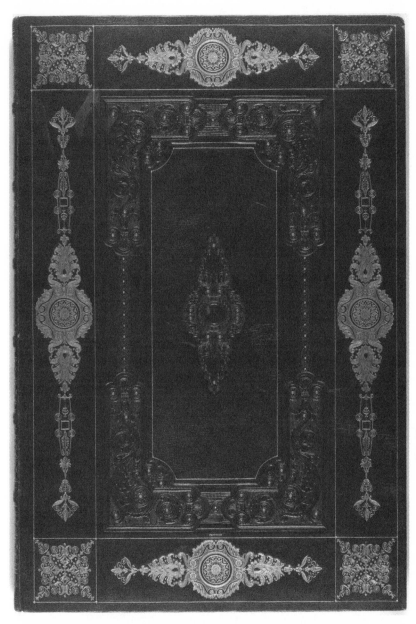

Fig. 5. A Paris binding by Joseph Thouvenin (l'aîné), *c.*1826. P. C. Tacitus, *Opera*, 4 vols (Paris, 1826). Purple straight-grain goatskin over paste boards, blocked and tooled in blind and gold. 549 × 367 × 36 mm. British Library, Davis 712

'the Art of Bookbinding', calling the binder 'the workman . . . in the . . . manipulations of his Art' and says that 'the trade of a Bookbinder has been ranked among the most difficult of the arts'. In a later (1865) edition he calls bookbinding 'the art and science of composing books, and their subsequent embellishment'.

If the English binders and other lovers of bookbinding designate this craft an art, are the German and French writers on the subject of a like mind? Johann Gottfried Zeidler, *Buchbinder-Philosophie oder Einleitung in die Buchbinder Kunst* (Hall im Magdeburgschen, 1708), agreed with Arnett in calling bookbinding a 'complex art', but he also refers to it as a 'noble art', a 'necessary and useful art' and a 'mechanical art', while distinguishing it from the free or beautiful [our fine] arts. Others[13] all call bookbinding an art, or a mechanical art,[14] while Halle adds that he understands the word art to mean such mechanical dexterity (or expertise) through which, with the help of certain tools, a natural substance is converted into a commodity, which can then be traded. Greve, while repeatedly talking about the art of bookbinding, calling binders 'fellow artists', refers to himself as a manual worker or craftsman.

In French, Anselme Faust, in his bi-lingual description of bookbinding, *Cunste der boeckbinders handwerck. Artifice des relieurs de livres* (MS, 1612), uses the words art, craft and science practically at random and synonymously. Later writers, starting with the 1704 manuscript of J. Jaugeon, *Descriptions et perfection des arts et métiers*, talk about the art of binding books or the art of the bookbinder.[15] Dudin is interesting in his statement that 'bookbinders . . . practise an art which, though classified as a mechanical art, is nevertheless entitled to a certain consideration since it is in some ways linked with The Arts,' while Diderot's *Encyclopédie* also refers to binding as a mechanical art, emphasizing (under the word art) that mechanical arts, being the work of the hand are not inferior to liberal arts, being the work of the mind. Lesné's poem 'celebrates his art', comparing it with poetry and insisting that, in order to practise a mechanical art, one follows a number of steps in the same way as these are followed when practising fine art. The binding processes, of which he mentions ten, can be considered as 'ten little arts.' He also assures his readers that the art of bookbinding has become more complex as it has become more perfect [during the eighteenth century], 'embellishment having become the most scientific part of the art.' Lenormand introduces one more designation, that of 'industrial art', but throughout his work he calls the binder an artist and his trade an art. E. Thoinan, *Les relieurs français (1500–1800)* (Paris, 1893), a combination of history and biography, uses the word art throughout, triumphantly ending his historical part with a quotation from M. de Laborde: *'la Reliure est un art tout français!'*

In the same year Sarah Prideaux, herself a binder who had received part of her training with Gruel in Paris, agreed with M. de Laborde, at least as far as the art of gold-tooling was concerned,[16] which she felt 'attained almost at once its highest perfection' during the reigns of Francis I and Henri II, explaining that 'though the artistic inspiration came from [Italy], it was in France that it took root as a fine art' (Figs 1, 2). Sarah Prideaux had taken up bookbinding in 1884, only a year after Mrs Morris persuaded Thomas James Cobden-Sanderson to try his hand at bookbinding, arguing 'That would add an Art to our little community, and we would work together'.[17] William Morris's first lecture 'On the Lesser Arts' also inspired Cobden-Sanderson 'with ardour, and made [his] own projected handicraft seem beautiful'.[18] In his *Journals* Cobden-Sanderson talks almost always about binding as a 'handicraft' or a 'handicraft trade,' sometimes calling himself 'a plodding artisan', several times quoting William Morris's view of binding as one of 'the minor arts', and once referring to it as among the 'lesser arts'.[19] Cobden-Sanderson's 'higher aim' was 'to dignify labour in all the lower crafts . . . and so to lift all the arts and crafts . . . to consecrate the arts and crafts to the well-being of society as a whole'[20] (Fig. 3). He definitely had no pretensions to be an artist, although his followers thought otherwise. In July 1888 Miss Nichols wrote to Miss Leigh Smith: 'could you mention my name as an aspirant in the art of which he is the head?'[21]

H. P. Horne, *The Binding of Books: An Essay in the history of gold-tooled bindings* (London, 1915), states in the preface: 'In France, alone, has bookbinding been continuously practised, and encouraged, as a fine art, since the Revival of Learning.' In his not-always-very-accurate history of bookbinding, Horne seems to be making a distinction between the technical processes, which he describes in a chapter entitled 'The craft of binding', and 'the art of finishing books in gold tooling'. Later on he classifies binding among the 'decorative arts', judging that from the Italian Renaissance onwards it has been all down hill: 'a decadence, which has, in the art of bookbinding, continued to the present time . . . in the binder's art . . . this gradual decadence was accompanied by a gradual approach towards greater perfection of workmanship, the one diminishing as the other increased',[22] a pessimistic point of view with which most nineteenth-century binders manuals disagree.[23]

However, looking at the near perfect gold-finishing of many French eighteenth-century bindings and of those made in England and France during the nineteenth century, their very perfection and lack of

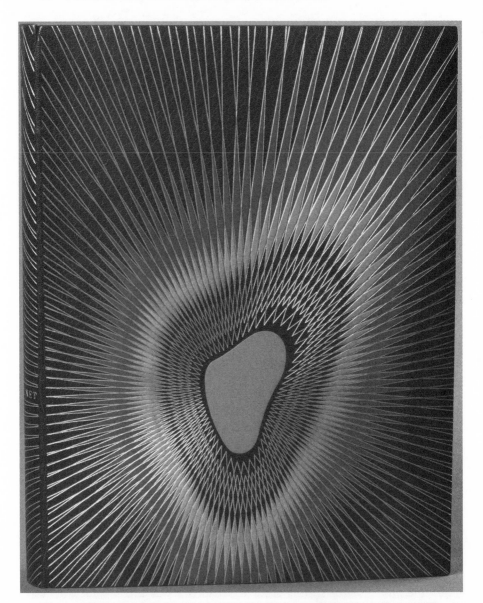

Fig. 6.   A Paris binding by Paul Bonet, 1962. Paul Valéry et al., *Paul Bonet* (Paris, 1945). Green goatskin over paste boards, onlaid in orange, red and pale blue-green calf and tooled in gold to a sunburst design. 331 × 254 × 43 mm. British Library, Davis 415. (See Plate II.)

Fig. 7. A binding by Philip Smith, 1985. William Shakespeare, *Macbeth* (Guildford, 1970). Red goatskin over boards, with multi-coloured feathered and maril sunk onlays, showing a portrait of Macbeth and the castle scene with three witches; blind-tooling on the spine. 508 × 363 × 30 mm. British Library, C.188.c.1

spontaneity make them seem more mechanical, more industrial even, than artistic (Figs 4, 5). Spontaneity, albeit a strictly controlled spontaneity, came back during the twentieth century, giving birth to such masterpieces of both perfection and artistry as the work of Pierre-Lucien Martin or Paul Bonet in Paris and of that of some of the English Designer Bookbinders, the latter striving to move bookbinding 'away from the realms of traditional decorative, or applied, art' to a more creative level, and, especially in England, to find a closer connection between the content of a book and the 'imagery' of its binding[24] (Figs 6, 7).

Kipling's devil clearly whispered about fine art, but had he ever considered bookbinding, and was he right?

References

1. R. Kipling, 'The Conundrum of The Workshops' (1890), in R. Kipling, *Collected Poems* (with an introduction and notes by R. T. Jones) (Ware, Herts, 2001), pp. 348–9.
2. For the result of some of this research see M. M. Foot, *Bookbinders at work, their roles and methods* (London and New Castle DE, 2006).
3. The *Oxford English Dictionary*, 2nd edn (Oxford, 1989), 'Art'.
4. Examples *c*.888 and 897; see *OED*, 'Craft'.
5. E. Chambers, *Cyclopaedia: or, an universal dictionary of arts and sciences* (London, 1728); J. Barrow, *A new and universal dictionary of arts and sciences* (London, 1751); W. Owen, *A new and complete dictionary of arts and sciences* (London, 1754–5); S. Johnson, *A Dictionary of the English Language* (London, 1755) (the only one to have craft meaning 'Manual art; trade'); *A new universal history of arts* (London, 1759); T. H. Croker, *The complete dictionary of arts and sciences* (London, 1764–6); *Encyclopaedia Britannica: or, a dictionary of arts and sciences* (Edinburgh, 1771); J. Cooke, *A new and universal dictionary of arts and sciences* (London, 1772, 71); E. Middleton, *The new complete dictionary of arts and sciences* (London, 1778); G. S. Howard, *The new royal cyclopaedia and encyclopaedia; or, complete, modern and universal dictionary of arts and sciences* (London, n.d. [1788]); A. Rees, *The Cyclopaedia; or, Universal dictionary of arts, sciences, and literature* (London, 1819); A. Ure, *A dictionary of arts, manufactures and mines* (London, 1839).
6. Barrow's earlier *Dictionarium Polygraphicum: or, the whole body of arts regularly digested* (London, 1735) does not list abstract concepts, but only mentions practical matters and people.
7. Where we are told that 'The application of skill to the arts of imitation and design: painting, engraving, [etc.] does not occur in any English Dictionary before 1880'.
8. Johnson has no entry for bookbinding, but includes '*To bind a book*. To put it in a cover' under the verb to bind.
9. See, for example, P. Smith, *New directions in bookbinding* (London, 1974), p. 12: 'the handbinder he is thrown . . . into the realm of "art"'; p. 13: 'the artist as bookbinder', and so on.
10. The only-known Swedish manual, J. A. Flintberg, *Borgerlige förmoner och skyldigheter, i stöd af författningar* (Stockholm, 1786), calls binding a craft and two Dutch manuals, M. van Loopik, *Volkomen handleiding tot de boekbindkonst* (Gouda, 1790) and H. de

Haas, *De Boekbinder of volledige beschrijving van al het gene wat tot deze konst betrekking heeft* [etc.] (Dordrecht, 1806), both speak of the noble art of bookbinding. De Bray's *Kort onderweijs* (MS, 1658) is purely practical.

11. Earlier English 'manuals' are either descriptions in Encyclopaedias and Dictionaries or deal only with gilding edges, marbling paper or edges, and colouring skins, except for J. Bagford who, in *Of Booke Binding Modourne* (MS *c*.1700), simply describes the various processes with a bit of history thrown in.

12. T. F. Dibdin, *The Bibliographical Decameron* (London, 1817), vol. II, p. 519, refers to bookbinding as 'the bibliopegistic art'.

13. J. S. Halle, *Werkstäte der heutigen Künste* (Brandenburg & Leipzig, 1761–79), vol. II (1762); *Anweisung zur Buchbinderkunst* (Leipzig, 1762); J. J. H. Bücking, *Die Kunst des Buchbindens* (Stendal, 1785); C. F. G. Thon, *Neuer Schauplatz der Künste und Handwerke* (Ilmenau, Weimar, 1820 (1832)); E. W. Greve, *Hand- und Lehrbuch der Buchbinde- und Futteralmache- Kunst* (Berlin, 1822).

14. The *Neue Buchbinder Ordnung* (Ludwigsburg, 1719) and J. H. Zedler, *Grosses vollständiges Universal-lexicon aller Wissenschaften und Künste* (Halle & Leipzig, 1732–50), vol. IV (1733), call binding a craft ('Handwerck').

15. E.g. D. Diderot and J. le Rond d'Alembert, *Encyclopédie ou dictionnaire raisonné des sciences, des arts et des métiers* (Paris ('Neuchatel'), 1751–80), vol. XIV (1765); P. Macquer, *Dictionnaire portatif des arts et métiers* (Paris, 1766); R. M. Dudin, *L'art du relieur-doreur de livres* ([Paris], 1772); M. M. Lesné, *La Reliure, poëme didactique en six chants* (Paris, 1820); L. S. Lenormand, *Manuel du relieur* (Paris, 1827).

16. S. Prideaux, *An Historical Sketch of Bookbinding* (London, 1893), p. 26, writing about gold tooling: 'the art is especially a French art'; the next two quotations are from pp. 27 and 35.

17. *The Journals of Thomas James Cobden-Sanderson 1879–1922*, (New York, 1969), vol. I, p. 94, diary entry for 24 June 1883.

18. Ibid., p. 97, diary entry for 21 July 1883; see also W. Morris, *On Art and Socialism. Essays and lectures* (selected and introduced by Holbrook Jackson) (London, 1947), pp. 17–37: 'The Lesser Arts'. Delivered before the Trades' Guild of Learning, 4 December 1877.

19. See Cobden-Sanderson, *Journals*, vol. I, p. 97, entry for 17 July 1883; p. 98, entry for 22 July 1883; p. 205, entry for 30 December 1884; p. 212, entry for 21 March 1885; pp. 243–4 entry for 6 April 1886.

20. Ibid., p. 268, entry for 11 June 1888.

21. Quoted in Cobden-Sanderson's *Journals*, vol. I, p. 269, entry for 3 July 1888.

22. H. P. Horne, *The binding of books* (London, 1915), pp. 55, 56.

23. E.g. Cowie (1828) and Lesné (1820) both say how much binding has improved in their own time or during the end of the previous century. Lenormand (1827) also refers to the eighteenth century during which the industrial arts have made a tremendous leap towards perfection, while Thon (1832) judges the German binders of his own time to be as good as, or even better than those in Paris and London.

24 P. Smith, *New directions*, pp. 12, 13.

Metal-cut Border Ornaments in Parisian printed Books of Hours as design sources for sixteenth-century English works of art

Malcolm Jones

In a pioneering article published as long ago as 1936, J. S. Purvis drew attention to the use of continental prints (and the blockbook *Biblia Pauperum*) as design sources for a number of English misericords of late fifteenth- and early sixteenth-century date[1] – and some years ago I was able to extend his work, particularly with regard to the sources of the misericords in St George's Chapel, Windsor.[2] But it is to M. D. Anderson that the credit goes for first pointing out that the carver of three misericords of the Bristol series of 1520 took his designs from border-scenes in early Parisian printed Books of Hours, and she was subsequently able to point to copies of the same designs carved on another contemporary set of misericords at Throwley in Kent.[3]

I extend Anderson's discoveries further here, showing that it was not just in carved woodwork that these tiny French metal-cut border designs proved so popular, but in other media too.

Thanks to surviving Customs records and books of rates, we know that thousands of printed *Horae* or 'primers' as they were known in the contemporary vernacular – *Vnes hevres, a primer or a mattyns boke* (Palsgrave, *Lesclarcissement* (1530), 183) – were entering the country in the decades either side of 1500. Parisian publishers were issuing printed Hours on an industrial scale, including many editions adapted to the Sarum Use clearly designed for mass export to England

In the present study, we are concerned with four principal subjects (here termed *Linear Motifs*), and several less common ones, mainly smaller vertical motifs – and we should further note that some of these designs exist copied in reverse. I take as my image-base the Sarum Use Hours printed in Paris by Philippe Pigouchet for the publisher Simon Vostre in the late 1490s and early 1500s, e.g. STC 15887 (1498), 15896 (1501) and 15905 (1507) – all of which are available in the British Library – the cuts reproduced here being taken from the 1501 edition.

The dependence on this design of misericords at Bristol (1520) (Fig. 2) and Throwley was noticed by Anderson (above), who also noted

Fig. 1.   Linear Motifs 1 and 2 from *Horae ad usum Sarum*, Pigouchet for Vostre, Paris, 1501 (STC 15896), sig. b.iii verso and b.iiii. British Library

a slight adaptation at the latter site where the carver has reduced the number of *antique* or *naked boyes* – contemporary vernacular terms for these early Renaissance *putti*[4] – to one. A rather more radical truncation of the design is now to be recognized at Beverley (1520) where the distinctive dragon appears alone. For further examples of the motif see Fig. 1.

Again Beverley is to be added to the misericords deriving from this design already noted by Anderson – the inclusion of the plant motif on the Throwley seat is striking proof of the source cut in *manière criblée* (this refers to the dotted background appearance of the metal-cuts). Just as textual scholars have come to terms in recent decades with the phenomenon of 'late' literary manuscripts deriving from early printed editions, we should perhaps not be surprised to observe the same process with regard to visual materials in late illuminated manuscripts. A manuscript Book of Hours sumptuously illustrated in England in the early sixteenth century was sold at auction in 1983 as part of the Bute Collection. Christopher de Hamel identified the full-page miniatures of the Passion sequence as deriving from Schongauer's series, and surmised that 'Many of the splendid little marginal scenes [were] based on engravings or continental pattern-books, to judge from the originality and incongruity of the little scenes'.[5] It is pleasing to be able to identify at least one such marginal subject that derives from a printed Parisian *Horae* in the Bute Hours, and it is probable that more could be recognized if the book itself, now in the Berger Collection on loan to the Denver Art Museum, were scrutinized by someone familiar with the Parisian printed *Horae*. One of the border scenes on folio 103r. is described in the catalogue as 'a putto chasing a monkey riding a donkey, and another monkey playing the bagpipes' (Fig. 3). The main subject certainly derives from our Linear Motif 2, and again the floral motifs confirm the derivation. Consulting the printed *Horae*, however, reveals that the 'monkey playing the bagpipes' in fact derives from a boar so occupied, one of the several small vertical cuts of interest to us. This capacity to 'mix and match' is instructive and can be found elsewhere:

Fig. 2. Misericord, Bristol Cathedral, carved 1520 (dragon chases putti). Photo: www. misericords.co.uk

curiously, the combination of the same two separate motifs – to which a third has been added (monkey playing pipe and tabour (Fig. 11 top)) – is found in a *bas-de-page* of the Helmingham Herbal and Bestiary (Oxford, Bodleian Library, MS Ashmole 1504), f. 23v, of the 1520s.

By the 1520s the English printer, Peter Treveris,[6] was using a wood-cut copy of our *criblée* Linear Motif 2, and it is to be seen in the 1529 edition of *The Grete Herball* (STC 13177) and in his contemporary edition of Barclay's *Egloges* (STC 1384). A woodcut copy of our Linear Motif 1 is also to be found in both the 1526 and 1529 Treveris editions of *The Grete Herball*. It is a pity that Hodnett omitted such 'ornaments' from his *English Woodcuts 1480–1535* (1935), though he admitted two as used in books printed by Treveris to the second, 1973 edition of his work, i.e. *2385a[7] and *2385b. The latter motif, the return from the Stag-Hunt, is also a woodcut copy of an Hours cut in *manière criblée*, and – though missed by Hodnett – is again found in the 1526 edition of *The Grete Herball* (STC 13176). More intriguingly both these motifs are also found as fillers on the earliest known 'portent and prodigy' sheet, *This horryble monster is cast of a Sowe . . .*, issued by Treveris in 1531. In fact, this is a German sheet – the conjoined piglets were born near

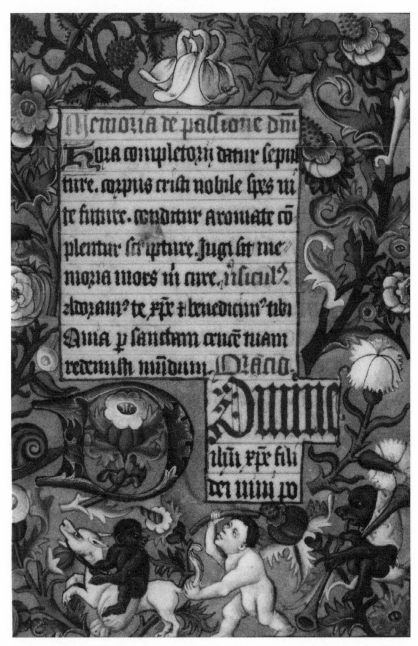

Fig. 3.   Illuminated page from the Bute Hours (f. 103r), English, early sixteenth century.
Photo: courtesy of Sothebys

Fig. 4.   Linear Motifs 3 and 4 from *Horae ad usum Sarum*, Pigouchet for Vostre, Paris, 1501 (STC 15896), sig. d. [v. verso] and d. [vi] British Library

Königsberg in Prussia – originally published in Nürnberg in 1531, on which an English translation and two English printer's ornaments have been superimposed, carefully interpolated between the back and front views of the animals.[8] The two known impressions in the British Library and British Museum have been cropped top and bottom removing all the German text and the imprint information. The two ornament blocks, being English, are, of course, lacking from the monolingual German edition preserved uniquely in Gotha, bearing the imprint of Hans Meldeman [Nürnberg]. The stencilled, ready-coloured sheets were clearly imported by Treveris, and then overprinted by him, and perhaps he was also responsible for cutting away all signs of their German origin. Though perhaps most significant as a very early example of such Anglo-German co-operation, it is curious that the text of the German sheet, *Diß Monstrum ist auff Natange[n] zu Preüssenn &c.*, is entirely neutral in tone, objectively descriptive – there is no hint, surprisingly, of the usual moralization. Treveris was equally indisposed to moralize, but could not resist adding the catchpenny epithet *horryble* to the imported sheet.

The Bristol misericord carved in 1520 (Fig. 5) is the only example of this motif in another medium known to me, but clear and un-equivocal.

A site we have not noticed so far, and a significant one, is Henry VII's chapel in Westminster Abbey. It has long been known that some of the misericords here, carved *c.*1512, derive from Continental prints (including Dürer and Van Meckenem), but the presence of Linear Motif 4 (Fig. 6) is the earliest certain instance I know of in England of an applied use of these Parisian *Horae*-derived motifs – and interesting testimony to the range of sources available to craftsmen employed on this royal commission.

A single paragraph appended to Purvis's 1936 paper by C. J. P. Cave noted that Boxgrove church, Sussex, a chantry chapel erected *c.*1532 to the memory of Thomas West, Lord De La Warr, known as the De La

Fig. 5.   Misericord, Bristol Cathedral, carved 1520 (mermaid between beast and bat-
winged devil). Photo: www.misericords.co.uk

Warr chantry, includes sculptural designs 'taken directly from woodcuts
[*sic*] which appear in books of hours published in Paris by Simon Vostre,
Thielman Kerver, and others round about the year 1500'. Having
explicitly noted panels carved with the present motif and also our Linear
Motif 1, Cave ends his *Note* by stating, 'I have little doubt that most of
the designs on the other panels could be traced to similar woodcuts
[*sic*].'[9] I have not yet had the opportunity to make a detailed inspection
of the chantry in person, but I have been able to draw on the evidence of
some excellent photographs taken by Michael Greenhalgh and posted
on his website,[10] and I am thus able to add a few further identifications
below which amply confirm Cave's confidence.

Though there can be no doubt about the origins of the confronted
wild men sculpted in stone on the De La Warr chantry (Fig. 7), or those
in another *bas-de-page* of the Helmingham Herbal and Bestiary (f. 24v),
the similarly battling wodewoses in the lower margin of BL, MS Cotton
Titus D.IV. f. 1, the presentation copy of Thomas More's Latin epigrams
celebrating the Coronation of Henry VIII and Catherine of Aragon
(1509), are only shown from the waist up, and this may be a derivation
too far for many readers, and not one I should want to insist on, not

Fig. 6. Misericord, Westminster Abbey, carved *c.*1512 (confronted wild men). Photo: author

Fig. 7. Sculpted stone panel, De La Warr chantry chapel, Boxgrove, Sussex (confronted wild men). Photo: author

having seen the rest of the manuscript – though it is indeed true in this area, as in others, that 'birds of a feather flock together' – that is, if we can be as certain as we may that we have identified one of these *Horae*-derived motifs in a manuscript, sculptured monument, or set of misericords, it heightens the probability that the artist has used other motifs of the same origin. A similarly partial waist-up only derivation seems much more likely in my opinion for the wild men battling on a bench-end in the church at Crowcombe, Somerset, which we know to have been carved in 1534. Although the carver has given both wild men the flower-shaped shield – only one bears the hexafoil shield of Linear Motif 4 – the presence of other certainly *Horae*-derived motifs at Crowcombe (see further below) makes this identification all but certain.

We have already noted that Treveris was using a woodcut copy of our Linear Motifs 1 and 2 by the late 1520s, but John Rastell was also contemporaneously using a presumably different set of woodcut copies of our motifs *c*.1525. A dozen ornamental 'fillers' arranged in three rows of four and framed with other woodcut border units appear *en masse* on the final page of his *Calisto and Melibea* (STC 20721) – several are complete designs (e.g. the cat washing itself on the bellows – used as the pattern for a French misericord now preserved in the Musée du Moyen Age in Paris, which also holds a contemporary glass quarry painted with the same design), but at least four are halves only of our Linear Motifs 1 (dragon alone), 2 (pursuing wild man alone), and 4 (both armed wild men – though separately). One of the confronted wild men of Linear Motif 4 reappears on the titlepage of the copy of Rastell's *A. C. mery talys* (1526) preserved in Göttingen (STC 23663) – the British Library copy has a different set of motifs on its titlepage.

Another strikingly bold carved bench-end in Crowcombe consists of three panels of carved ornament, a tall vertical panel above two smaller square panels. The large panel shows two (?wild) men battling against a two-headed dragon which, I feel certain, derives ultimately from our Linear Motif 1, a derivation confirmed by the origin of the lefthand smaller panel (Fig. 8). Beyond the fact that some sort of gaping monster is depicted, it is difficult to make out the subject of this panel clearly until one recognizes the *Horae* cut from which it was evidently derived (Fig. 9). From the mouth of a monster which is nothing but a gaping jaw on legs, emerges a long-necked creature with a collar-like mane, from whose neck is suspended a basket containing four birds. The composition is so very peculiar – in both senses of that word – that the derivation must be regarded as certain.

A contemporary series of bench-ends in another Somerset church,

Fig. 8. Bench-end, Crowcombe church, Somerset, carved 1534 [birds hanging from basket round monster's neck]. Photo: courtesy of Jacqueline Ross

those at East Lyng, were carved *c*.1530 and similarly betray the influence of *Horae* models. One of them depicts a man riding a horse but holding a sack on top of his head with his right hand (Fig. 10). I suggest this derives from the same design which is found as one of the smaller vertical *criblée* cuts (Fig. 11), though I believe his mount is intended to be the proverbially foolish ass, rather than a horse – not least, because this is a traditional proverbial folly which I have termed elsewhere the Humane Rider, that is, the foolish rider who, from the best of intentions, thinks he can save his beast some of the burden by carrying the sack on his own head/back – as he rides![11] A folly of precisely this type was per-petrated by the ironically-styled Wise Men of Gotham – and the woodcut appearing on the titlepage of *The Fool's Complaint to Gotham College* (1643) depicts a fool riding on an ass which ironically remarks, *The fool rides me.*

Fig. 9. Criblée source of fig. 8 from *Horae ad usum Sarum,* Pigouchet for Vostre, Paris, 1501 (STC 15896), sig. a.iiii verso. British Library.

Be that as it may, given the number of *Horae*-derived motifs known from Bristol, it would seem that the rider with the sack on her (?his) head on a misericord in the cathedral there (carved 1520) is another example of this derivation. Indeed – given the widespread diffusion of Parisian printed *Horae* – it is not improbable that the very similar Humane Rider on a contemporary misericord in the Spanish monastery of San Salvador de Celanova in Ourense is yet another.

Fig. 10.   Bench-end, East Lyng church, Somerset, carved *c*.1530 (humane rider). Photo:
courtesy of Dave Bown

Another 'one-off' – as far as I can see – is one of the misericords of
Beverley Minster (also carved in 1520), again a somewhat puzzling
composition until one recognizes the source. The central carving shows
what appears to be a rabbit riding on the back of a dragon, the reins
attached to the monster's neck appearing to pass behind the rabbit. The
original piece of engraved grotesquerie shows what looks very like the
forequarters of a rabbit emerging from a snail-shell – unless what I

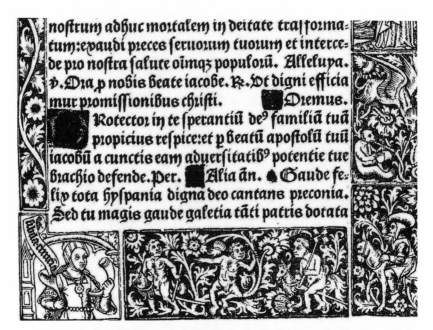

Fig. 11.   Criblée source of fig. 10 from *Horae ad usum Sarum*, Pigouchet for Vostre, Paris, 1501 (STC 15896), sig. h. [vi]. British Library

understand as the rabbit's ears are meant to be the snail's horns – though surely no snail should have paws! Again, it is only the presence of other undoubtedly *Horae*-derived motifs amongst the Beverley misericords that makes me bold to suggest such a derivation for this carving too.

Another of the East Lyng bench-ends is also certainly derived from one of the smaller vertical *criblée* cuts, but one I have not noted used elsewhere as yet. The carving shows a boy wearing only a pair of shorts with one foot on the back of another naked kneeling boy and the other on the trunk of a tree, a branch of which he holds onto as if to steady himself (Fig. 12). In his other hand he holds what many a visitor will have interpreted as a cross – are we not, after all, in a Christian church? – but recognizing the *Horae* cut source (Fig. 13) shows the item to be a child's whirligig or toy windmill. It is interesting to note that the Crowcombe carver has provided a pair of shorts to preserve his boy's modesty – a strategy not felt necessary by the original French engraver who has depicted his *putto* stark naked.

It is the supporters rather than the central carving of another of the Westminster Abbey misericords carved *c*.1512 that brings me to my final suggestion for a *Horae*-derived motif in the corpus of early sixteenth-

Fig. 12.   Bench-end, Crowcombe church, Somerset, carved 1534 [putto stands on back of kneeling putto]. Photo: courtesy of Jacqueline Ross

Fig. 13. Criblée source of fig. 12 from *Horae ad usum Sarum*, Pigouchet for Vostre, Paris, 1501 (STC 15896), sig. h. [viii]

century English carved woodwork. The misericord in question features as its main subject (though damaged) what has been convincingly shown to be a children's game, known in more recent centuries as 'cock-fighting' (as in Kipling's *Stalky and Co*), but in Medwall's early sixteenth century interlude, *Fulgens and Lucres* (printed by Rastell between 1512 and 1516), named somewhat alarmingly, *farte pryke in cule*,[12] a game also depicted as one of the supporters of a late fifteenth-century misericord in St George's Chapel, Windsor. But it is the righthand supporter of the Westminster seat that is at issue here – it depicts a (clothed) boy riding a hobbyhorse – two such *putti* riding hobbyhorses (separated by a third seated on a flower stem) occur as another of the linear *criblée* cuts in the Parisian *Horae* which are the subject of this essay (Figs 12 and 13). I have not noticed the children's 'cock-fighting' game in any printed Hours to date, and I would not absolutely insist that the cut must be the source for the supporter carving, but again, the certainty that the Westminster carver made use of our Linear Motif 4, must, I feel, strengthen the probability – to state it no more forcefully.

A very rare item to survive from the early sixteenth century, and in a quite different medium, is the chased silver pax made around 1510 bearing a central image of the Crucifixion and now preserved at New College, Oxford. Marian Campbell drew attention to the fact that the engraved decoration in its lower border 'closely parallels the upper border motif of daisies and backward-looking beasts' in a Pigouchet *Horae* of *c*.1500 – as indeed it does – but so too do its upper border and the two lopped-branch side-borders.

But to return to the De La Warr chantry: one of the sculpted panels depicts a backward-looking beast with a second head in its hindquarters and a long tail/trunk, which again derives from one of the smaller *Horae* cuts – the surprise here, as throughout the monument – is the extraordinary disparity in scale between these tiny engraved units, only about an inch wide, and the carved stone panels deriving from these designs well over two feet wide. The slender columns which are part of the chapel's architectural structure are also adorned with carved work – one of them clearly derives from the long vertical strip found in the *Horae* which depicts two men climbing an apple-tree and dropping the picked apples down into the oustretched lap of the dress of a woman waiting at the foot of the tree.

The Parisian *Horae* were also an important channel by which the imagery of the *Danse Macabre* was conveyed into England.[13] A Sarum Use Hours printed by Bignon in Paris in 1521 for Richard Fa(w)kes includes by far the earliest illustrated edition of Lydgate's poem, the *Daunce of Machabree* (though the sole surviving copy is imperfect, having only ten cuts with their accompanying verses, from a sequence which would probably have contained about thirty).[14] But excerpts from the personnel of the *Danse* – with French-language captions given to each of the dancers – are also found in earlier Sarum Use *Horae* – and another of the columns of the De La Warr chantry reproduces the confrontation between *lescuyer* [The Squire] and Death with his grave-digger's shovel, his skeletal hand on the sleeve of the youth who tries in vain to pull away from him.

We have only been concerned here with the *border* cuts in the Parisian *Horae* – were we to enlarge our investigation to include the full-page subjects, we would very soon come across the Beaton panels now in the National Museum of Scotland, one of which bears the arms of Beaton over an abbot's crozier flanked by the letters *D.B.*, for David Beaton, who became Abbot of Arbroath on his uncle's resignation in his favour in 1523, receiving a papal dispensation permitting him to post-pone taking holy orders until 1525, so that the panels may well belong to the 1520s,[15] and may have originally come from Arbroath Abbey. The Tree of Jesse panel derives from the version of the subject as represented in the Parisian *Horae* printed by Thielman Kerver, e.g. that dated 23 June 1507, which includes, for example, a crescent moon beneath the Virgin & Child, and the dreamer's left hand placed against his cheek, unlike the version in Pigouchet's books. Some art historians, however, have suggested that the 'style suggests Flemish workmanship', so that we may be mistaken in considering the panels examples of 'English' woodwork at all.

Fascinating confirmation that these early printed *Horae* were indeed valued especially on account of their border cuts, is afforded by two of the three manuscripts which make up the autograph copy of the 'New Chronicles of England and France' by Robert Fabyan (commonly known as *Fabyan's Chronicle*), completed in November 1504. The first volume, Earl of Leicester, Holkham MS 671, contains many small woodcuts and printed borders, pasted into it and coloured, from two Sarum *Horae* printed in Paris by Pigouchet. The earlier is the edition he printed in 1494 for Jean Richard of Rouen (STC 15879), from which no fewer than 36 borders were taken, including several which feature the designs in which we are particularly interested here, and the other, that dated 20 October 1501, printed for Vostre (STC 15896). The use of this latter edition, printed only three years before Fabyan completed his second volume, is interesting testimony both to the speed with which these Parisian books of Hours entered England, and to the apparent ease with which their images, at least, might be 're-cycled'.

The study of the surprising influence exerted by these tiny metal-cuts on artwork in sixteenth-century England (and the rest of Europe, indeed[16]) is still in its infancy, but I hope this short investigation of those derivations known to me, may prompt a rather more thorough-going survey of these disproportionately important prints.

References

1. J. S. Purvis, 'The use of Continental woodcuts and prints by the "Ripon School" of woodcarvers in the early sixteenth century' in *Archaeologia* LXXXV (1936), 107–28. I first discussed the importance of these humble stereotyped designs as the models for artworks in a variety of genres in my unpublished doctoral thesis, 'Iconography & design-sources of the Beverley Minster misericords' (University of Plymouth, 1991).
2. 'German and Flemish prints as design-sources for the misericords in St. George's Chapel, Windsor (1477x84)' in L. Keen and E. Scarff (eds), *Windsor. Medieval*

Archaeology, Art and Architecture of the Thames Valley (*The British Archaeological Association Conference Transactions 1998*, XXV (2002)), 155–65.

3. T. Cox [M.D. Anderson], 'Twelfth-Century Design Sources of the Worcester Cathedral Misericords' in *Archaeologia* 97 (1959) 165–6; the Throwley examples are noted in G. L. Remnant, 'A catalogue of misericords in Great Britain' (Oxford, 1969).

4. Note the interesting use of the term in Skelton's description of Wolsey's *Triumph of Death* tapestry from the suite of Petrarchan *Trionfi* he bought for Hampton Court from the executors of the estate of Bishop Thomas Ruthall: *unycornes/ With theyr semely hornes;/ Upon these beestes rydynge,/Naked boyes strydynge* . . . (*Collyn Clout* 964–7), J. Scattergood, *John Skelton: The Complete English Poems* (Harmondsworth, 1983), 477, where it is noted that in the tapestry in question, which still remains *in situ*, 'the car of Chastity is drawn by unicorns on which ride naked boys'.

5. *Catalogue of the Bute Collection of forty-two illuminated manuscripts and miniatures*, Sotheby Parke Bernet & Co., 13 June 1983, lot 34, 118–30, here 122. I am grateful to Christopher de Hamel for supplying me with a photocopy of the relevant entry, for correspondence concerning it a decade later, and for supplying the photograph of folio 103r.

6. I style him 'English' as he was printing in Southwark, but his surname suggests that his family were originally natives of Trier in Germany. As the evidence discussed later in this paragraph makes clear, he continued to have connections with at least one German printer.

7. Treveris was using this panel of apes jousting as early as 1527, e.g. in STC 15574, STC 25489.7 and STC 25471.5. It is another motif derived from imported early French Sarum Use primers printed by Pigouchet – but in this instance as found in a *Horae* for the Rouennais publisher, Jean Richard, issued in 1494 [STC 15879]. I am grateful to Nathan Flis for drawing my attention to this derivation.

8. See the very full treatment in S. O'Connell and D. Paisey, '*This horryble monster*. An Anglo-German Broadside of 1531', *Print Quarterly* 16 (1999), 57–63.

9. Purvis, 'Continental woodcuts', 127–8.

10. http://dspace.anu.edu.au/handle/1885/11179/browse?type=subject&order=ASC& rpp=20&value=de+la+warr+chantry+chapel

11. M. Jones, *The Secret Middle Ages* (Stroud, 2002), 136–7.

12. M. Twycross et al., 'Farte Pryke in Cule' in *Medieval English Theatre* 6 (1984), 30–9; ibid., 23 (2001), 100–21.

13. The contemporary vernacular term was 'Dance of Paul's', i.e. the Dance of Death as seen in St Paul's Cathedral, London.

14. H. S. Herbrüggen, 'Der Schäfer-Kalender . . .' in M. von Arnim (ed.), *Festschrift Otto Schäfer* . . . (Stuttgart, 1987), 237–88.

15. The Arbroath Abbey provenance is disputed in David H. Caldwell, 'The Beaton Panels – Scottish Carvings of the 1520s or 1530s' in John Higgitt (ed.), *Medieval Art and Architecture in the Diocese of St Andrews* (Leeds, 1994), 174–84.

16. The influence of such full-page *Horae* cuts as design sources for continental artworks was discussed by Geneviève Souchal, 'Un grand peintre français . . .' in *Revue de l'Art* 22 (1973), 22–86.

Publishing Palladio in England, 1650–1750

Charles Hind

With a readership that I suspect knows more about publishing than architecture, it might be helpful to begin with an explanation of why the history of publishing the works of an Italian Renaissance architect in England in the century following the Restoration of King Charles II might be of interest. So I begin with two incontrovertible statements. Andrea Palladio is the most influential architect in the world. And Palladio's influence and reputation rely heavily on his book, *I Quattro Libri dell'Architettura*, first published in Venice in 1570.

Some biographical information will help place Palladio's book in context and explain why it was republished, first partly, then wholly in English in the seventeenth and eighteenth centuries.[1] Andrea di Pietro, known as Palladio,[2] was born in 1508 in Padua but his professional career as a stonemason and later as architect was based in Vicenza. The turning point in his life came in 1537 when his firm, in which he was already a partner, won the contract to rebuild the villa near Vicenza of Giangiorgio di Trissino, a distinguished Vicentine scholar and amateur architect. Trissino took a liking to the young man, gave him the name Palladio and allowed him the run of his library. He also introduced him to his intellectual circle not only in Vicenza but even more importantly in the university city of Padua. One of the most important introductions was to Daniele Barbaro, a Venetian patrician who promoted Palladio tirelessly for all manner of projects in Venice over the next 25 years. Trissino also took Palladio to Rome in 1541, giving him his first opportunity to study the major ruins of antiquity at first hand, rather than from the often inaccurate woodcuts in books by authors such as Sebastiano Serlio.

Between 1537 and the mid-1560s, Palladio built a solid reputation as an endlessly inventive designer of villas that combined elements of traditional villa design infused with a deep understanding of Roman architecture adapted to suit contemporary needs. This experience stood him in good stead when he began major ecclesiastical commissions in Venice from the early 1560s, on which work continued until his death in 1580. A lifetime of thought, study and design experience went into

I Quattro Libri dell'Architettura, which appeared in print when he was over 60 years old, and which codified his views for a very wide audience.

So why did Palladio become influential and what differentiated him from his contemporaries in Renaissance Italy? He is inextricably linked to an idea of architecture that is based on simplicity, proportion and integration into the landscape, which culminated in a series of outstanding buildings. He brought theory and practice together in publications and buildings as no other Renaissance architect had. He democratized architecture, proclaiming the value of domestic structures, believing that farmhouses, barns and bridges were works of as much value as churches and palaces and that any building could be beautiful without the use of costly materials. It was an appealing and potent combination.

As an author, Palladio wrote rather more than just the *Quattro Libri* for which he is remembered, although not much of it was translated into English. His first two works, both published in Rome in 1554, were the *Antiquitates Urbis Romae*, evidently written in Latin, and the Italian *Descritione de le Chiese, Stationi, Indulgenze & Reliquie de Corpi Sancti, che sonno in la Citta de Roma*. These were two small guidebooks, the first a brief study of the antiquities of Rome, digested by Palladio from a number of sources but including a lot of new material. The second describes the history, treasures and services of the seven most important ancient churches, with a list of other churches, festivals and indulgences. Both were published by Vincentio Lucrino. Only three copies of the first edition of the church guidebook are known[3] and as much of it was plundered by other authors it survives in works by other hands.[4] Only the guide to the antiquities maintained a separate existence and numerous editions were published in Rome and Venice into the seventeenth century. It finally reached an English edition in 1709 (though not *in* English), published in Oxford, edited and translated by Charles Fairfax for Henry Aldrich, Dean of Christ Church. Dean Aldrich (1648–1710) was an early advocate of Palladian architecture and was himself a talented amateur architect, being responsible amongst other buildings for Peckwater Quadrangle and the Library of Christ Church. The Antiquuities were published in parallel Latin and Italian texts.[5]

Palladio's next involvement in publishing was as an illustrator rather than as a writer. I have mentioned one of his key patrons and supporters – Daniele Barbaro, a student at Padua in the late 1530s and a friend of Trissino. Barbaro was a polymath who, in due course, wrote a standard history of the Venetian Republic, edited the work of Vitruvius and served as Venetian Ambassador in England during the reign of Edward VI before being appointed Patriarch Elect of Aquileia. He also founded the Botanical Garden in Padua, the oldest surviving in the world. Palladio worked with Barbaro on publishing the new edition of Vitruvius (in 1556), translated into Italian and thus making it more widely available, and he provided the illustrations, some of which operate with flaps, a bibliographical novelty.[6] A second edition appeared in 1567. Vitruvius was the author in the first century BC of the only treatise on architecture to survive from antiquity.

Palladio's third book was *I Quattro Libri* to which I shall return, but his fourth and final works were on unlikely topics, an illustrated Italian edition of Julius Caesar's Commentaries,[7] and, left incomplete at his death in 1580, an edition of Polybius's Histories, which would have included 43 engravings of armies deployed in various battles. Both texts were, or would have been abundantly illustrated and the key feature of the Commentaries was how Palladio devised what are almost film stills to explain the movement of the armies. The illustrations were again fully integrated into the texts, as we have seen with the Vitruvius and will see with *I Quattro Libri*.

Palladio's most important work, *I Quattro Libri dell'Architettura*, forms the basis of his subsequent reputation (Fig. 1). The four books (Palladio hoped to publish a further four but only one partly survives and that in rough draft) sum up his knowledge and experience of both Roman architecture and contemporary building. Book one deals with the basic components of architecture and the rules governing them, the orders, room shapes, vault types, doors, windows and stairs. Book 2 tells the reader how to put them together to design palaces and villas (cleverly his views are illustrated with his own works (Fig. 2). Book 3 discusses public buildings, starting with roads and bridges before moving on to piazzas and basilicas; and Book 4 contains general observations on religious buildings followed by a discussion of antique temples and a detailed analysis of particular examples.

I Quattro Libri was also an effective work of graphic design and in its integration of texts with measurements and illustrations, it formed a model for all subsequent architectural books. Palladio aimed it at a wide readership, ranging from literate craftsmen, scholars, architects and potential clients to cultivated gentlemen. It went into numerous Italian editions (Inigo Jones owned a copy of the 1601 edition).[8] The first full translation out of the original Italian was published in French in Paris in 1650 by Roland Fréart de Chambray (1606–76).[9] In due course, this was followed by four English editions, the first by Giacomo Leoni in 1715–20. The second was begun by Colen Campbell but left incomplete

Fig. 1.   Titlepage to *I Quattro Libri dell'Architettura*, published in Venice in 1570. This copy belonged to Lord Burlington. (Courtesy of RIBA British Architectural Library)

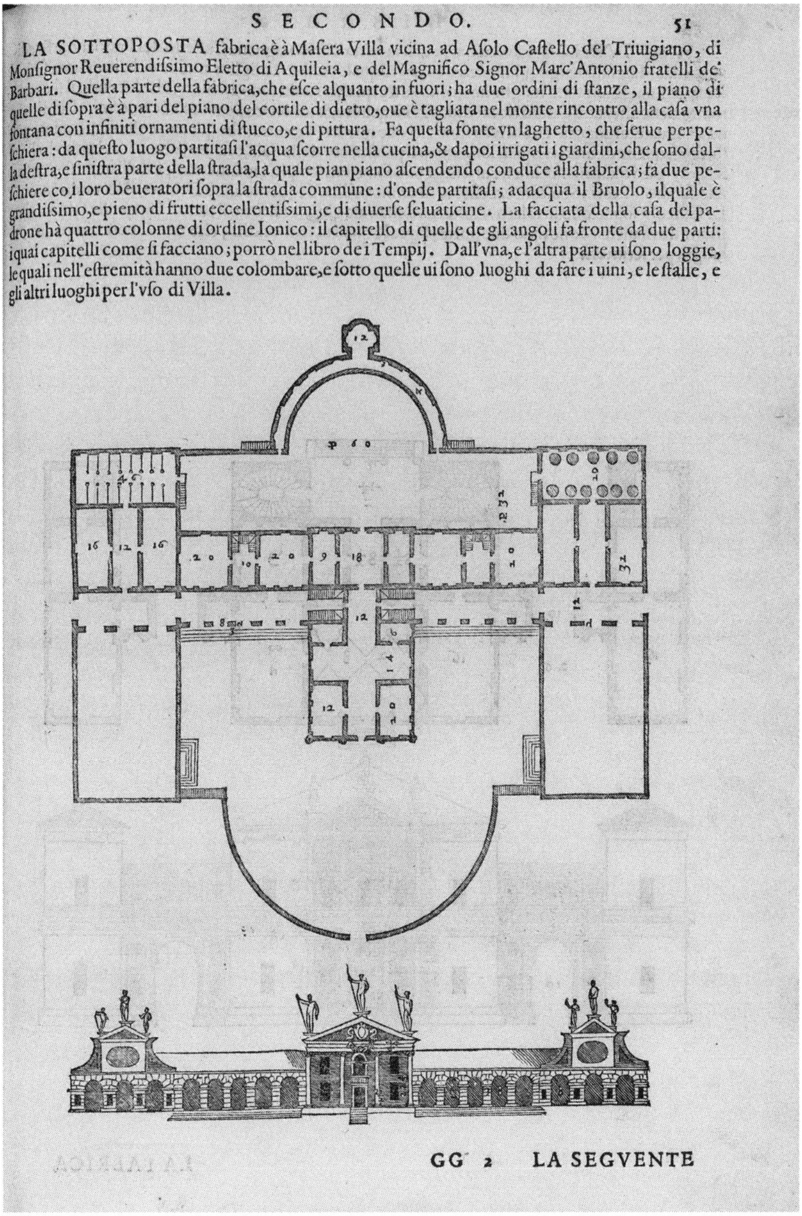

S E C O N D O.   51

LA SOTTOPOSTA fabrica è à Mafera Villa vicina ad Afolo Caftello del Triuigiano, di Monfignor Reuerendifsimo Eletto di Aquileia, e del Magnifico Signor Marc'Antonio fratelli de' Barbari. Quella parte della fabrica, che efce alquanto in fuori; ha due ordini di ftanze, il piano di quelle di fopra è à pari del piano del cortile di dietro, oue è tagliata nel monte rincontro alla cafa vna fontana con infiniti ornamenti di ftucco, e di pittura. Fa quefta fonte vn laghetto, che ferue per pefchiera: da quefto luogo partitafi l'acqua fcorre nella cucina, & dapoi irrigati i giardini, che fono dalla deftra, e finiftra parte della ftrada, la quale pian piano afcendendo conduce alla fabrica; fa due pefchiere co, i loro beueratori fopra la ftrada commune: d'onde partitafi; adacqua il Bruolo, ilquale è grandifsimo, e pieno di frutti eccellentifsimi, e di diuerfe feluaticine. La facciata della cafa del padrone hà quattro colonne di ordine Ionico: il capitello di quelle de gli angoli fa fronte da due parti: iquai capitelli come fi facciano; porrò nel libro de i Tempij. Dall'vna, e l'altra parte ui fono loggie, le quali nell'eftremità hanno due colombare, e fotto quelle ui fono luoghi da fare i uini, e le ftalle, e gli altri luoghi per l'vfo di Villa.

GG 2   LA SEGVENTE

Fig. 2.   Woodcut of the Villa Barbaro, remodelled and extended by Palladio in the 1550s and shown in a woodcut from *I Quattro Libri dell'Architettura* (Venice, 1570) (courtesy of RIBA British Architectural Library)

at his death in 1729. The third was the morally dubious version of 1732–4 by Benjamin Cole and the last remained the definitive English version, edited by Isaac Ware and published from 1737. Otherwise there was a clear preference for republishing Book I as a separate item. I shall revert to this later.

The first full English edition, of which Book I appeared in 1715, marks a turning point in English architectural history. The editor was Giacomo Leoni (c.1686–1746), who described himself as a Venetian but of whose early life nothing is known.[10] He is first recorded in 1708, when a manuscript now in McGill University, Montreal, indicates that he was in Düsseldorf.[11] His later claim that he was 'Architect to the Elector Palatine', whose court was at Düsseldorf, was probably exaggerated but Leoni was certainly involved in building work for the Elector. The earliest evidence for his presence in England is his edition of Palladio, which appeared in five instalments between 1715 and 1720.[12] The text was in Italian, French and English and claims to be a translation of Palladio's original text. But in fact the English text is a revised translation of Fréart's French edition of 1650 translated by Nicholas Dubois, a French soldier, military engineer and architect who probably left France at the Revocation of the Edict of Nantes in 1685 and made his subsequent career in England. Leoni also took considerable liberties in adapting the illustrations. Fig. 3 shows his version of the Villa Rotonda on the outskirts of Vicenza.

Leoni explicitly drew attention to his work on the plates:

Such as are true judges will, by comparing the Draughts of Palladio with mine, easily discern a vast difference. His Wooden Cuts I have chang'd in Copper Plates, which for the greater perfection of the work, tho' much to my own loss, I have procur'd to be engrav'd in Holland by the famous Monsieur Picart . . . I have not only made the draughts myself, and on a much larger scale than my Author, but also made so many corrections with respect to shading, dimensions, ornaments &c. that this Work may in some sort be rather consider'd as an Original, than an Improvement.[13]

The plates are certainly of high quality, though Picart probably engraved very few of them. Of the 52 bearing his name, all but nine are signed 'direxit' and were doubtless engraved in his Amsterdam studio. The frontispiece in Fig. 4 was engraved after a drawing or painting (now lost) by Leoni's fellow Venetian Sebastiano Ricci (1659–1734). Interestingly, given Lord Burlington's later interest in Palladio, his mother was one of the subscribers and the book must have been delivered to Burlington House about the time that Lord Burlington returned home from his first grand tour, in which architecture did not feature very large.

Fig. 3. Elevation and section of the Villa Rotonda from Leoni's edition of Palladio
(London, 1715) (courtesy of RIBA British Architectural Library)

Fig. 4.   Frontispiece after Sebastiano Ricci from Leoni's edition of Palladio, showing
the bust of the architect surrounded by allegorical figures (London, 1715)
(courtesy of RIBA British Architectural Library)

Lord Burlington and his circle reviled Leoni's work, partly because the plates do have a somewhat baroque flavour, which doubtless prompted Colen Campbell's unfinished edition of 1729. But Leoni's Palladio remained one of the standard textbooks of the English Palladian revival and it had a considerably larger circulation (and therefore influence) in North America than Isaac Ware's later and more accurate edition. It went into three editions, of which the second (1721) kept the English text only and dropped the Italian and French. There had evidently been a considerable and immediate demand for the first edition, as Leoni announced in the *Daily Courant* on 5 March 1720 that he was willing to buy back any unwanted copies of Books 1 and 2 and was preparing a second edition.[14] In both first and second editions, Leoni promised to include Inigo Jones's annotations to his copy of the 1601 edition, but the owner of that copy, the Oxford academic Dr George Clarke, refused to allow him to copy them and they only appeared in Leoni's third edition of 1742, six years after Clarke's death, by which time the volume was owned by Worcester College, to which it had been bequeathed by Clarke.

Colen Campbell (1676–1729), who was the next to essay a sound English edition, was a Scottish lawyer turned architect responsible for that other harbinger of the Palladian Revival, *Vitruvius Britannicus* (1715–20).[15] He was also the architect of a number of key Palladian buildings such as Wanstead House, Essex, and Stourhead in Wiltshire. It was probably *Vitruvius Britannicus* that sparked Burlington's interest in architecture, so it was not surprising that it was Campbell who sought to replace Leoni's edition with something a little closer to Palladio's original. He only got as far as editing Book I,[16] which appeared the year before his death in 1728, with the result that the publisher, Samuel Harding, abandoned it incomplete. There is no evidence that Burlington was directly involved, but as Campbell, the publisher Harding and the engraver Paul Fourdrinier were all connected with Burlington's circle, it seems likely that the project at least enjoyed his passive support. The text was still derived from the French, however, rather than from Palladio's original and it is probably true for the titlepage to describe Campbell as the reviser rather than the editor. The prime mover seems to have been the publisher, as Samuel Harding's *Proposals*, published in late 1727, indicated that Harding was the 'Undertaker [who] has already at his own expence printed the first Book and he intends to go on with the other Three at Michaelmas next'.[17] The book was cheaper than Leoni's, but not intended to be really cheap. Large paper copies were to be two and a half guineas, while small paper were to be one and a half guineas. Book I seems to have been reissued before Campbell's death in September 1729, with the addition of five plates of designs by Campbell himself. His death stopped the publication, which is puzzling as there would obviously have been public interest in seeing the work completed and perhaps Harding had a problem finding a replacement for Campbell. As he had not succeeded in replacing Campbell by 15 November 1732, his plans were superseded by the less dilatory and certainly very businesslike Benjamin Cole.

Cole's prospectus, published on that date, proposed publishing Book I at a cost of 5s., less than half the price of Harding's, or issuing it in sixpenny parts. Harding responded by slashing his own price to 5s. and then engaged in a bitter exchange of propaganda in the press.[18] Cole won by getting out his Book 2 at the end of 1733, silencing Harding, whose plates ended up being sold to Robert Sayer and recycled as illustrations for *The Modern Builder's Assistant* (1757), a compilation work indicative of the conservative nature of such pattern books.

Cole's edition appeared over three years, 1732–5, in sixpenny parts and was finally available for £1 10s. complete[19]. Cole was an unscrupulous publisher, and the plates were largely copied either from Harding's edition or from Leoni, with additional material lifted from Isaac Ware's *Designs of Inigo Jones and Others* (London, 1731). Cole did not even bother to prepare special drawings for his edition, and he copied the Leoni plates exactly, so that when printed off the copper plate, they appeared as mirror images (although in far smaller format). The additional material came from *Designs of Inigo Jones and Others*, with drawings by Burlington's protégé, Isaac Ware; all the full plates were chimneypieces, with other designs as space fillers (Fig. 5). Copyright having been established in the text, Edward Hoppus (d.1739) was employed to rework the wording to disguise its origins and avoid the charge of plagiarism but until the Engravers' Copyright Act of 1735, there was no legal copyright in images so Cole's theft of the intellectual property of others could go unchallenged. It was either an act of unparalleled cheek or an attempt to curry favour that made Cole add a dedication to Lord Burlington that can scarcely have impressed the Earl but may have forced him to encourage Ware to take on the task of preparing a truly authoritative text. But with all its faults, Cole's edition appears to have achieved its aim of bringing Palladio to those who could not afford the expensive editions by Leoni, to the extent that ESTC records fewer surviving copies of Cole's two editions together than for each of Leoni's three editions.

Isaac Ware (1704–66) was a member of Burlington's circle and an

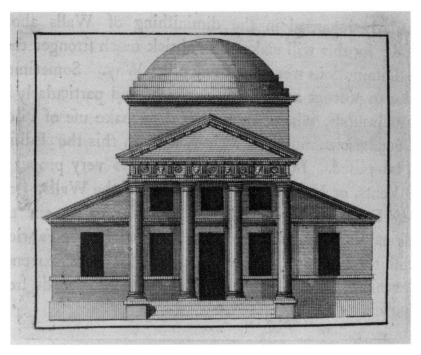

Fig. 5. An endpiece in Cole and Hoppus's edition of Palladio, showing a temple design
. . . lifted from Isaac Ware's *Designs of Inigo Jones and Others* (London, 1731)
(courtesy of RIBA British Architectural Library)

official in the Office of the King's Works for over 30 years.[20] His first
publication was the octavo volume looted by Cole, *The Designs of Inigo
Jones and Others*, the others being Burlington and William Kent. Ware's
edition of *I Quattro Libri*[21] was a careful and scholarly work in which
'particular care' was taken 'to preserve the Proportions and Measures
from the Original, all the plates being engraved by the Author's own
hand'. As Ware had a personal grievance against Cole for pirating the
designs from Inigo Jones (indeed, Ware was one of the petitioners for the
Engraver's Copyright Act), it must have given him particular pleasure
to see off Cole's edition. In the *London Evening Post* announcement that
the book was in the press in April 1737, Ware promised subscribers that
there would be no liberties taken with the 'Beautiful Proportions of
that Correct and incomparable author, no deviations from the drawings
(Ware of course had access to drawings in Burlington's collection and
reminded subscribers of this) . . . no fanciful decorations introduced'.
Cole was explicitly attacked for his dedication to Burlington without the
latter's 'Approbation and Knowledge or his so much as having heard of

the author . . . or seen his Book'. He was also flattened by the statement that the book was 'done with so little understanding and so much negligence, that it cannot but give great offence to the judicious, and be of very bad consequence in misleading the unskilful, into whose hands it might happen to fall'.[22]

Presumably with Burlington's considerable financial support, the price of a copy of this work was kept down to £1 10s., the same as Cole's, and was also available in weekly parts costing sixpence. Ware was helped by eight agents, who happened to include Samuel Harding and the engraver Paul Fourdrinier, who had both lost so much in Campbell's abortive edition. Burlington's assistance was acknowledged in the dedication for having revised and corrected the text with his own hands and Ware's authentic edition (a second edition appeared in 1753–4) survived as the authoritative English text until the late twentieth century.

I mentioned earlier that Palladio's Book I, dealing with the orders, vaults, doors and windows and so forth, remained a popular single publication. The first English edition was Godfrey Richards of 1663.[23] The format, plates and general design was based on Pierre Le Muet's Paris edition of 1645[24] and the frontispiece was a direct copy. The titlepage claims that Richards translated Le Muet's French text but in fact he seems to have worked from both Le Muet and the original Italian text, as he includes material in Palladio but omitted by Le Muet and some of the later parts of the book include material evidently written by Richards himself. Some of the chimneypiece designs added by Richards and taken from Le Muet were chosen because they were 'most agreeing to the present practice both in England and France'.[25] A second edition was issued because of the need for such works after the Great Fire of London and went into numerous further editions until superseded by the cheap Cole and Hoppus edition.

The mixing in of other material in the dissemination of Palladio started by Richards in 1663 was standard by the eighteenth century. Francis Price's *A Treatise on Carpentry* (London, 1733), from its second edition of 1735 called *The British Carpenter*, claimed it was a compilation of 'the most approv'd methods of connecting timber together' given by Alberti, Serlio, Palladio and others. From the second edition onwards it included a supplement that extracted Palladio's work on the orders, with doors and windows from Book I, together with a proportional system of his own devising that preserved the proportions of Palladio whilst offering a simpler way to arrive at them.

William Salmon's *Palladio Londinensis* (first published in 1734) remained the standard builder's manual through eight editions until

1773 and whilst it nodded in the direction of Palladio, Salmon used what he wanted and discarded the rest. Salmon was a carpenter who advertised in *The Builder's Guide* (London, 1736) that he 'draws Draughts or Designs for Gentlemen, and estimates the same' but no works of his have been identified and his reputation is based on the large numbers of modestly priced and eminently practical builders' manuals that he wrote. *Palladio Londinensis* is a compendium of material, ranging from the carpentry of roofs and stairs to a summary of the London building acts. Palladio's name is being used as a marketing tool but the book does include an easy method of calculating proportions of the five orders of architecture and by these means, and in other works, Palladio's rules on the orders were popularized and made accessible to eighteenth-century builders and craftsmen, who rarely read, or had access to, translations of the original Renaissance treatise. One feels that Palladio would not have disapproved![26]

I will conclude with a unique tribute to Palladio, in fact one not as far as I am aware accorded to any other architect before the late nineteenth century. It was a private venture by Lord Burlington and relates to his own collection of drawings by Palladio and in particular the measured drawings and reconstructions of the imperial bath complexes in Rome. But first I must explain why Burlington owned drawings and how they had arrived in England. In 1613–14, Inigo Jones made an extended tour of northern Italy in the company of the Earl and Countess of Arundel. Jones took with him a copy of the 1601 edition of *I Quattro Libri*, which he annotated with his observations.[27] In Venice, probably from Vincenzo Scamozzi, Palladio's former pupil, he acquired a trove of about 150 drawings. These formed the bedrock of Jones's architectural development over the next thirty years and after his death they passed through the hands of successive architects until they were sold by John Talman to Burlington in 1720 for £170.[28] The previous year, Burlington had made his second grand tour to Italy specifically to look at Palladio's buildings and acquired, in Venice according to a letter he wrote to Sir Andrew Fountaine,[29] a further block of drawings, mostly it seems to do with baths and public buildings. British holdings of these two collections, now mostly belonging to the RIBA, are larger than survive for every other Italian Renaissance architect put together.

In *I Quattro Libri*, Palladio referred to his hope that he would soon be able to put out further books dealing with amphitheatres, baths and other ancient edifices but these never appeared. It would have been perfectly reasonable for Burlington to assume that his fresh haul of drawings related to this project and cherish a hope that a manuscript might

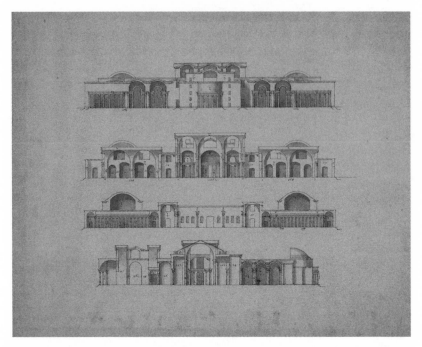

Fig. 6.   Isaac Ware after Andrea Palladio, 'The Baths of Nero', *c.*1730 (courtesy of RIBA
British Architectural Library)

turn up containing Palladio's text. As it did not, Burlington considered
doing it for him, using his drawings. The titlepage of *Fabbriche Antiche
Designate da Andrea Palladio Vicentino e date in luce da Riccardo Conte
di Burlington* depicts a Doric aedicule said to have been invented by
Palladio. On its base stands a depiction of the bust of Palladio, made for
the Earl by John Michael Rysbrack.[30] The design of the titlepage is
William Kent's and it is engraved by Paul Fourdriner.

On the evidence of George Vertue,[31] who visited Chiswick in 1734,
the engraving of the plates was still underway, despite the titlepage being
dated 1730. Vertue subsequently engraved the headpiece to Burlington's
preface in which he promised that a further volume of ancient triumphal
arches, theatres, temples and other ancient buildings would follow the
baths. This never appeared and *Fabbriche Antiche* was still unpublished
in 1736, when Burlington's collections were described by the Italian
antiquarian Marchese Francesco Scipione Maffei.[32] Indeed, it was never
published for sale and Burlington apparently only gave away copies to
friends.

During the 1720s, Burlington commissioned copies of his drawings from Henry Flitcroft and Isaac Ware. Some of the originals were very large, so some of the copies were reduced, as in Ware's drawing of the Baths of Nero (Fig. 6). Using elements from other drawings of the same building, Ware produced a convincing assemblage, while other drawings were copied absolutely faithfully and to the same scale. Fourdrinier then engraved the sheets, which were printed in bistre, enhancing the effect of the prints being original drawings. This was a technique already established for the reproduction of Old Master drawings, but had not so far been applied to reproducing architectural drawings. So far as I am aware, there was no other attempt to reproduce drawings like this until the late nineteenth century so Burlington was far ahead of his time.

Although the presence of Palladio's drawings in England was the key to the development of Anglo-Palladianism in the more elevated circles of English architects, the Palladian message trickled down the social scale via the pattern books rather than the translations of *I Quattro Libri dell'Architettura*. The endless editions of builders' manuals by William Salmon, Batty Langley and others taught even country carpenters how to inject a memory of Palladio's vision of classical antiquity into the Georgian buildings that we so revere and seek to protect today.

References

1. The best general accounts of Palladio's life and career are J. S. Ackerman, *Palladio*, 3rd edition (Harmondsworth, 2006) and B. Boucher, *Andrea Palladio* (New York &c., 1998). The catalogue to the recent exhibition on Palladio in Vicenza, London, Barcelona and Madrid is indispensable. The English edition is G. Beltramini and H. Burns (eds), *Palladio* (London, 2008).

2. Palladio was born simply Andrea di Pietro, Andrew son of Peter, sometimes in Paduan records referred to as Pietro della Gondola. The name Palladio means wise or trustworthy.

3. One is in London (at the Royal Institute of British Architects, British Architectural Library), whilst the other two are in Rome.

4. Both are now available in translation. See V. Hart and P. Hicks (eds), *Palladio's Rome* (New Haven and London, 2006).

5. A Palladio, *Antiquitates Urbis Romae. L'Antichita di Roma* (Oxford, 1709).

6. *I dieci libri dell' architettura di M. Vitruvio / tradutti et commentati da Monsignor Barbaro . . . Con due tauole, l'una di tutto quello si contiene per i capi nell' opera, l'altra per dechiaratione di tutte le cose d'importauza* [sic] (Venice, 1556).

7. *I Commentari di C. Giulio Cesare, con le figure in rame de gli alloggiamenti, de' fatti d'arme, delle circonvallationi della città, & di molte altre cose notabili descritte in essi. Fatte da Andrea Palladio per facilitare a chi legge, la cognition dell'historia* (Venice, 1575).

8. Now in the Library of Worcester College, Oxford.

9. R. Fréart, sieur de Chambray, *Parallele de l'Architecture Antique et de la Moderne. Avec un Recueil des Dix Principaux Autheurs Qui Ont Ecrit des Cinq Ordres* (Paris, 1650).

10. The best brief description of his life and career is in H. Colvin, *A Biographical*

Dictionary of British Architects 1600–1840, 4th edition (New Haven and London, 2008), pp. 642–5.

11. P. Collins, 'The McGill Leoni', in *Journal of the Royal Architectural Institute of Canada*, vol. 34, January 1957, pp. 3–4.

12. The best description of Leoni's edition (and indeed of all the books discussed later, citations below) is E. Harris, *British Architectural Books and Writers 1556–1784* (Cambridge, 1990), pp. 355–9.

13. *The Architecture of A. Palladio: in Four Books, Revis'd, . . . Design'd, and Publish'd by Giacomo Leoni, . . . Translated from the Italian Original* (London, 1715–20), Book IV, part II, preface.

14. Harris, *Architectural Books*, p. 356.

15. Colvin, *Dictionary*, pp. 213–17.

16. *Andrea Palladio's Five Orders of Architecture. With his Treatises of Pedestals, galleries, . . . Faithfully translated, and all the plates exactly copied from the first Italian edition printed in Venice 1570. Revised by Colen Campbell, . . . To which are added, five curious plates . . . invented by Mr Campbell* (London, 1728). It was reissued the following year with a slightly revised title.

17. Royal Institute of British Architects, *Early Printed Books 1478–1840, Catalogue of the British Architectural Library Early Imprints Collection* (London, 1994–2003) (hereafter RIBA), vol. 3, p. 1371.

18. Harris, *Architectural Books*, pp. 361–3.

19. RIBA, vol. 3, p. 1351.

20. Colvin, *Dictionary*, pp. 1087–9.

21. I. Ware, *The Four Books of Andrea Palladio's Architecture* (London, 1738 [1737]). Despite the titlepages being dated 1738, there is clear evidence that the book was available for sale the previous year (see Harris, *Architectural Books*, p. 691).

22. Ware, p. [xi].

23. G. Richards, *The First Book of Architecture by Andrea Palladio: translated out of Italian, with an Appendix Touching Doors and Windows by Pr Le Muet; Translated out of French by G.R.* (London, 1663).

24. *Traicte des Cinq Ordres d'Architecture: desquels se sont seruy les anciens traduit du Palladio; augmente de nouuelles* [sic] *inuentions* [sic] *pour l'art de bien bastir par le Sr. Le Muet* (Paris, 1745).

25. Richards, *First Book of Architecture*, p. [vii].

26. See also C. Hind and I. Murray, 'Publishing Palladio and the spread of Anglo-Palladianism', in C. Hind and I. Murray (eds), *Palladio and His Legacy: A Transatlantic Journey*, catalogue of an exhibition held at the Morgan Library & Museum, New York and elsewhere, 2010–11 (Verona, 2010), pp. 110–13 and catalogue entries 38–51.

27. See footnote 8.

28. See C. Hind, 'Provenance of the Palladio Drawings in the British Architectural Library of the Royal Institute of British Architects', in Hind and Murray, *Palladio and His Legacy*, pp. xii–xiii.

29. Quoted in J. Harris, *The Palladian Revival. Lord Burlington, His Villa and Garden at Chiswick* (New Haven and London, 1994), p. 62.

30. Now at Chatsworth.

31. George Vertue, *Vertue Note Books*, vol. 3 (Walpole Society, London, 1933–4), p. 73.

32. Harris, *Architectural Books*, p. 349.

The Young-Mans Time Well Spent: *Learning to Draw from a Master*

MEGHAN DOHERTY

A DIVERSE CROSS-SECTION OF ENGLISH people in the seventeenth century were interested in learning to draw.[1] In particular, members of the Royal Society understood that drawing was a necessary skill for the study of nature, and that learning to draw was important for the study of natural philosophy. The writings of Fellows and book reviews in the Society's journal, the *Philosophical Transactions,* show their interest in the fine arts. In 1668 John Evelyn, a founding member, published a translation of Roland Fréart's *Idée de la Perfection de la Peinture* as *An Idea of the Perfection of Painting.* One of the Society's aims in the early days was to create a history of trades and Evelyn, who was an active member, often contributed to it, writing articles about improvements made to the plough, among other everyday implements, as well as books on the history and practice of painting, engraving, and architecture.[2] The review of Evelyn's translation of Fréart's text in the *Philosophical Transactions,* in addition to giving an account of the book, encouraged readers to learn to draw, paint, and engrave for themselves.

All this is now represented in *English* with so much perspicuity, and rendered so weighty by every Period of the Excellent Interpreters addition, that it justly deserves high recommends, and will doubtless animate many among us to acquire a perfection in Pictures, Draughts and Chalcography, equal to our growth in all sorts of Optical Aydes, and to the fullness of our modern Discoveries. *Painting* and *Sculpture* are the politest and noblest of Antient Arts, true, ingenuous, and claiming the Resemblance of Life, the Emulation of all Beauties, the fairest Records of all Appearances, Divine or Humane. And what Art can be more helpful or more pleasing to a Philosophical Traveller, an Architect, and every ingenious Mechanician? All which must be lame without it.[3]

The reviewer sees drawing as a necessary adjunct to new discoveries and emphasizes the importance of drawing for the pursuits of Fellows of the Royal Society. Just as learning to draw was important in the education of the gentleman, so it was considered fundamental to the education of the naturalist, one of whose tasks was to create a record of his observations.[4] Such a record was both visual and verbal, with text and images combined to provide a more complete profile of the object of study. Similarly, drawing manuals which included intaglio printed images provided those who sought to draw nature with detailed instructions and extensive visual material, providing the would-be draftsman with both textual and visual instruction.

Early modern students were taught to draw by looking at prints with the result that their drawings tended to look like prints. In his article on the authority of prints, William MacGregor was concerned with their rôle in the education of young artists.[5] I would like to expand this to include the importance of prints in the education of naturalists. Although MacGregor focused primarily on early eighteenth-century France, I believe that the observations he makes about the place of prints in visual education was well established in the seventeenth century, as witness the burgeoning trade in printed drawing manuals aimed at the amateur learner.

In the only monograph on this subject in an English context, Ann Bermingham has argued that 'the scientific embrace of drawing at the end of the seventeenth century, in the form of scientific illustration, assisted in sanctioning drawing as a social practice, for it countered the Protestant suspicion of images and the belief that drawing and painting were frivolous and corrupting aristocratic pastimes'.[6] While she sees the growth in the production of 'scientific illustrations' as a step toward drawing as an accepted practice among gentlemen, I would like to suggest that it was the spread in the teaching of drawing and the publication of printed manuals that helped to make natural philosophers and naturalists focus on the printed images in their books. They had to be trained to see the world and to translate what they observed accurately and in a recognizable style. I take issue with her contention that learning to draw fell out of favour during the Civil War – I maintain that, on the contrary, publication of drawing manuals continued throughout the seventeenth century, from the later years of James I's reign, through the critical years of the Civil War and the Interregnum.

I take as my exemplar *A Book of Drawing, Limning, Washing or Colouring of Mapps and Prints*, first published in 1647 and later subtitled *Albert Dürer Revived*.[7] It shows us what drawing manuals taught and what visual source material was made available to those learning to draw. I choose it partly for its long publication history, extending from the first edition of 1647 at least as far as 1731 (the latest printing I have found) (see Appendix 1). I argue that the longevity of the publication is owing to its association with Albrecht Dürer (1471–1578), which its author was at pains to emphasize. It was the only drawing manual of the period to be repeatedly reissued over such a long period. In contrast none of the

Fig. 1. Frontispiece portrait of Albrecht Dürer, from *A Book of Drawing* (London, 1660).
(See Plate III.)

popular manuals of Alexander Browne (d.1706), for example, published
in the 1660s and 1670s, not even his *Ars Pictoria: or An Academy Treating
of Drawings, etc.* (London, 1669) went through more than two editions or
survived after the height of his career; yet he was well known in his day,
and his pupils included Samuel Pepys's wife.[8] Moreover, the content of
his books was quite similar to *A Book of Drawing*, but I would argue that
it was Albrecht Dürer's name and reputation which accounts for the
enduring popularity of *A Book of Drawing*.

Albrecht Dürer, though long dead, is made the book's source of
inspiration and a model for a method of learning to draw. His portrait,
as 'the very prime painter and graver of Germany' is used as the
frontispiece to all the editions of the book (Fig. 1). His reputation as a
great artist and observer of nature was well known in England during the
seventeenth century.[9] I argue that his name, rather than being the literal
source of instruction on how to draw, indicates a set of practices and a
method for learning to draw, which involved studying prints that offered
a systematic approach for those wishing to learn to depict nature. These
books were intended to be used by those who were learning on their own

without a drawing master and I argue that 'Albert Dürer' filled that rôle as he looked out from the beginning of the book.

This paper concentrates on the long publishing history of *A Book of Drawing*, tracing the use and state of the plates as they passed through the hands of a number of London publishers; then the content of the book is examined together with a scrutiny of its method of teaching the young gentleman how to draw. I shall discuss the book's sources and identify the numerous masters that the author makes use of and reproduces for the benefit of the young pupil. The last part of my paper will examine the importance of 'Albert Dürer' as the book's figurative patron and surrogate master. I will explore the way Dürer is used as a marker for a set of practices although he had no part in the source material for the book.

A Young-Mans Time Well Spent: *An Early Modern Drawing Manual*

At least ten editions of *A Book of Drawing, Limning, Washing or Colouring of Mapps and Prints, or The Young-Mans Time Well Spent* were published over the course of 84 years. The first edition was printed by Joseph and James Moxon for Thomas Jenner in 1647 and sold at Jenner's shop at the South Entrance of the Royal Exchange (see Appendix 1). Jenner (fl. 1618 – d.1673) is best known as a publisher of religious and political tracts and single sheet engravings by English and foreigner engravers. He published subsequent editions of *A Book of Drawing* in 1652,[10] 1660, and 1666. After his death in 1673, his shop, together with the plates of *A Book of Drawing* were bought by John Garrett who published further editions in 1679, 1685, 1698 and 1718.[11] Garrett's first issue of the text and plates, the 1679 edition, has the additional title of *Albert Dürer Revived*. Thomas Glass took over Garrett's shop in 1720 and continued to publish the *Book of Drawing* from the same address, 'at his Shop, as you go up the Stairs of the Royal Exchange in Cornhill'.[12] The latest edition I have found is that of 1731.

A Book of Drawing, under that title, first appeared in 1647, but its source, according to Arthur Hind, was *A Booke of the Art of Drawing According to ye Order of Albert Dürer, Jean Cozÿn and Other Excellent Picture-makers, Describing ye True Proportions of Men, Women & Children*, published in London between 1616 and 1620 by Compton Holland.[13] It is considered to be the first drawing manual in English, but little is known about its contents because all that has survived are two copies of the engraved titlepage, one in the British Museum and the other in the Huntington Library.[14] This engraved titlepage is an early state of the

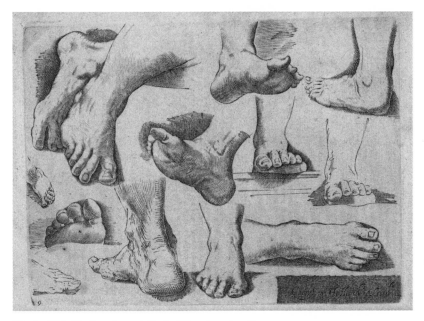

Fig. 2.   Life-like feet, from *A Book of Drawing*, plate 9

portrait of Dürer that appears in every subsequent edition of the book (see, for example, Fig. 1). The *c.*1616 titlepage is signed 'Compton Holland excudit', and it seems likely that Holland published at least some of the plates before his death in 1621; the one (Fig. 2) which depicts various life-like feet, for example, is signed 'Compton Holland excudit' in the lower right-hand corner. If we accept Hind's assertion that the whole book was published between 1616 and 1620, then the examples in *A Book of Drawing* would have been available in various forms for over 100 years, providing generations of amateur artists with instruction in the art of drawing.

The titlepage of the first edition of *A Book of Drawing* (1647) explains whom the book is intended for and what the author considers its usefulness for those learning to draw.[15] The subtitle, *The Young-Mans Time Well Spent*, makes it clear that it was an educational tool for young gentlemen and that learning to draw was not just an idle waste of time, but a most worthwhile pursuit. The titlepage promises the young man 'the Ground-work to make him fit for doing any thing by hand, when hee is able to Draw well'.[16] The titlepage goes on to state that the book is 'very usefull for all Handicrafts, and Ingenuous [ingenious] Gentlemen, and Youths', increasing the sense that this book is aimed at young gentlemen of leisure. The titlepage concludes with a moral Latin epigram, '*Infælix qui pauca, sapit spernitque Doceri*' which can be translated as '[He is] unfruitful who knows little and refuses to be taught'.[17] It emphasizes the importance of education for a useful member of society and that learning to draw is a part of the educational process. The titlepage gives the impression that this book will provide a young man with a useful occupation and prepare him for whatever lies ahead.

A Book of Drawing is organized to make it easy for the beginner to learn to draw by following the steps described. The author begins by listing the tools (pens, charcoals, leads, a feather, compasses) needed and explaining how each is to be used. He asserts his own and his text's authority by giving clear instructions on which tool to use for which task, recommending those which 'are the onely necessary ones' and explaining that the pieces of charcoal should 'have a pith in the middle of them, which is the best token to know them by' (2). He cautions that 'Your compasses are not to be used constantly, for they will spoyle you that cannot draw without them . . .' (2). In these early sections he is at pains to develop good working habits in his readers and to establish his text's credibility.

Having given a survey of the equipment needed, the first half of the book is devoted to taking the readers through the steps needed to learn how to draw faces, hands and feet, bodies, bodies in perspective, garments, and landscapes. The second half explains how to prepare colours for washing and the art of limning. The author must have intended the images to follow in sequence, as most of them are numbered in the lower left-hand corner.[18] There seems to have been no set order in which the plates appeared within the book as it varies between different editions.[19] Ideally, the images began with how to draw faces, then hands and feet, and finally complete bodies, according to the order of the text, training the mind's eye and the physical eye through the juxtaposition of text and image. The text taught the reader to perform the prescribed step and the plates showed him how to carry it out. In some cases image and text are on facing pages, the image illustrating the text, but in many of them text and image are unrelated. Whether in tandem or in parallel, text and image were meant to work together to teach the young gentleman how to see the world around him and how to record what he saw.

However, a number of the plates are self-explanatory, with a great deal of description engraved on them as, for example, that of a man standing with a staff, titled 'The proportion of a Man to be seene standing forward', includes a lengthy caption:

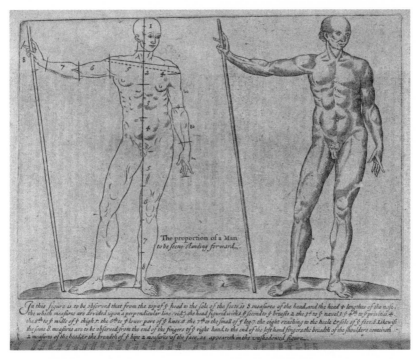

Fig. 3. 'The proportion of a Man to be seene standing forward', from *A Book of Drawing*,
plate 16

In this figure is to be observed that from the top of ye head to the sole of the
feete, is 8 measures of the head, and the head 4 lengthes of the nose, the which
measures are divided upon a perpendicular line vid the head figured with 1. ye
second to ye breasts, 2. the 3^d. to ye navel 3. ye 4th. to ye privities. 4. the 5th. to ye
middle of ye thigh 5. the 6th. to ye lower part of ye knee. 6. the 7th. to the small
of ye leg. 7. the eight reaching to the heele & sole of ye feet. 8. Likewise the same
8. measures are to be observed from the end of the fingers of ye right hand, to
the end of the left hand fingers: the breadth of the shoulders containeth 2 measures of the head, & the breadth of ye hips 2 measures of the face, as appeareth in
the unshadowed figure. (Fig. 3).

The caption not only provides a key to the labels on the man's body, but
also illustrates the text which explains how to draw a man in proportion
by dividing up the 'unshadowed figure' proportionally; the caption on
the plate describes the relationship between the parts and the whole: the
body 'is 8 measures of the head, and the head 4 lengthes of the nose'.
The image and the caption work together to teach the student how to
construct a perfectly proportioned body. The process described on this
plate was and still is the standard method for drawing the human body.

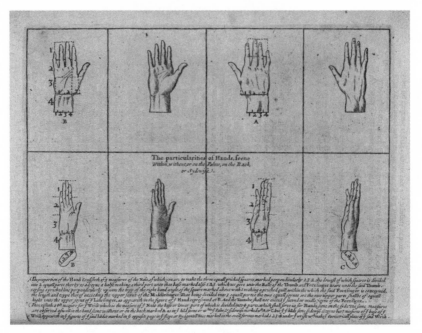

Fig. 4. 'The particularities of Hands, seene Within, without, or on the Palme, on the Back, or Sydewise', from *A Book of Drawing*, plate 6

Although only a few of the plates relate directly to the text, they still manage to teach different aspects of learning to draw; and where text and image do match, they reinforce each other to help in the learning process. For instance, in the section 'Of Drawing Hands and Feet', the author tells his reader to practice drawing hands and feet a great deal before progressing to drawing whole bodies, and refers him to one of the plates so that he will see how it is done:

> For the proportions of a hand, you have it sufficiently set downe in the print, by lines and figures, which shews the equalities of proportion in a hand, and how many equall measures there are in it, which you should endeavour to be acquainted with, that so you might know when a hand is well proportioned, with just and equall distances (8).

Here text and image work together for a complete understanding of 'the equalities of proportion'. The text, for example, explains that the hand is made up of equal measures, while the plate shows 'The particularities of Hands, seene Within, without, or on the Palme, on the Back, or Sydewise' (Fig. 4) and illustrates that 'the four equal measures in the height of a hand and three in the width', each being equal to

Fig. 5.   Views of hands working, from *A Book of Drawing*, plate 7

one measure of the nose'. Thus neither text nor image can stand alone.

The nineteen plates in *A Book of Drawing* may be divided into two categories. The first group consists of eleven diagrammatic plates showing how to draw hands and feet and the full bodies of men, women, and children. Heavily labelled, unshaded figures are paired with unlabelled, shaded versions of the same figures. Examples of this usage are 'The proportion of a Man to be seene standing forward' (discussed above) and 'The particularities of Hands, seene Within, without, or on the Palme, on the Back, or Sydewise' (Figs 3 and 4). The second category of images, which I will call life-like[20] show the diversity of the human form which the draftsman can expect to encounter. For instance, a plate of eyes, ears, noses, mouths, arms, and torsos shows the diversity of the human form in nature; another shows eight sets of hands performing different tasks (Fig. 5). These two types of illustration, the diagrammatic and the lifelike, combine to train the student in the fundamentals of drawing the infinite variety of nature's forms.

Considered all together, the nineteen plates in *A Book of Drawing* provide a variety of well-selected images to be copied. The author emphasizes that only approved masters should be used as models: '. . . which you must diligently observe, and you shall by little and little finde out, in good Masters workes which you should chiefly desire to imitate, and not botchers' (6). Good judgement is to be inculcated by studying illustrations from 'good Masters workes'. The images used are 'patterns' which should be scrutinised closely and copied exactly; the term is used eleven times (as the phrase 'according to your pattern' six times).[21] Success can only be achieved 'by imitating your patterne exactly' (12), which serves as the ultimate guide as to what the final drawing should look like; the final drawing thus should 'resemble the patterne you draw it from'. 'Your pattern' should be consulted to better understand how to show the mass of the body through covering draperies (14). In these instances the pattern is clearly another image and the young draftsman is to rely on the skill of others to perfect his own technique.

'Nature' is the ultimate pattern of all patterns for drawings of the human body, above even the 'good Masters works', and in the final, eleventh, use of the term nature is the pattern to be followed:

. . . yet must neither the one nor the other be drawne in such a posture as will not agree with the motion of nature, that is, to draw such a posture which a man cannot imitate with his naturall body, and so for any thing else whatsoever nature must be the patterne of all kind of drafts (14).

The student is warned that the various poses of the body must be kept in mind when drawing the human figure. Nature must be followed, within the constraints set by the pattern; fancy must not be given free rein.

The plates provide models for different types of drawings and help the student to imitate man and his 'naturall body'. They should be consulted in order to learn how to express the grace and stature of the subject properly. One of the plates shows a group of unrelated figures, one representing a type that the student should learn to draw.

. . . and so to make a Souldier, to draw him in such a posture, as may betoken the greatest courage, boldnes and valour . . . and so for every thing, that the inward affection and disposition of the mind be most lively exprest in the outward action and gesture of the body (12).

The plate showing a man in armour resting his head on his hand provides one example of how a master would represent the bravery and valour of a soldier. The student is encouraged to study the work of a master, not nature, because the master has done this for him.

Now that you might attaine to a skill herein; I would counsel you diligently to observe the works of famous Masters, who doe use to delight themselves in seeing those that fight at cuffs, to observe the eyes of privy mutherers, the courage of wrestlers, the actions of Stage-players, the intising allurements of Courtesans, and those who are led to execution, to mark the contraction of the brows, the motions of their eyes, and the carriage of their whole body, to the end they might express them to the life in their drawings and works (12).

Diligent observation of masters' works is a necessary precursor to the direct observation of nature. Close scrutiny of the work of 'famous Masters' is insisted on and students are advised to take note of 'the contraction of the brows, the motions of their eyes, and the carriage of their whole body', in order to learn to recognize these gestures.

Taken as a whole this slim volume provides both visual and written guidance in the art of drawing. The method depends on repeated copying of 'the works of famous Masters' before proceeding to draw from nature itself. The author realizes that the young get impatient and are reluctant to keep practising. His message is reinforced by an opening Latin tag, mentioned above in my discussion of the titlepage, about the joys of learning: '*Infælix qui pauca, sapit spernitque Doceri*' ([He is] unfruitful who knows little and refuses to be taught). This moral is matched with a closing rhyming precept on the necessity for patience and diligence to achieve skill in draftsmanship:

Be patient, thou that seekest for this skill,
By grace and art so mayst thou have thy will (40).

'Good Masters Workes': Identifying the Sources of A Book of Drawing

In its first (suggested *c*.1616) instance *A Book of Drawing* advertised itself as *A Booke of the Art of Drawing according to ye order of Albert Durer, Jean Cozÿn and other excellent Picture-makers*. Two named artists are given as the sources for this book: Albrecht Dürer (1471–1528) and Jean Cousin (*c*.1500–*c*.1560). We are left to wonder at the identity of the 'other excellent Picture-makers', but can assume that their work was deemed good enough to stand alongside Dürer and Cousin although they did not merit individual mention. Aside from the frontispiece portrait, there are no references to Dürer in the editions published between 1647 and 1660. After 1679 the book has a new beginning to its title, *Albert Durer Revived*. Jean Cousin is not mentioned by name in any of the editions published between 1647 and 1731. The disappearance and reappearance of Dürer's name in the title might lead one to assume that he was the 'good Master' consulted in the production of the plates.

However, this was not the case, instead the plates owe their largest debt to Cousin. In this section, I trace the sources, where possible, for the nineteen plates in *A Book of Drawing* showing the way in which the plates combine a range of images from a number of available sources.

First it is important to note that the illustrations from Dürer's *Vier Bücher von Menschlicher Proportion* (*Four Books on Human Proportion*) were known in England at least by 1598 when Richard Haydocke published a translation of Giovanni Paolo Lomazzo's *Tratttato dell'Arte de la Pittura* as *A Tracte Containing the Artes of Curious Paintinge, Carvinge & Buildinge*. Dürer's *Vier Bücher* was probably finished as early as 1523 but not published until a few months after his death in 1528.[22] A Latin version by Dürer's friend Joachim Camerarius came out between 1532 and 1534.[23] Lomazzo's treatise was first published in Milan in 1584[24] and although Haydocke at first had difficultly acquiring a complete copy of the work, he was eventually given one by a friend who wished him, in an inscription, 'every felicity in translating this author'.[25] In its original Italian, a portrait of the author was the only illustration in Lomazzo's book and although he called for images, none was supplied.[26] Haydocke fulfilled the promise of the text with woodcuts based on Dürer's treatise. As John Pope-Hennessy notes, Haydocke used Dürer's figures without attribution even though he preferred Lomazzo's theory of proportion to Dürer's.[27] He asserts that the Latin edition of Dürer's *Vier Bücher* as well as a French edition of 1557 would have been available in London in the sixteenth century.[28] Any number of editions, then, would have been available for Haydocke to use as a source for his illustrations.

The illustrations accompanying Lomazzo's theory on the proportion of man are directly related to those included in Dürer's *Vier Bücher*. The figure accompanying the section of Haydocke's translation concerning 'The Proportion of a Man of Eight Heads' replicates both the overall format of Durer's plate on the same topic and specific details.[29] The stance of the men in both images is the same: the men who are facing forward stand with their feet apart and their right hands behind their backs. Haydocke also adopted the detailed system of dividing the body into parts that dominates Dürer's work and also uses similar notations, such as the arc across the mid-section that ends with two pointing arrows. The woodcuts in Haydocke's treatise were not directly trans-ferred from the 1528 edition of *Vier Bücher*, as there are differences in the physiognomy of the men facing forward, but the hair- line in both the profile and full views shows a clear relationship between Dürer's illus-trations and Haydocke's, as the men in both images have a steep widow's peak and tufts of hair sticking up in the profile view. There is both a superficial connection between the images and a content-based relationship that clearly indicates that some version of Dürer's illustrations was available in London and used as a source by Haydocke.

While it is clear from this example that Dürer's *Vier Bücher* would have been available in London at the beginning of the seventeenth century, either in its original form, in a later edition, or in Haydocke's repurposing, the plates detailing how to draw the human body in proportion in *A Book of Drawing* do not rely on Dürer's example or a derivative of it. Instead they draw on Jean Cousin's *Livre de Pourtraiture*. In 1595 Jean Cousin, the younger (*c.*1525–*c.*1595), published, in French, 'The Book of Portraiture of M. Jean Cousin, Excellent Painter and Geometrician'.[30] Cousin, the younger, was following through with a plan his father had announced for a work on the human body in his *Livre de Perspective* published in 1560.[31] The *Livre de Pourtraiture* consists of 34 woodcuts with text on the facing pages that describe the images and detail how to construct them. The order of the images is fixed between editions and the reader builds up his skill by first learning to draw the head, the hands, and the feet before moving on to the torso, arms, and legs and finally full bodies. After each body part is presented and learned, Cousin provides the reader with directions on how to draw foreshortened versions of that part. The same is true for the whole bodies of differing shapes and sizes. The book provides a clear program for those wishing to learn to draw the human figure and each plate builds upon what was learned in the previous ones.

While the precise ordering of the images is not preserved in *A Book of Drawing*, eleven of its nineteen plates are copied directly from Cousin's *Livre de Pourtraiture*.[32] These are the eleven plates earlier identified as diagrammatic. A comparison of one of them in *A Book of Drawing* with its source in the *Livre de Pourtraiure* shows how closely Cousin's designs and text were followed (Figs 3 and 6). Comparison of the plate of 'The proportion of a Man to be seene standing forward' and Cousin's 'Pour la figure de l'homme veüe de front, ou par devant' shows that not only were the basic forms and structures copied, but also the minute details such as the placement of the man's fingers on the staff he leans on and the contours and shading of the ground on which he stands. The fidelity to Cousin's material extends to the caption on the plate in *A Book of Drawing*, which is a complete translation of the text page facing Cousin's image.[33]

Although Dürer is the artist most closely associated with *A Book of Drawing* over the course of its publication history, it is actually chiefly based on Jean Cousin's *Livre de Pourtraiture*. While Cousin's work may

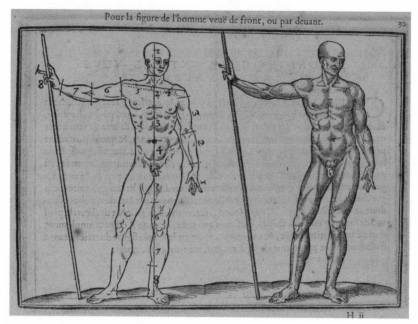

Fig. 6. 'Pour la figure de l'homme veuë de front, ou par devant', from Jean Cousin, *La vraye science de la pourtraicture* (Paris, 1635), p. 30. © V&A Images

itself owe a debt to Dürer's, he uses a system of proportion that is much simpler and easier to follow than Dürer's complex system. Cousin's system is based on an eight-part division of the body and omits Dürer's very detailed calculations. Instead of using images directly from the *Vier Bücher*, *A Book of Drawing* presents its young readers with a much easier system for drawing the human body in proportion.

While Jean Cousin's *Livre de Pourtraiture* was the primary source for the plates that show how to draw bodies and their parts in proportion, *A Book of Drawing* relied on Italian sources for the less diagrammatic plates. There are two main sources for the other eight plates – Odoardo Fialetti's *Il vero modo et ordine per dissegnar tutte le parti* (Venice, 1608) and the manual based on the drawings and teachings of Agostino Carracci, *Scuola perfetta per imparare a disegnare tutto il corpo humano* (Rome, before 1616).[34] Visual comparisons would make it appear that Fialetti's work was known through Joannes Janssonius's *Diagraphia*, which was published in Amsterdam in 1616. This book used Fialetti's *Il vero modo* and *Scuola perfetta* as its sources.[35] However, as we will see, it seems that the *Scuola perfetta* was available in London as the details in the plates that are related to it in *A Book of Drawing* are closer to the

Fig. 7.   How to draw a face, from *A Book of Drawing*, plate 1

original than the copies in the *Diagraphia*. The *Diagraphia* seems a likely source as Compton Holland had close ties to the Netherlands and it has been suggested that he was responsible for bringing the Dutch engraver Simon de Passe (1595–1647) to London.[36] In addition, John Astington has shown that Thomas Jenner had access to a great deal of visual material from the Low Countries, which he repurposed in his emblem books.[37] Based on my research it appears that Italian drawing manuals were known both in their original forms and in copies, and they served as sources, either directly or indirectly, for a number of the plates in *A Book of Drawing*.

Material from Fialetti's *Il vero modo* was used in two of the plates in *A Book of Drawing*. In both of these plates, material from multiple plates in Fialetti's work is combined into a single plate in *A Book of Drawing*. For example, in the plate that is usually first in *A Book of Drawing*, which shows how to use a series of circles to construct a face, three of Fialetti's plates have been combined into a single composite plate (Fig. 7). From this plate, the young gentleman learns how the face of a child or putto, either in profile or straight on, can be built up through a series of circles and a triangle for profile faces and a square for faces drawn from the front and how to draw a man's face in profile looking up and down at different angles. In this case the selection and assemblage of images was completed not for *A Book of Drawing*, but instead by Janssonius for *Diagraphia*. Two plates from the *Diagraphia* integrate the material from three plates in Fialetti. The plate from *A Book of Drawing* is made up of two plates from the *Diagraphia* reversed. Of particular interest is the addition of the square connecting the four circles of the child's face in the centre of the left-hand part of one of the two plates (Fig. 8). This square was not present in Fialetti's original. This example shows how the material in Fialetti's drawing manual was recombined in the *Diagraphia* and further reorganized in *A Book of Drawing* to provide the young draftsman with more detailed instructions on how to draw faces.

The same techniques of recombination and adaptation were used in the incorporation of material from the *Scuola perfetta*. There are four plates in *A Book of Drawing* that draw on material from the Carracci drawing book. In each of these plates, multiple plates from the *Scuola perfetta* are combined to provide the young draftsman with good examples to study. For instance, plate two of *A Book of Drawing* combines a plate that shows a young boy in profile with another of a series of sketches of faces in profile.[38] Plate three brings together two fairly complete images: one of an old man, thought to be based on a bust of Socrates and another of a young woman.[39] The two other plates in *A Book of Drawing* that rely on material from *Scuola perfetta* show hands and feet performing different actions (see Figs 2 and 5). These plates draw figures from a number of different plates and recombine them to fit the format of *A Book of Drawing*. Specifically, the plate of hands uses all of the images from one plate from the *Scuola perfetta*, maintaining the orientation of the images, and uses three hands from another plate in reverse (Fig. 5 and *Illustrated Bartsch*, nos 50 and 55). A comparison of the plate of hands from the *Scuola perfetta*, the *Diagraphia*, and *A Book of Drawing* shows that the *Scuola perfetta* was used as a source for *A Book of Drawing*. The plate in the *Diagraphia* has left out the artist's signature whereas this has been retained in *A Book of Drawing* (Fig. 9). Much like the use of the images in *Diagraphia* based on Fialetti's book, the *Scuola perfetta* is treated as a repository of source images from which the author/illustrator picks and chooses.

While I have discussed these three sources, earlier scholars have suggested other possibilities. After stating that Cousin's *La Vraye Science de la Pourtraicture*[40] was the main source for *A Book of Drawing*. Arthur Hind goes on to credit another source:

But nearest of all in detail are some of the designs by Abraham Bloemaert, engraved for a Drawing Book (*Tekenboeck*) by Frederick Bloemaert. These,

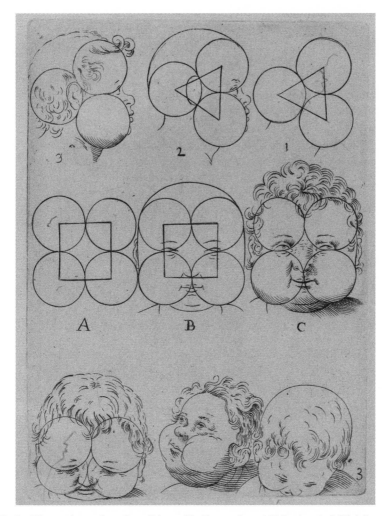

Fig. 8.   How to draw a face, from *Diagraphia* (Amsterdam, 1616), plate 3. © V&A Images

however, could hardly have appeared till after 1620, but Abraham Bloemaert's designs were probably well known by artists and teachers of drawing earlier than the engraved publication.[41]

Given recent research on Bloemaert's career and the publication of the *Tekenboek* this assertion seems unlikely. In his catalogue raisonné of Abraham Bloemaert's painting and prints, Marcel Roethlisberger states that the drawings that were eventually published in Bloemaert's *Tekenboek* were executed 'between *c.*1620 and 1650, mainly 1625–35'

Fig. 9.   Hands working, from *Diagraphia*, plate 15. ©V&A Images

and the engravings were completed by his son Frederick by 1650/56.[42] The *Tekenboek* contained only plates and no text. The images included are not complete compositions, but are instead individual figures or parts of bodies to help the student learn the vocabulary of the human form. Roethlisberger argues that the impetus for Bloemaert's publication was Crispin de Passe's 1643 drawing manual bringing together a range of examples by Utrecht masters.[43] De Passe's book also used images from Italian and French drawing manuals as well as Dürer's works. Comparison of the plates from *A Book of Drawing*, the *Scuola perfetta*, and Bloemaert's *Tekenboek* shows that while there are similarities in subject, the plates from *A Book of Drawing* are clearly closer to the *Scuola perfetta*.[44] A comparison of the *Tekenboek*, *A Book of Drawing*, and the works discussed here as sources for *A Book of Drawing* shows that the illustrations more closely resemble those in Fialetti and the *Scuola perfetta* than they do those in the *Tekenboek*. Therefore not only does the timing of the preparation and publication of the *Tekeenboek* prove problematic, but the visual comparison also shows that Bloemaert was not the basis for *A Book of Drawing*.

Three texts, Cousin's *Livre de Pourtraiture*, Fialetti's *Il vero modo*, as it was known through the *Diagraphia*, and the *Scuola perfetta* are the primary sources that were used to produce the images for *A Book of Drawing*. Together these sources provide both diagrammatic images of how to draw a body in proportion and more life-like ones of men, women, and child. These figures give the young draftsman a range of models and examples of 'good Masters workes' on which to base their own practice. *A Book of Drawing* then is an assemblage of images drawn from different sources that begin to educate the young gentleman in the practice of copying from appropriate models which is the foundation for the method of learning to draw proposed by the text.

'Albert Dürer Revived': Branding a Method

I hope I have shown that Dürer's book on human proportion cannot have been a direct source for *A Book of Drawing*, despite the use of his portrait as the frontispiece and his name in the subtitle. It is my claim that his name represents an early form of branding for a set of practices and a method for learning to draw (paradoxically learning to draw nature by studying prints). The image of a well-known Old Master artist is used as a surrogate tutor in a student's guide. Careful examination of *A Book of Drawing*'s images of how to draw figures in proportion shows that Dürer's methodology of studying and measuring individual bodies is not the model (see, for example, Fig. 3) A simplified method is employed and Dürer's scrupulous working methods are cited merely to lend credibility to a practical teaching manual. Far from 'englishing' Dürer, *A Book of Drawing* merely pays lip service to his method while relying on those of the Italian masters. But whereas the Italian books are collections of engraved plates without text, *A Book of Drawing* uses the structure of Dürer and Cousin's manuals, which combine text and image, for a teaching manual on drawing the human form. This combination stresses the connection between prints and drawings in learning to draw, as the text reminds the student to copy the prints provided before attempting to draw nature himself.

Dürer's pre-eminence is established by the caption to his portrait: 'the very prime painter and graver of Germany' (Fig. 1), although ironically, the portrait used is, according to Giulia Bartrum, based on Peter Killan's *Portrait of Albrecht Dürer* of 1608, which in turn derives from Johann Rottenhammer's copy of Dürer's self-portrait included in his painting *Feast of the Rose Garlands*.[45] This 'true portraiture' of Dürer then, is in fact quite removed from Dürer's original image. I would argue that the portrait is meant to provide a symbolic link with Dürer, and is part of 'The Dürer Renaissance', the term applied to the revival of interest in Dürer's work between 1570 and 1630.[46] Bartrum identifies this resurgence with the Continent; but I believe the use of his name and portrait in *A Book of Drawing* shows that England too was already alive to this renaissance; and the importance of this particular book for the history of art and art education is bound up with Dürer's popularity in the seventeenth century. I am suggesting, finally, that *A Book of Drawing* is evidence that the Dürer Renaissance had reached England by the 1640s and it was his name and reputation that account for the astonishing, long-lasting popularity of this book. *A Book of Drawing* provided the young gentleman with 'the Ground-work to make him fit for doing any thing by hand', combining diagrammatic and life-like images with didactic text all under the watchful eye of Albrecht Dürer.

Appendix 1: Editions of *A Book of Drawing* Examined

List of abbreviations:

BL: British Library
EEBO: Early English Books Online
Folger: Folger Shakespeare Library, Washington, DC
HEH: Henry E. Huntington Library
LOC: Library of Congress, Washington, DC
NAL: National Art Library, UK
NGA: National Gallery of Art Library, Washington, DC
YCBA: Yale Center for British Art

The following list contains the title and imprint for each edition of *A Book of Drawing* that I consulted in preparing this paper as well as the location of the copies consulted. If EEBO is listed first, then I have not viewed the physical copy from that collection. If EEBO is listed in parentheses, then I consulted the copy at the library where the original is held. The spelling and use of italics have been maintained from the originals.

1. A Book of Drawing, Limning, Washing or Colouring of *Mapps* and *Prints*. Or, The Young-Mans Time well spent. *LONDON*. Printed by *James* and *Joseph Moxon*, for *Thomas Jenner*; and are to be sold at his Shop, at the South Enterance of the *Royal Exchange*. 1647. YCBA.

2. A Book of Drawing, Limning, Washing Or Colouring of Maps *and* Prints: And the Art of Painting, with the Names and Mixtures of Colours used by the Picture-Drawers. Or, The Young-mans Time well Spent. *LONDON*. Printed by *M. Simmons*, for *Thomas Jenner*; and are to be sold at his Shop, at the South Enterance of the *Royal Exchange*. 1652. HEH (EEBO), LOC, NGA.

3. A Book of Drawing, Limning, Washing or Colouring of Maps and Prints: And the Art of *Painting*, with the Names and Mixtures of Colours used by the Picture-Drawers. Or, *The Young-mans Time well Spent.* *LONDON*, Printed by *M. Simmons*, for *Thomas Jenner*, and are to be sold at his Shop at the South Entrance of the *Royall Exchange*. 1660. BL (EEBO), YCBA.

4. A Book of Drawing, Limning, Washing Or Colouring of Maps and Prints: And the Art of *Painting*, with the Names and Mixtures of Colours used by the Picture-Drawers. Or, *The Young-mans Time well Spent.* *LONDON*, Printed by *M. Simmons*, for *Thomas Jenner*; and are to be sold at his shop, at the south entrance of the *Royal Exchange*. 1666. BL, EEBO (Folger), NAL.

5. Albert Durer Revived: or, A Book of Drawing, Limning, Washing or Colouring of Maps and Prints: and the Art of Painting, with the Names and Mixtures of Colours used by the Picture-Drawers. Or, *The Young-mans Time well Spent. LONDON*, Printed by S. and B. *Griffin*, for *John Garrett* at his Shop, as you go up the Stairs of the Royal Exchange in *Cornhill*: where you may have choice of all sorts of large or small Maps; coloured, of uncoloured, variety or *Dutch* Prints: as also Colours ready prepared and ground, to colour Prints with, and very good *Indian* Ink to draw withal, 1679. LOC.

6. Albert Durer Revived: or, A Book of Drawing, Limning, Washing or Colouring of Maps *and* Prints: and the Art of Painting, with the Names and Mixtures of Colours used by the Picture-Drawers. Or, The Young-mans Time well Spent. *LONDON*, Printed by *H. Hills*, Jun. for *John Garrett* at his Shop, as you go up the Stairs of the Royal Exchange in *Cornhil*: Where you may have choice of all sorts of large and small Maps, coloured or uncoloured; variety of *Dutch* and *French* Prints, and Prints done in *Metzo Tincto* ; very good *Indian* Ink to Draw withall; and all sorts of the best Copy-books; and *Cocker's* Tutor to Writing and Arithmetick, being a new and most easie Method, so easie that the meanest Capacity may understand it at first sight, 1685. LOC, NAL.[47]

7. Albert Durer Revived: Or, a Book of Drawing, Limning, Washing, Or Colouring of Maps and Prints: And the Art of *Painting*, with the Names and Mixtures of Colours used by the Picture-Drawers. With Directions on how to lay and Paint Pictures upon Glass. Or, *The Young-Man's Time well Spent. LONDON*, Printed by *I. Dawks*, for *John Garrett*, at his shop as you go up the Stairs of the *Royal Exchange* in *Cornhill*, where you may have choice of all sorts of large and small Maps, Coloured or Uncoloured, variety of *Dutch* and *French* Prints, and Prints done in *Metzo Tincto*, very good *Indian* Ink to Draw withal, and all sorts of the best Copy-Books, and *Cocker's* Tutor to writing and Arithmetick, being a new and most easie Method, so easie that the meanest Capacity may understand it at the first sight, and several sorts of Coloured Sashes to set before Windows [*c.* 1697]. EEBO (Folger).

8. Albert Durer Revived: Or, a Book of Drawing, Limning, Washing, Or Colouring of Maps and Prints: And the Art of *Painting*, with the Names and Mixtures of Colours used by the Picture-Drawers. With Directions how to lay and Paint Pictures upon Glass. Or, *The Young-Man's Time well Spent. LONDON*: Printed by *F. Collins*, for *John Garrett*, at his Shop, as you go up the Stairs of the *Royal Exchange* in *Cornhill*: Where you may have choice of all sorts of large and small Maps, Coloured or Uncoloured; variety of *Dutch* and *French* Prints, and Prints done in *Metzo Tincto*; very good *Indian* Ink to Draw withal; and all sorts of the best Copy-books; and *Cocker's* Tutor to Writing and Arithmetick, being a new and most easie Method, so easie that the meanest Capacity may understand it at first sight; and several sorts of Coloured Sashes to set before Windows. 1698. LOC, YCBA.

9. Albert Durer Revived: Or, a Book of Drawing, Limning, Washing, Or

Colouring of Maps and Prints: And the Art of *Painting*, with the Names and Mixtures of Colours used by the Picture-Drawers. With Directions how to lay and Paint Pictures upon Glass. Or, *The Young-Man's Time well spent*. *LONDON*, Printed for *John Garrett*, at his Shop as you go up the Stairs of the *Royal-Exchange* in *Cornhill*, where you have Choice of all Sorts of large and small Maps, Coloured or Uncoloured, Variety of *Dutch* and *French* Prints, and Prints done in *Metzo-Tincto*, very good *Indian* Ink in draw withal, and all Sorts of the best Copy-Books, and *Cocker's* Tutor to Writing and Arithmetick, being a new and most easie Method, so easie that the meanest Capacity may understand it at the first Sight, and several Sorts of Coloured Shashes to set before Windows. Where is also sold 3 half Sheets of black Lines to lay under paper, to help any one to write even, the Lines being of the Height of the Letters, 1718. LOC.

10. Albert Durer revived: Or, a Book of Drawing, Limning, Washing, or Colouring of Maps and Prints: And the Art of *Painting*, with the Names and Mixtures of Colours used by the Picture Drawers. With Directions how to lay and paint Pictures upon Glass. Or, the Young Man's Time well spent. *LONDON*, Printed for Thomas Glass, at his Shop as you go up the Stairs of the *Royal-Exchange* in *Cornhill*: Where you may have Choice of all Sorts of large and small Maps, coloured or uncoloured, Variety of *Dutch* and *French* Prints, and Prints done in *Metzo-Tincto*, very good *Indian*-Ink to draw withal, and all sorts of the best Copy-Books, and *Cocker's* Tutor to Writing and Arithmetick, being a new and most easy Method, so easy that the meanest Capacity may understand it at the first Sight; and several Sorts of coloured Sashes to set before Windows. Where is also sold three half Sheets of black Lines to lay under Paper, to help any one write even, the Lines being the Height of the Letters. M.DCC.XXXI [1731]. BL,[48] LOC, YCBA.

11. Albert Durer Revived: Or, a Book of Drawing, Limning, Washing, Or Colouring of Maps and prints: And the Art of *Painting*, with the Names and Mixtures of Colours used by the Picture-Drawers. With Directions how to lay and Paint Pictures upon Glass. Or, *The Young-Man's Time well Spent*. *LONDON*: Printed for *John Garrett*, at his Shop as you go up the Stairs of the *Royal-Exchange* in *Cornhill*, where you may have Choice of all sorts of large and small Maps, Coloured or Uncoloured, Variety of *Dutch* and *French* Prints, and Prints done in *Metzo Tincto*, very good *Indian*-Ink to Draw withal, and all sorts of the best Copy-books, and *Cocker's* Tutor to Writing and Arithmetick, being a new and most easy Method, so easy that the meanest Capacity may understand it at first

Sight, and several sorts of Coloured Sashes to set before Windows. Where is also sold 3 half Sheet of black Lines to lay under Paper, to help any one to write even, the Lines being of the Height of the Letters. [no date]. LOC.[49]

References

1. Others have noted that a wide range of amateurs were concerned with the art of draw-ing in the seventeenth century. See, for example, Kim Sloan, *'A Noble Art:' Amateur Artists and Drawing Masters, c.1600–1800* (London: The Trustees of the British Museum, 2000), pp. 11–18.

2. A representative article in the *Philosophical Transactions* is: John Evelyn, 'A Letter . . . Concerning the Spanish Sembrador or New Engin for Ploughing', *Philosophical Transactions* 5.60 (1670): 1055–65. On painting: Evelyn, *An Idea of the Perfection of Painting* (London: Henry Herringman, 1668). On engraving: Evelyn, *Sculptura: or the History, and Art of Chalcography and Engraving in Copper* (London: G. Beedle and T. Collins, 1662). On architecture: Evelyn, *A Parallel of the Antient Architecture with the Modern* (London: John Place, 1664).

3. Throughout this paper I have maintained the spelling, grammar and word choices of my seventeenth-century sources; none of these aspects has been modernized. 'An Account of Some Books', *Philosophical Transactions* 3.39 (1668): 779–88, p. 785.

4. I say young men throughout because in the seventeenth century these manuals were billed as being an essential part of a young man's education. It was not until the eighteenth century that drawing became a lady's occupation. Compare, for instance, chapters 2 ('Complete Gentlemen') and 5 ('Accomplished Women') in Ann Bermingham, *Learning to Draw: Studies in the Cultural History of a Polite and Useful Art* (New Haven: Paul Mellon Centre for Studies in British Art, 2000).

5. William B. MacGregor, 'The Authority of Prints: An Early Modern Perspective', *Art History* 22.3 (1999): 389–420.

6. Bermingham, *Learning to Draw*, p. 34.

7. As I will discuss in more detail later in this paper, the text is anonymous and there is no clue as to its authorship.

8. Samuel Pepys, *The Diary of Samuel Pepys: A New and Complete Transcription*, ed. Robert Latham and William Matthews, 11 vols (London: G. Bell & Sons, 1970–83) vol. 6, p. 98. Browne published three different manuals and only claimed *Ars Pictoria* as his own work. The other two were: *The whole art of drawing, painting, limning, and etching* (London: Printed by Peter Stent, 1660) and *A compendious drawing-book. Composed by Alexander Browne limner* (London: Printed for Austin Oldisworth, 1677?).

9. Giulia Bartrum, *Albrecht Dürer and his Legacy: The Graphic Work of a Renaissance Artist* (Princeton: Princeton University Press, 2002), p. 89.

10. In his *Descriptive Bibliography*, Howard Levis writes that his copy of the 1652 edition, 'has 40 pages of text and illustrations numbered from 1 to 40 (about 8 × 12 in.)': *Descriptive Bibliography of the Most Important Books in the English Language, Relating to the Art & History of Engraving and the Collecting of Prints* (London: Ellis, 1912), p. 25. Arthur Hind repeats Levis's account of the 1652 edition as unverified and states that it 'appears to differ from the later editions': *Engraving in England in the Sixteenth and Seventeenth Centuries: A Descriptive Catalogue with Introductions* (Cambridge: Cambridge University Press, 1952–64), vol. 2, p. 233. Based on my examination of

Levis's copy of the 1652 edition now in the Rosenwald Collection of the Library of Congress and my correspondence with Daniel de Simone, Curator of the Rosenwald Collection, I believe Hind misreads Levis's sentence to mean that the illustrations themselves were numbered 1 to 40 instead of the text pages (which are numbered 1–40 except that the plates are unnumbered so only every other page has a number). The 1652 edition therefore does not differ from previous or later editions in its contents or format. Daniel de Simone, e-mail message to author, 23 September 2009.

11. Antony Griffiths, *The Print in Stuart Britain, 1603–1689* (London: British Museum Press, 1998), p. 17. The inventory of Jenner's shop is to be included in a volume edited by Giles Mandelbrote of inventories of seventeenth-century printers and stationers. This inventory includes '18 plates for Albertdu[r]ers draweing book att 5s. per plate'.

12. Michael Hunter and Malcolm Jones, *British Printed Images to 1700 (bpi1700)*, accessed 2 September 2009.

13. Hind, *Engraving in England in the Sixteenth and Seventeenth Centuries*, vol. 2, pp. 233–4, pl. 134.

14. Bartrum, *Albrecht Dürer and his Legacy*, p. 89.

15. While this section considers the titlepage of the 1647 edition of *A Book of Drawing, Limning,Washing and Colouring of Mapps or Prints*, it should be noted that this text was reprinted (with additions) through the book's long publication history. I want to stress that although Jenner is often listed as the author of this text in library catalogues, I will not refer to him as the author in this chapter. In light of the fact that the text of the Holland edition of 1616–20 is unknown to us, it is unclear to me whether the text in the 1647 edition, and all subsequent ones, is Jenner's work, or Holland's, or some other anonymous author's.

16. Throughout this paper I am using the text from the 1652 edition at the Huntington Library, which is available as part of Early English Books Online (Wing (2nd edn, 1994)/B3705AB). I have compared this text with the 1647 and the differences are only in the typesetting, not in the content. References to pages in the text are given parenthetically following subsequent quotations.

17. George Shuffelton, 'Latin Epigrams'. *Codex Ashmole 61: A Compilation of Popular Middle English Verse* (Kalamazoo, Michigan: Medieval Institute Publications, 2008). The Camelot Project at the University of Rochester, accessed 10 September 2009.

18. Ideal order (titles taken from plates where available): 1) how to draw a face; 2) selection of sample heads in profile; 3) head of an old man and a young woman; 4) sample ears, eyes, noses, mouths, arms, and torsos (I have not found this plate with a number on it, but 4 is the only number missing); 5) 'The perticularities of Hands, seene Within, Without or on ye Palme, on the Back, or Sydewise forshorten;' 6) 'The particularities of Hands, seene Within, without, or on the Palme, on the Back, or Sydewise;' 7) hands performing actions; 8) 'To foreshorten feete seene forwards;' 9) life-like feet; 10) 'The proportion and measure of a Childe standing forward;' 11) 'The proportion of a Childe behinde;' 12) 'The proportion of a woman to be seene afore;' 13) 'The proportion of a woman standing backe;' 14) 'The Whole figure of Mans body foreshortened a little on the Syde;' 15) 'The Whole figure of Mans body foreshortened a litle & seene by the Sole of the Foot, the Back upwards;' 16) 'The proportion of a Man to be seene standing forward;' 17) 'The 3. whole Anatomique figures Before Behind & Sydewise;' 18) a collection of heads and figures; 19) a collection of standing figures.

19. The order of the plates was consistent within editions because the text pages went

through the press twice so that each page had type-set text on one side and an engraved plate on the other.

20. For arguments about use of the terms 'life-like' and 'from the life' see, for example, Peter Parshall, '*Imago Contrafacta*: Images and Facts in the Northern Renaissance', *Art History* 16.4 (1993): 554–79 and Claudia Swan, '*Ad vivum, Naer het leven*, From the Life: Defining a Mode of Representation', *Word and Image* 11.4 (1995): 353–72.

21. From *A Book of Drawing*: '. . . lightly draw the out-stroak, or circumference of the face just according to the bignes of your pattern, making it to stand fore-right, or to turn upwards or downwards according to your patterne . . .' (6); '. . . but onely make it at first but a bare circumference, turning this way, or that way, according as the pattern doth . . .' (6); '. . . always make your curle to bend, and turne exactly according to the patterne . . .' (6); '. . . then if you have done that right, part the fingers asunder, or close, according to your pattern, with the like faint stroake . . .' (8); and 'last of all draw the armes, and then the hands, either joyned to the body or separated from the body, according to your patterne' (10).

22. Walter L. Strauss (ed.), *Albrecht Dürer, The Human Figure: The Complete 'Dresden Sketchbook'* (New York: Dover Publications, Inc., 1972), p. v.

23. Erwin Panofsky, *The Life and Art of Albrecht Dürer* (Princeton: Princeton University Press, 1955), p. 270.

24. Ackerman lists four editions of the book that were published in Milan in 1584 and 1585. Gerard Ackerman, 'Lomazzo's Treatise on Painting' *The Art Bulletin* 49.4 (1967): 317–26, p. 317, see especially footnote 1.

25. Lucy Gent provides an account of the copy of Lomazzo's *Trattato* in the British Library (561*.a.1.(1.)) and translates sections of the Italian inscription from Thomas Brett to Haydocke. Lucy Gent, 'Haydocke's Copy of Lomazzo's *Trattato*', *The Library* s6-I 1(1979): 78–81.

26. Ackerman, 'Lomazzo's Treatise on Painting', p. 318.

27. John Pope-Hennessy, 'Nicholas Hilliard and Mannerist Art Theory', *Journal of the Warburg and Courtauld Institutes* 6 (1943): 89–100, p. 93.

28. Pope-Hennessy, 'Nicholas Hilliard and Mannerist Art Theory', p. 93.

29. Haydocke's book is available in a modern reprint published by Gregg International Publishers in 1970. Dürer's preparatory drawings have been published in Strauss. See Strauss, no. 31, for a comparison with the image on page 47 of Haydocke.

30. The Bibliothèque Nationale de France lists an edition that was published in Paris by J. Le Clèrc in 1595. I have consulted an edition from 1608 at the National Gallery of Art Library in Washington, DC that was also published by Jean Le Clèrc. I have found further editions that were published in 1618 (British Library), 1635 (National Art Library, UK), and 1656 (National Gallery of Art Library, Washington, DC).

31. Henri Zerner, 'Jean Cousin, (i) and (ii)'. *Grove Art Online*, accessed 9 November 2009.

32. Hind noted the connection between these two texts but did not discuss the link in any detail. Hind, *Engraving in England in the Sixteenth and Seventeenth Centuries*, vol. 2, p. 234.

33. The caption on the plate in *A Book of Drawing* reads: 'In this figure is to be observed that from the top of ye head to the sole of the feete, is 8. measures of the head, and the head 4 lengthes of the nose, the which measures are divided upon a perpendicu-lar line. vid. the head figured with 1. ye second to ye breasts. 2. the 3d. to ye navel 3. ye 4th. to ye privities. 4 the 5th. to ye midle of ye thigh 5. the 6th. to ye lower part of ye knee. 6. the 7th. to the small of ye leg. 7. the eight reaching to the heele & sole of ye

feet. 8. Likewise the same 8. measures are to be observed from the end of the fingers of ye right hand, to the end of the left hand fingers: the breadth of the shoulders containeth 2 measures of the head, & the breadth of ye hips 2 measures of the face, as appeareth in the unshadowed figure.'

The text facing Cousin's image reads: 'En ceste premiere figure veuë par le devant nous declarons les mesures qu'il faut observer depuis la sommité de la teste, iusques à la plante des pieds, qui sont en nombre de huict mesures de test, & la teste quatre mesures de nez, lesquelles huict mesures faut marquer sur une ligne perpendiculaire, dont la teste fait la 1. marque, la seconde iusques aux tetins 2. la tierce iusques au nombril 3. la quatre iusques aux genitoires faisant la moitié du corps 4. la cinqiemse à la moitié de la cuisse 5. la sixiesme au dessous du genouil 6. la septiesme au dessous de la ratte 7. la huictiesme iusques au talon & planted du pied 8. Semblablement les mesmes huict mesures s'observent depuis les extremitez des doigts de la main dextre, iusques à l'extremité des doigts de l'autre main senestre: la largeur des espaules contient deux mesures de teste, & à l'endroit des hanches deux mesures de visage, qui sont 6. longueurs de nez, comme il appert en la simple presente figure, où il n'y-a que la traict, qui nous sert d'ordonnance ou esbauchement, pour venir aux ombres & perfection de l'autre figure, y observant le mesme traict & mesure qu'à la premiere. Et quand aux particularitez, nous en avons declare plus amplement les proportions & mesures cy-devant.'

34. In her catalogue raisonné of the prints by the Carracci family, Diane DeGrazia Bohlin states that the *Scuola perfetta per imparare a disegnare* was never formally published. Diane DeGrazia Bohlin, *Prints and Related Drawings by the Carracci Family: A Catalogue Raisonné* (Washington, DC: National Gallery of Art, 1979), p. 410. The date given in most library catalogues for the publication of the *Scuola perfetta* is *c*.1620. However, given the inclusion of plates from this book in *Diagraphia*, which was published in 1616, this date is too late.

35. Jaap Bolten, *Method and Practice: Dutch and Flemish Drawing Books, 1600–1750* (Landau, Pfalz: PVA, 1985), p. 119.

36. Hunter and Jones, *British Printed Images to 1700 (bpi1700)*, accessed 2 September 2009.

37. John Astington, 'Thomas Jenner: English Emblems and their Models from the Low Countries', in *The Bookshop of the World: The Role of the Low Countries in the Book-Trade, 1473–1941*, ed. Lotte Hellinga (Goy-Houten, Netherlands: Hes & De Graaf, 2001), p. 169.

38. Diana DeGrazia Bohlin (ed.), *The Illustrated Bartsch. Italian Masters of the Sixteenth Century*, vol. 39 (New York: Abaris Books, 1980), nos 42 and 12.

39. Bohlin (ed.), *The Illustrated Bartsch*, nos 32 and 38.

40. This is an alternate title for Cousin's *Livre de Pourtraiture*.

41. Hind, *Engraving in England in the Sixteenth and Seventeenth Centuries*, vol. 2, p. 234.

42. Marcel G. Roethlisberger, *Abraham Bloemaert and His Sons: Paintings and Prints* (Doornspijk, The Netherlands: Davaco Publishers, 1993), p. 389.

43. Roethlisberger, *Abraham Bloemaert and His Sons*, p. 390.

44. For example, compare Figure 5 with *Illustrated Bartsch*, no. 50 and Roethlisberger, *Abraham Bloemaert and His Sons*, T60.

45. Bartrum, *Albrecht Dürer and his Legacy*, p. 89.

46. Bartrum, *Albrecht Dürer and his Legacy*, pp. 266–7.

47. The National Art Library's catalogue gives *c*.1675 as a date for their copy with the call number, G.30.A.1. The imprint, however, exactly matches the imprint for the copy at the Library of Congress, so I am listing this copy as being from 1685.

48. Based on the extant portion of the titlepage, I think that British Library 536.l.21.(2.) should be dated 1731.
49. Although the imprint of this edition is very similar to the 1718 edition, there are slight differences in the typography of the titlepage and imprint.

Building a Library: Evidence from Sir John Soane's Archive[1]

SUSAN PALMER

SIR JOHN SOANE (1753–1837) is familiar to many as a great architect and a great collector, who left his house in Lincoln's Inn Fields, London and his collections to the nation as a museum, to be left as nearly as possible as it was when he died.[2] Born the son of a bricklayer, he came from humble circumstances, but he had a good education at a school in Reading, and there is evidence of books in the family – school books which survive in the collection have inscriptions which show how they came to him from his brother and sisters.[3] Having gone into the family business on leaving school, Soane was later able to go to London to be apprenticed as an architect. He also studied at the Royal Academy Schools and at the end of his time there won a travelling scholarship which enabled him to make a two-year Grand Tour between 1778 and 1780.[4]

Amongst his extensive collections of paintings, sculpture and antiquities, Soane left a library of almost 7,000 books, and it is noteworthy that in the portrait he had painted by William Owen in 1804 (Fig. 1), two years before he was elected Professor of Architecture at the Royal Academy, he chose to have books featured prominently. In front of him is Desgodetz's *Les Edifices Antiques de Rome* (1682), open at the plate showing one of his favourite buildings – the Temple of Vesta at Tivoli. In the background can be seen the Galiani translation of Vitruvius (1758), given to him when he was in Rome by his first patron, the Bishop of Derry. At the same time the Bishop also gave him the Consul Smith facsimile edition of Palladio's *I Quattro Libri* (c.1775), with a magnificent binding bearing the Hervey coat of arms in gold on both the front and back boards. As was his usual practice, Soane duly recorded this on the flyleaf: 'From the Bishop of Derry to J.Soane, at Rome/ Oct^{r}1778'.[5]

Soane began the process of building up a library from the time of his return to London in 1780, his ability to do so being boosted considerably by the money he inherited from his wife's uncle and guardian in 1790, and the growing success of his architectural practice, which enabled him to build a country home – Pitzhanger Manor at Ealing –

Fig. 1.   Portrait of John Soane by William Owen, 1804. By courtesy of the Trustees of Sir
          John Soane's Museum

from 1800.[6] He patronized all the well-known London booksellers (see
Appendix 1) and also bought at many auction sales. A rough calculation
based on entries in his account Journal shows that he spent just over
£400 with Robert Faulder over the sixteen years between 1784 and
1800 and just short of £1,500 with Thomas Boone over the 27 years
between 1804 and 1831. His 'Estimate of Annual Expenditure' of
21 December 1802[7] shows that at that date he was spending £100 a year

on books. Sometimes one can detect patterns in his buying – for instance there is a high level of book purchasing around the time of his election as Professor of Architecture at the Royal Academy in 1806, when he was starting work on the preparation of his professorial lectures. In the mid-1820s he bought heavily, taking advantages of the many books for sale because of the depressed economic conditions. At other times his book-buying reflected practical needs, such as when, on 23 December 1813, he purchased from James Asperne for one guinea William Preston's *Illustrations of Masonry* (1812), just after he had been elected Grand Superintendent of Works to the United Grand Lodge of England.

It is not my intention in this paper to dwell on the scope of Soane's library or his motivations for assembling it.[8] Instead I want to focus on the vast mass of surviving documentation that underpins it – bills, receipts, sale catalogues, prospectuses and correspondence – which reveals what Soane was buying, from whom and for how much, and affords us insight into the London book trade at the beginning of the nineteenth century. The recataloguing of Soane's library to modern bibliographical standards is nearing completion and the entries include all this archival evidence.[9] Once the catalogue is complete it will be possible to perform detailed analysis and produce statistics about buying patterns and sources. This paper will provide an outline of the range of the archival evidence.

Soane understood the importance of keeping detailed and meticulous business accounts and this extended to his personal expenditure. His account Journals, which contain his transactions with his clients, include a chronological record of personal expenditure. One such entry for 2 March 1799 records: 'Paid Mr Faulder for Sir W. Hamilton's *Campi Phlegraei* £20.0.0'.[10] The reason for the high price of this copy is its sumptuous binding by Staggemeier and Welcher.

The Soane archive also includes an almost unbroken series of the small, marbled-paper-covered pocket memorandum books which he carried everywhere, in which he recorded appointments and daily expenditure. The entry for 1 January 1802 reads: '. . . At Taylor's subscribed to Repton's . . .',[11] and the receipt for that subscription survives,[12] as does a bill from Josiah Taylor which records for 8 July 1803: 'Repton's Landscape Gardening, balance subscription £2.4.0'.[13] Fig. 2 shows another of the many receipts for subscriptions to part-works in the Soane archive, this one for a coloured copy of the *Gallery of the Louvre*, dated 1802.[14]

Notes in Soane's account Journals and memorandum books also record the return of books not wanted. On 22 August 1799 he wrote in

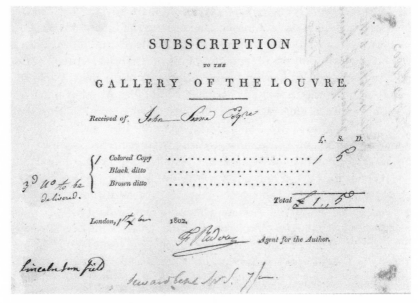

Fig. 2.   Receipt for a subscription to the *Gallery of the Louvre*, 1 December 1802. By courtesy of the Trustees of Sir John Soane's Museum

his Journal: 'Mr Bell, left at his shop Collins Ode, sent by mistake';[15] on 15 January 1807: 'Returned this day 2 vols of Pocock's Description of the East to Mr Faulder';[16] and on 22 July 1813: 'Joseph [his butler] returned to Messrs Boydell in Cheapside a large Book which had been sent to Mr S sometime since'.[17]

He made similar notes to keep track of his books when he moved them between his various houses or when he loaned them to people. On 22 November 1803 he noted in his memorandum book: '. . . Mrs S went to Ealing took 4 parcels of books making together 6 containg. the whole of the Scotch Encylopedia';[18] on 11 May 1806 he notes : 'At Ealing . . . brought from Ealing Pans. 2 vol, Desgodetz, Lewis's Palladio';[19,20] and on 19 October 1812: 'At Chelsea with Mrs S. brot away d'Aviler's dict d'architecture and delanvilles French dictionary'.[21,22] On 20 November 1800 he recorded: 'Lent the Revd Mr Sennett the first vol of Newton's Vitruvius for 3 or 4 days';[23] on 5 February 1805: 'Lent Mr Mylne "Stato presente degli edifice Siciliani" thin folio';[24] and on 4 September 1810: 'Lent Mr Hase Fontana's St Peters. NB Bishop of Asaph has Evelyn's Parallel'.[25] Surviving correspondence reveals that requests for loans from Soane's library came not just from friends and professional colleagues but also from strangers or more distant acquaintances seeking sight of copies of books that were scarce. On 3 December 1823, for instance, Lord Colchester wrote to him enquiring whether he had in his library 'the work of Louis upon the Salle des Spectacles at Bourdeaux, published at Paris in f[oli]o 1782', adding that 'the Book is not to be found at The British Museum, nor in The King's Library at Buckingham House'.[26] A similar, undated (but post-1831), request from an H. Billendentter of Lincoln's Inn, seeks 'a French work, the title of which I have forgotten but it is picturesque travels in Istria and Dalmatia, and contains some views of Pola'; he adds that 'It is not in the B. Musm.'.[27] It is annotated by George Bailey, Soane's clerk, '67 Voyage Pittoresque et Historique de l'Istrie et Dalmatie par Joseph Lavallee. Paris 1802, folio'. Both correspondents were seeking to consult the book in question *in situ*, rather than to borrow it.

Finally, Soane also bought books to give away and recorded these purchases in his account Journals and memorandum books. On 26 April 1815 he notes: 'Bought Mrs Soane a prayer book, & ordered the beauties of Shakespeare for Miss Patteson'.[28,29] A similar note on 8 September 1817 records: 'Gave John the 4th volume of Britton's Antiquities. Gave Miss Keate 3 vols Botarelli's dictionary'.[30,31] A correspondence with the Bishop of St Davids in May 1827 further reveals Soane's generosity.[32] The Bishop wrote on 8 May to say: '. . . that if you really do not want the Burman's Phaedrus (1727) which I yesterday saw at your house, when you were so good as to offer it to me . . . and if you will have the kindness to fix some price on it, or allow Messrs Payne & Foss or any other Bookseller you approve of to do so, and will permit me to pay you for it whatever the price may be, it will be a great pleasure to me to have the Book'. A copy of Soane's reply is appended to the letter in his own hand: 'Mr Soane is honoured with the Lord Bishop/ of St David's letter, & has great pleasure in being able to/ comply with his Lordship's request – Mr Soane/ met with the book by chance he paid £1.5.0/ for it, and at that price it is at the service/ of the Lord Bishop of St Davids. Mr S. has/ only to observe that his Lordship, as a relative of Lord Liverpool, would confer a favour/ on Mr Soane by doing him the favour to accept of the Book.'[33]

Printed prospectuses for new or forthcoming books so rarely survive that Soane's collection of some 200 titles has particular consequence, covering a range of works from the most lavish and important downwards. Sometimes such prospectuses are the only evidence for the proposed work or for a particular edition or variant. One particularly notable example is a proposal of 1813 for William Hazlitt's projected

History of English Philosophy.[34] The work was never published, but Duncan Wu has shown that this prospectus, given to Soane by Hazlitt when they became acquainted in 1818, reveals that the work came closer to publication than had previously been thought and that 'far from being an obscure non-event . . . [it] was well-known to numerous overlapping circles in London society . . .'.[35] Soane's copy of the prospectus includes two manuscript emendations in Hazlitt's hand showing changes to the cost and to the terms of the subscription. It also includes a list of all those who had subscribed by April 1813, with subsequent manuscript deletions of two names, again in Hazlitt's hand.

Another of the prospectuses in the Soane archive is for Ledoux's *L'Architecture Considerée* of 1804, sent to him by Josiah Taylor.[36] In the event Soane purchased the work not from Taylor, but from Dulau and Co. of Soho Square, the specialists in foreign books. Their bill, dated 13 December 1804, shows that he bought it as soon as it appeared, paying £18 0s. and becoming one of the first people in the country to own a copy.[37] The stub for the cheque on Praed's Bank with which he paid for the book also survives.[38] Later, in 1819, he had the work bound 'Russia bands Gilt', as a bill from Thomas Boone shows.[39]

Soane was a regular patron of Dulau and Co. Amongst his large collection of architectural drawings is a view of their bookshop – a water-colour done by one of Soane's architectural pupils *c.*1809 as an illustration to one of his Royal Academy lectures (probably to make a point about the use of the order on the façade) (Fig. 3).[40] Fig. 4 shows a bill from Dulau and Co. dated 1806 for a book by Gondoin on the Ecole de Chirurgie in Paris, published in 1780.[41] The bookseller's notes on the bill make it particularly interesting: '1° Messrs Dulau and Co. received the above only yesterday from Paris where it is exceeding scarce. 2° Palais Maisons &c dessinés à Rome – our correspondent has not been able to meet with one copy, but still hopes to find it [Soane had evidently requested a copy of this work of 1798 by Percier and Fontaine]. 3° The 2d volume of Le Doux architecture is not yet published'.[42]

A bill from Josiah Taylor shows that Soane eventually managed to buy a copy of the Percier and Fontaine eight years later on 3 November 1814, paying £3 13s. 6d.[43] Then, in 1818, Sotheby's sale of the 'Library of a Foreigner of Distinction Imported from Malmaison' included a copy (Lot 281) of *Palais Maisons* with hand-coloured plates, bound in green morocco, presented by the authors to Josephine Bonaparte.[44] Soane, with his great interest in Napoleon, could not resist purchasing this handsome volume.

The 1818 Sotheby sale catalogue is one of some 600 to survive in

Soane's collection. A number of these are marked up with the prices fetched by all the lots, as is the case with his copy of the sale catalogue of John Nash's Library of July 1835.[45] A bill from John Williams lists the 28 lots that he bid for on Soane's behalf, at a total cost of £57 16*s.*, including £2 10*s.* commission.[46] Unusually, in this case we also have a record of Soane's purchases made at this sale by his chief clerk, George Bailey, in a little marbled-paper-covered notebook, presumably in an effort to keep track of his 82-year-old employer's vast and ever-expanding library. Bailey described the books in more detail than Williams's bill does, listing Lot 378 as 'Lafitte Description de l'Arc de Triomphe de l'Etoile, in green morocco with silk linings and gilt leaves . . .', and this sumptuous binding is a rare example in the collection of the name of the binder appearing on the spine.[47]

As a young man, Soane did the rounds of the bookshops and the auction rooms in person. But as he got older he often employed someone to do so for him. The antiquarian, John Britton, who acted as his agent on many occasions, became a valued acquaintance and friend, and

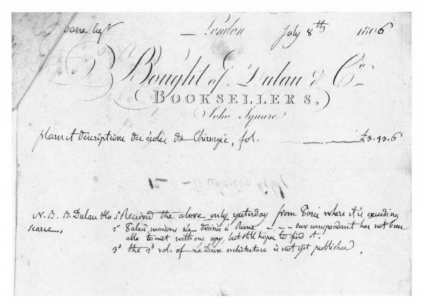

Fig. 4.   Bill from Dulau and Co., 13 December 1804. By courtesy of the Trustees of Sir John Soane's Museum

an extensive correspondence survives in the archive.[48] One of Britton's most celebrated purchases for Soane was a copy of Shakespeare's First Folio which had formerly belonged to the actor Charles Kemble.[49] Soane's copy of the catalogue of the sale of Kemble's Library held in 1821 includes manuscript annotations which reveal that the First Folio (Lot 1657) was purchased by James Boswell for £112 7s.[50] In 1825 Boswell's library in turn came up for sale at Sotheby's and it was at this sale that John Britton bought the First Folio on Soane's behalf for £105, as he wittily describes in the following letter to his friend and client:

June 4 1825
My dear Sir
By extraordinary good luck/ I just arrived at the death. The game was started when I/ entered the field, – tho' *hot* in the pursuit I was/ *cool* and collected at each leap, and not only was the/ first in, when caught, but immediately bag'd the/ prize. It is now sent for your larder, where it will/ long keep, be always in good flavour, and honor/ to the possessor. It will afford a perpetually standing/ dish on the table of genius & Talent – never create/ surfeit, but 'increase of appetite', by its almost/ miraculous qualities. Hoping to live long, *with you,*/ to participate in 'the feast of reason & flow of soul', which/ such a banquet is calculated to afford, is the sincere,/ & not unreasonable wish of/ Your confirmed friend/ John Britton/ Burton Street

The London booksellers occasionally competed for Soane's favour. In April 1825 Sotheby's sold the Library of Henry Fauntleroy, who had been convicted of forgery and hanged the previous year. Lot 587 in this sale comprised a handsomely bound extra-illustrated copy of Thomas Pennant's *Some Account of London* of 1805 in six volumes in which Soane had evidently expressed some interest to John Weale, who wrote to him on 11 April:

Sir

Since I had the honour of an interview/ with you yesterday morning, I have seen/ several persons from whom I have learnt/ something relative to the Pennant; which, should you make up your mind to bid for,/ would be of some guide. It is said that the/ City intend bidding for it for a new Library, a Mr Martin a man of great wealth at the west / end of the town intends to bid – Thorpe the/ bookseller has also a commission – I call'd this/ morning upon Dyer the printseller, who was/ employ'd for years in collecting drawings/ & prints for it, he is considered to have a/ good knowledge in these matters, & he gave/ it as his opinion that the book is worth to/ any gentleman 500 G^s – to the several/ persons I have spoken I have not in the least hinted that I knew of anyone who/ had an idea of bidding for it.// Should you make up your mind/ to bid for it & will interest me/ with the commission I will discharge the duty faithfully . . .'[51]

Perhaps rather unfairly, in the light of these diligent enquiries, Soane engaged John Britton to bid on his behalf, securing it for 650 Guineas.[52]

Soane hardly ever travelled abroad again after his return from Italy in 1780; but in 1819 he made a two-week trip to Paris and took full advantage of the opportunity to buy French books on the spot. One representative entry in his memorandum book for 3 September 1819 reads: 'Went book-hunting'.[53] Evidence of some of his purchases is afforded by a bill of 9 September 1819 from a Monsieur J. Salmon of No. 1 Boulevard Montmartre (Fig. 5).[54] It is probable that the survival among Soane's collection of sale catalogues of one of the stock of Firmin Didot of 24 rue Jacob can also be ascribed to the 1819 Paris trip.[55]

Bills dated the month after his return from Paris show that he had his book purchases shipped home: one for the necessary customs procedures for a box of books which had come over on the *Penryhn Castle*[56] (Fig. 6) and another for the delivery to Lincoln's Inn Fields.[57]

The trip to Paris in 1819 was Soane's last foray abroad, but a small number of bills indicate that he continued to order books directly from France. A bill of 1 September 1831 from a French bookseller, possibly Porquet (the signature is indistinct), details the purchase of eighteen volumes of the works of Rousseau, six volumes of Molière and 'Architecture de Sobry' for 303 francs 50 in total.[58] The bill is

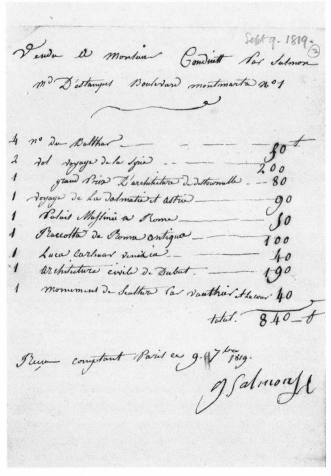

Fig. 5. Bill for books bought in Paris, 9 September 1819. By courtesy of the Trustees of Sir John Soane's Museum

accompanied by one in English from an unidentified agent, translating the whole into English pounds and adding 'Carriage, porterage, duty at Dieppe and Brighton, with case'.

Soane's library included a small but fine collection of illuminated manuscripts, the earliest being a thirteenth-century Bible, the evidence for the acquisition of which comes from a letter tipped in at the front of the volume – it was a Christmas present from his friend, Mr Herring of Norwich: 'Norwich Dec' 22 1829/ My Dear Sir/ I venture to beg/ your acceptance of a MSS. sent/ by this day's Mail as you expressed/ some

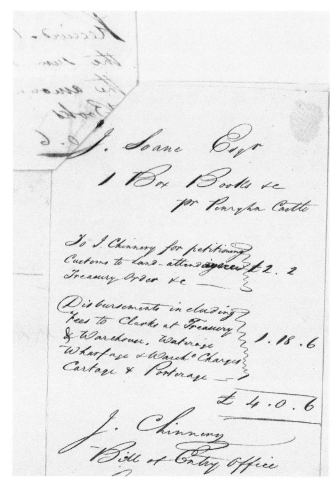

Fig. 6. Bill for customs charges for a box of books shipped from France, 16 October 1819. By courtesy of the Trustees of Sir John Soane's Museum

desire to possess it and/ in so doing I am the more gratified/ as it will fall into the hands of/ a gentleman who will value it/ according to its merits and place/ the same amongst his other/ valuable M.S.S.'

Several of Soane's other illuminated manuscripts came from the Duke of Buckingham (a client of Soane) in 1833 when financial difficulties forced him to sell many of his collections. Soane paid the Duke £735 for two books of hours and Cardinal Grimani's Commentary on the Epistle of Paul to the Romans with illustrations by Guilio Clovio, as is revealed by a copy of a letter to the Duke: 'Chelsea Hospital/

16 Septem^r 1833/ My Lord Duke/ I am honoured with your Graces/ letter naming the prices of the five Articles/ I wish to possess . . . The three last Articles I wish to possess and will pay the/ amount of £735 into your Graces banker or in any other/ way you please. The Grainger & Joan of Arc/ would far exceed my present means, & I must add/ however anxious I may be to possess the Grainger it/ would be impossible so thoroughly is my house already/ crowded, I should not be able to arrange them . . .'[59,60]

The details of this transaction are fleshed out by a letter of November 1864 from William James Smith, who had been Secretary to the Duke, to the Curator of the Museum, Joseph Bonomi.[61] After thanking him for a visit the previous Thursday he continues:

I find by reference to my Diary that it was in September 1833, that, on the part of the Duke of Buckingham, I sold to Sir John Soane, the Giulio Clovio, the Lucas van Leyden and another small illuminated book called the Marlborough MS. for £735. After having paid me for them, Sir John intrusted them to me for a week or ten days, in order that I might write for him a description of them . . . //Very soon after I offered the Collection of Cameos and Intaglios to Sir John for £1,000, and he paid me that sum for them, stipulating, however, that another small illuminated MS. should be thrown in to the bargain, to which I consented, this was probably the book which has some specimens of niello work on the cover.// In all my dealings with Sir John Soane, I always found in him the most princely liberality & kindness. I endeavoured to persuade him to purchase the Duke's extensive collection of British Portraits for £6,000, and I believe I should have been successful, but for the interference of the lawyers who thought they could manage Sir John better than I could.[62] This interference with me displeased Sir John, for he was afterwards so kind as to tell me that my zeal for the Duke's interest had not been properly appreciated, and therefore declined the purchase on the plea the he could not make room in his house for so many Portfolios.// On the 10th of October following, Sir John came to visit me at Stowe, and spent the whole day in going through the house, and making a particular inspection of some MSS. which he desired to purchase, but he declined paying the very large sums which were required for them, and I believe him to have acted wisely, for they were certainly not worth the large sums . . . asked . . .'

The archive reveals much about the workings of the book trade in early nineteenth-century London. One bill from John Williams of September 1830 is annotated: 'J W having found the above works marked in Mr Soane's Catalogue, has sent them for approval'.[63,64] Some 120 printed booksellers' catalogues survive in the collection, some of them dating back to the beginning of the nineteenth century. However, there is some evidence that their survival may be something of an accident. The greater proportion of them date from the late 1820s and

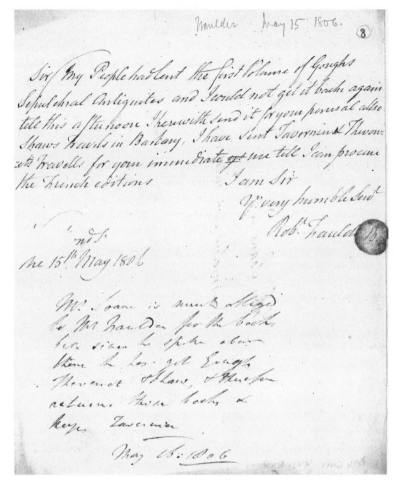

Fig. 7. Note from Robert Faulder to Soane, 15 May 1806, annotated with a copy of Soane's reply. By courtesy of the Trustees of Sir John Soane's Museum

1830s and are from firms that Soane rarely or never patronized. Many of them are unannotated and some are unopened. They were bound into volumes after Soane's death, though some retain the paper wrappers in which they were issued. It seems likely that they would generally have been thrown away and that this happened less as Soane got increasingly old and infirm.

A note from Robert Faulder to Soane, dated 15 May 1807 (Fig. 7) shows in a little more detail the relationship between bookseller and client.[65] It reads: 'Sir My People has lent the first volume of Goughs/

Sepulchral Antiquities and I could not get it back again/ till this after-noon. I herewith send it for your perusal also/ Shaw's Travels in Barbary. I have sent Tavernier & Thevon/ets Travells for your immediate use till I can procure/ the French editions.' Soane's reply is appended in his own hand: 'Mr Soane is much obliged/ to Mr Faulder for the books/ but since he spoke about/ them he had got Gough/ Thevonet & Shaw, & therefore/ returns these books &/ keeps Tavernier.' He paid 18 shillings for it, acquiring a French edition many years later in 1828 from Thomas Boone.

There are many letters from Soane's booksellers showing the good relationship he had with them and the deference with which such a good (though at times irascible) customer was treated. It was, of course, the job of the bookseller regularly to produce things with which to tempt his client. In a letter of 29 July 1824 John Weale wrote to Soane: 'Sir/ Mr Britton wrote to me stating that the Wiebelling/ was to come back – I have sent a person now/ for the purpose of receiving it should it be/ convenient if not he can call again./ Fearful of giving trouble, instead of sending,/ I have taken the liberty of informing you of/ the receipt of 'Count Cicognaris Fabbriche/ più cospicue di Venezia' Qt large folio with/ many plates, we have but just received it from Venice & should you wish a/ sight of it, I will immediately send it. . . .'[66] Soane eventually succumbed, paying £22.10.0 for the two volumes.

A month earlier, on 2 June 1824, Weale had written to Soane: 'Sir/ Upon looking at Mons Quatre/mere de Quincys work I discover'd/ that it cost us 9/15/-, we marked/ it in our catalogue 12/12/-,/ but I will sell it to you for/ the cost price. It was bought/ of the author about two years/ since, & I understand he charges/ now very high prices for them. . . .'[67]

Soane clearly, and unusually for his time, had a reputation as a prompt payer amongst the London book trade. In June 1818 James Moyes wrote: 'Agreeably to your request I enclose the receipt for Rees [Rees's Encyclopedia], and have below added two or three books, which were sent a short time ago, as I know you would censure me if allowed to stand over. . . .'[68] In similar vein John Britton, in a letter of 11 August 1818, wrote: '. . . As I know you dislike to keep open account I beg to state mine. . . .'[69]

Soane's generally cordial relations with those from whom he bought books is further borne out by the fact that he lent money to several of them, notably John Britton, John Weale, and James Moyes. Some of these booksellers also published (or rather printed) Soane's own works and his archive includes a large quantity of proofs for these various publications and also a number of copper plates that were used to produce the illustrations, besides the agreements for the work and the bills for the engraving, printing and binding.

Soane's occasional irascibility is well illustrated by a letter dated 26 March 1833 from S. Lewis and Co. of 87 Aldersgate Street:

Sir/ We were much surprised/ on being informed by our clerk that, on his presenting your subscription copy of our/ 'Topographical Dictionary of Wales', you/ refused to take it. In the publication/ of that work we have expended several/ thousand pounds, and as it is published/ exclusively for subscribers, we cannot/ suffer individual caprice to hinder the/ return of the capital which we have/ embarked in it on the faith of their/ signatures, but must insist upon the/ fulfilment of those engagements to which they are bound both in honour, equity, and/ law. We shall, therefore, feel obliged by/ a reply informing us whether or not it is/ your intention to abide by your contract;/ as, in case you persist in refusing to take/ the copy for which you have subscribed,/ we must, in justice to ourselves, place the matter in the hands of our solicitor.[70]

The letter is annotated with a copy of Soane's reply sent the following day:

Sir John Soane has to acknowledge the receipt of/ Messrs Lewis & Co's letter of the 26th Inst., and in answer/ thereto acquaints them that when he has given/ his name as a subscriber to any work it is not/ his custom to retract it: – the impertinence/ of their Clerk was the sole cause of his refusing to/ receive the Book and he requests it may be/ delivered to the Bearer, who will pay for/ it on receiving a proper receipt.

Soane's archive also includes a number of bills for bookbinding (see Appendix 2). A detailed analysis of the bindings has yet to be carried out, but preliminary investigation has revealed that Soane did not routinely have books rebound in a personal style, and that those, of which there are a number, in very fine bindings were purchased already so bound. A typical bill from Hood and McCullock dated 24 February 1826 is for: '. . . binding Annual Register 1804 to 1814 11 vols 8vo calf gilt to pat[ter]n 3/6 £1 13s'.[71] A bill of 22 June 1829 submitted by Edwin Hutchinson for a total of £16 3d lists 27 works almost all of which are described as being bound 'calf, Lett[ere]d, lined & grained & roll[e]d'.[72] There were more mundane tasks undertaken as well: a bill of 1822 from W. Boone includes the sums of one shilling and sixpence for 'Boarding Examiner Newspaper for 1821' and 4 shillings for 'binding Newspaper Scraps folio'.[73] Likewise, Edwin Hutchinson, in a bill of 29 September 1831, charged ten pence for rebacking and lettering '1 French Assistant 8vo', and resecuring its leaves, and added a sum of two shillings and six pence to the end of the bill for 'much mending of leaves'.[74] However, there are also a number of examples of slightly richer bindings. In November 1804, for instance, John Wingrave charged £2 8s. for binding Le Roy's *Ruines . . . de la Grece* 'Russia Gilt Atlas folio Bordered &c' and a further four shillings for 'Hot Pressing d[itt]o'. Similarly in 1822 T. & W. Boone charged £1 8s. for binding Soane's copy of Payne Knight's book on the worship of Priapus, which he had purchased from them three months earlier for £5 12s., 'Green Mor[occo] Gilt Leaves'.[75]

A bill dated 11 January 1803 from Paas & Co., engravers and printers of No. 53 Holborn, for printing 500 bookplates at a cost of £0 7s. 6d. is one of a number of such bills from different printers over the years.[76] Soane affixed bookplates to all of his books. Two versions of the bookplates exist, neither of which use arms to which Soane was entitled. The first features the arms granted to Thomas Some of Waversdon in the County of Suffolk, and the second also includes the arms of Wyatt used by Soane's wife's uncle's family.[77]

It is not only from papers in the archive that we learn more about Soane's library – inscriptions in the books themselves can also be revealing. Amongst Soane's books, as one would expect, are a number of presentation copies from authors, and some of the presentation inscriptions reveal further details about the book in question. A case in point is a copy of John Britton's *Remarks on the Life and Writings of William Shakespeare* (1814), in a handsome fawn morocco binding with a gilt tooled palmette border, in which, above the presentation inscription, the author has included the information: 'Only 5 copies of this sort printed/ none for sale.' Similarly, Soane's copy of *Jephtha's Daughter. A Dramatic Poem* by M. J. Chapman (1834) has a presentation inscription from the printer: 'From his grateful and obedient servant G. C. Levey of whose printing-press this is the first production.'[78] Levey was no doubt showing off his prowess in printing to Soane, who had by this date written several books of his own, a gesture which clearly paid off, as the next edition (1835) of Soane's *Description* was printed by Levey.[79]

Soane bought books on his travels around the country in the course of his work. One such was *Poems. By a Bird at Bromsgrove*, printed for Crane and Sons, Booksellers, Bromsgrove, which Soane inscribed on the front free endpaper: 'John Soane/ Bromsgrove/ 10 June 1815' and '0/4/0' [four shillings]. His pocket memorandum book records: 'Friday 9 June Left Butterton Hall at 2 in Mr S's carriage to Trentham, from thence in chaise to Bromsgrove, got there at 11.00 at night. Saturday coach to Bath.'[80]

Inscriptions on the flyleaves of other volumes in the library also give us rare glimpses of the taste of Soane's wife Eliza, one example being *The Peacock at Home; and Other Poems* by Mrs Dorset (1809), in which she has inscribed her name 'Eliz^th Soane' on the inside of the front board, followed by the date '1815' – rather poignant in that this was the last year of her life.[81] This volume is also an example of the many books in Soane's collection which have booksellers' printed advertisements bound in at the back, in this case a list of medical books published by John Murray. These advertisements survive in somewhat greater numbers than usual in Soane's library: they would often be discarded at a later rebinding. The March 1807 issue of *The Gentleman's Magazine* has bound into it three printed single-sheet advertisements for forthcoming publications.[82] The first reads: 'Just published, The rising sun, a serio-comic satiric romance . . . Finely printed on foolscap octavo, embellished with two elegant humorous coloured engravings, by O'Keefe. Printed for Appleyard's Wimpole Street . . .' The other two announce the publication of 'Madame Cottin's Popular New Novel, Elizabeth; or the Exile of Siberia', in one duodecimo volume, price 4s. 6d. in boards; and the publication 'in a few days' of 'Gabriel Forrester; Or, the Deserted Son. A Novel in Four Volumes'. Such ephemera were almost certainly slipped loose into the pages of that issue of *The Gentleman's Magazine* in much the same way as printed fliers are inserted into newspapers and magazines today, and would normally have been lost or thrown away.

It is fitting to end with a watercolour of Soane's Library by one of his pupils (Fig. 8), probably produced as a preparatory sketch for the first edition of his *Description* of the Museum which came out in 1830. In the same year, Charles James Richardson, one of two remaining assistants in Soane's office, started work on a complete catalogue of the library.[83] Finished in 1831, it is the earliest surviving catalogue of Soane's books.[84] It includes plans of the various rooms and locations around the house where books were kept, including the passage between the bedchambers on the second floor, showing the position of the bookcases in each space. The entries, some of which include corrections in Soane's hand, are arranged room by room in numerical order of bookcase and cite author, title, size (i.e. folio etc.), and place and date of publication.[85] At the back is a list of books kept at Soane's house at the Royal Hospital, Chelsea, where he was Clerk of Works, and lists of the books in piles on the tables in the Study and the Library. A companion, paper-bound volume, also compiled by C. J. Richardson, bears a label in Soane's hand on the front cover: 'LIF/ Library 23^d Jan.1831/ Books arranged under/ each Letter/

.PLATE.12

Fig. 8.   Watercolour view of Soane's Library at 13 Lincoln's Inn Fields, by one of the
pupils in his office, *c.*1830. By courtesy of the Trustees of Sir John Soane's
Museum

with references to the several Cases' – in practice, a crude subject index
to the library.

On 20 March 1821 the *Morning Chronicle* published the following
description of the collection: 'The Library is stored with almost every
known work in Architecture; no expence has been spared in procuring
the most scarce and useful, as well as the most splendid publications.
There is beside a very general selection of classical Authors, and some
valuable original manuscripts. The united collection is perhaps unrivalled, considered as belonging to an individual Artist, and the result
of his increasing application, talent, taste and liberality.' Twentieth-
century studies have demonstrated the importance of the library for the
evidence it provides of Soane's life and work. This article has sought to
show the important light the library sheds on the eighteenth- and early
nineteenth-century book trade, through the extensive archive that
underpins it.

Appendix 1: List of the London booksellers patronised by Soane[86]

James Asperne
Baldwin, Craddock and Joy
A. W. Barlace
Joseph Bell
Mr Besley
Black, Young and Young
Joseph Booker
Thomas Boone (later Thomas
  and William Boone)
Robert Bowyer
Boydell and Co.
John Britton
John Budd
James Carpenter (later and Son)
William Collins
John Cumming
John Curtis
J. Darling
Dulau and Co.
Thomas and John Egerton
Robert Faulder
Thomas Faulkner
Fisher, Son and Co.
R. Floyer
Hood and McCullock
Hurst, Robinson and Co.
Thomas King Jnr
Lackington, Allen & Co.
Edward Lawrence
Longman, Hurst, Rees, Orme and
  Brown

Edward Lumley
E. Macklew
Alexander Maxwell
John Maynard
John Miller
James Moyes
Mr Murphy
John Murray
Nornaville and Fell
Ogles, Duncan and Cochran
  (later Ogle, Duncan and Co.;
  James Duncan)
John and Richard Priestly (later
  Priestly and Weale)
Lupton Relfe
Thomas Roden
Rodwell and Martin
Robert Scholey
Josiah Taylor
Henry Torond
A. J. Valpy
Vernon and Hood
George Virtue
James Wallis
John Weale (later Priestly and
  Weale)
John White (later White,
  Cochrane and Co.)
John Williams
John Wingrave

Appendix 2: London bookbinders patronised by Soane[87]

Thomas and William Boone
Thomas Faulkner
Edwin Hutchinson
Christian Kalthoeber
Edward Lawrence
Leighton and Sons

Peter Low
Alexander Maxwell
Hood and McCullock
Staggemeier
John Wingrave

References

1. All references are to items in the archive of Sir John Soane's Museum unless otherwise indicated. I am grateful to my colleague Dr Stephie Coane with whom I have discussed aspects of this paper.

2. 3° Gul. IV, Cap. iv *An Act for settling and preserving Sir John Soane's Museum, Library and Works of Art, in Lincoln's Inn Fields.* . . . For further details of the Museum see Tim Knox, *Sir John Soane's Museum, London* (London: Merrell Publishers, 2009) and www.soane.org.

3. Pierre de la Ruffinière du Prey, *John Soane's Architectural Education 1753–80* (New York and London: Garland Publishing, 1977), pp. 12–14.

4. For full biographical details see Dorothy Stroud, *Sir John Soane Architect* (London: Giles de la Mare Publishers, second edition 1996) and Gillian Darley, *John Soane an Accidental Romantic* (New Haven and London: Yale University Press, 1999).

5. The 'e' was carefully added after he changed his name from Soan to Soane at the time of his marriage in 1783, a change he made meticulously in all the books in which he had inscribed his name up until that date.

6. Soane employed James Wyatt, a wealthy London builder, who had the contract for the City paving among other enterprises.

7. Account Book 1797–1803, Cupboard F/29. Sadly he did not continue the exercise of estimating or calculating his annual expenditure in later years. It seems to have been related to his purchase of Pitzhanger Manor as a country retreat in 1800.

8. This has been done before, by people much better qualified than the present writer – see Eileen Harris, 'Sir John Soane's Library. "O, Books! Ye Monuments of Mind"' in *Apollo*, April 1990; *Hooked on Books: the Library of Sir John Soane Architect 1753–1837*, Soane Museum exhibition catalogue, 2004 [out of print but a pdf available at www.soane.org/archive.html#hooked]; Nicholas Savage, 'Hooked on Books: Interpreting Sir John Soane's Library' in *The Private Library*, 5th ser., vol. 10:1 (Spring 2007); Margaret Willes, 'Building a Library: The Books of Sir John Soane', in *Reading Matters: Five Centuries of Discovering Books* (New Haven and London: Yale University Press 2008), chapter 5.

9. The records are currently being edited for online publication. New entries are added daily and just over 70% of the records have been published (January 2012) – see http://www.soane.org.uk/library/; the catalogue of The Soane Archive is currently in manuscript, but a programme of retroconversion and publication on the Museum's website is planned for 2012–13; for queries regarding the Library contact Stephie Coane (scoane@soane.org.uk) 020 7440 4253; for queries regarding the Archive contact Sue Palmer (spalmer@soane.org.uk) 020 7440 4245.

10. Journal 4, p. 145.
11. SNB 43.
12. Archives 7/2/24.
13. Private correspondence XVI.E.1.7.
14. Archives 7/4/6; Maria Cosway and Julius Griffiths, *Galerie du Louvre* (Paris, 1802).
15. Journal 4, p. 210.
16. Journal 5, p. 77.
17. Journal 6, p. 4.
18. SNB 58.
19. Between 1800 and 1810 Soane had a country house at Ealing – Pitzhanger Manor.
20. SNB 77.
21. Journal 5, p. 11.
22. The Royal Hospital Chelsea, where he was Clerk of Works from 1807 and had an official house.
23. Journal 4, p. 336.
24. Journal 5, p. 11.
25. SNB 100.
26. Archives 8/88.
27. Private correspondence XVI.H.91.
28. SNB 124.
29. Probably a member of the Patteson family of Norwich. Soane had met John Patteson on his Grand Tour and they remained life-long friends.
30. Journal 6, p. 261.
31. John was Soane's elder son and Miss Keate probably a sister or daughter of Thomas Keate, the Surgeon at Chelsea Hospital, a friend and neighbour of Soane at Chelsea.
32. Private correspondence II.S.1.1.
33. Lord Liverpool, the former Prime Minister, was a client of Soane.
34. Private correspondence I.H.11.2.
35. Duncan Wu, 'Hazlitt's Unpublished *History of English Philosophy*: The Larger Context', *The Library*, 7th ser., vol. 7, no. 1 (March 2006), pp. 25–64.
36. PC 53 (5).
37. Spiers Box (miscellaneous booksellers).
38. Archives 6/24. A number of cheque book stubs survive in the Archive, together with cheques returned by the bank after encashment – a practice only recently discontinued.
39. Spiers Box (Boone).
40. Drawings 27/6/8.
41. Spiers Box (miscellaneous booksellers).
42. Presumably in response to a further request from Soane. In the event this was not published in his lifetime.
43. Archives 7A/15/30.
44. A Mr Huybers. SC 12 (2).
45. SC 43. Soane went on adding to his collection right up until the time of his death on 20 January 1837.
46. Spiers Box (purchases through personal friends).
47. [R]EL P[AR] BOZERIAN J[EUNE].
48. Private correspondence III.B.1.
49. A copy regarded with horror by some because it is inlaid in larger paper, Kemble preferring his books to be like this so that he could write marginal notes. Sadly there are no marginal notes in Soane's copy.

50. SC 82 (10).
51. Spiers Box (purchases of MSS etc/9).
52. Private correspondence XVI.E.7.52.
53. SNB 154.
54. Private correspondence XIV.B.4.2. The bill is made out to 'Monsieur Conduitt' – the husband of Soane's friend and housekeeper Sally Conduitt. The couple had accompanied the 66-year-old architect on his travels.
55. SC 60 (4). Dated November 1817.
56. Envelope 1/45.
57. Envelope 1/46.
58. Private correspondence XVI.E.7.23.
59. Soane was Clerk of Works to the Royal Hospital, Chelsea, from 1807 and had an official residence there.
60. Spiers Box (Books and Illuminated MSS/7).
61. The letter is pasted into Trustees Minute Book I, 15 November 1864.
62. Presumably the Grainger referred to in Soane's letter quoted above.
63. Archives 7/14/33.
64. This is quite a late example, but there are many similar ones from earlier years.
65. Private correspondence XVI.F.8.
66. Archives 7/22/27.
67. Archives 16/12/71.
68. Private correspondence XVI.E.3.5.
69. Private correspondence XVI.E.3.8.
70. Private correspondence XVI.F.12.
71. Private correspondence XVI.E.6.3.
72. Private correspondence XVI.E.6.29.
73. Soane kept a series of albums of newspaper cuttings.
74. Private correspondence XVI.E.7.13.
75. Private correspondence XVI.E.4.5–6.
76. Archives 7/4/6.
77. Report from J. P. Brook-Little of the College of Arms, 24 May 1989.
78. George Levey, part of the firm of Levey, Robson and Franklyn, listed at 46 St Martin's Lane 1835–39 (William B. Todd, *A Directory of Printers and others in Allied Trades London and Vicinity 1800–1840*, London: The Printing Historical Society, 1972).
79. I am grateful to Robin Myers for this observation.
80. SNB 125. 'Mr S' was Thomas Swinnerton, a client, of Butterton, Staffordshire.
81. She died on 22 November 1815.
82. PC 14 (2).
83. The entry in the office Day Book for 17 August 1830 shows that he began 'Making rough catalogue of Mr Soane's Library'.
84. The earliest reference in Soane's notes to cataloguing his books dates from 1783, work carried out in connection with his imminent move to No. 12 Lincoln's Inn Fields. There are several subsequent references to catalogues being compiled.
85. The bookcases and drawers are numbered and lettered on small ivory disks.
86. Appendices 1 and 2 are based on surviving bills and correspondence, entries in his memorandum books and account Journals, printed catalogues and notes in the books themselves.
87. This list includes some booksellers who offered bookbinding as part of their service but farmed the work out.

Colour Printing and Design Reform:
Owen Jones and the Birth of Chromolithography

ABRAHAM THOMAS

OWEN JONES (Fig. 1), architect and designer, was also a passionate educator, theorist and one of the nineteenth century's leading protagonists within the design reform movement. Through his valuable work in the 1851 Great Exhibition and in the Government School of Design he was a leading figure in the foundation of the South Kensington Museum, later to become the Victoria & Albert Museum. Through his publication on the decoration at the Alhambra and his design sourcebook, *The Grammar of Ornament*, Jones became known as an expert on Islamic design, as well as a pioneer in drawing upon observed models of flat-patterning, abstraction and geometry, in the pursuit of a modern style for Victorian Britain. In this essay I shall describe the vital role that book publishing played in his career as a designer and will explain how his parallel practice of book illumination, through the relatively new technique of chromolithography, became an important factor in allowing Jones to refine his crucial theories on ornament, colour composition and architectural decoration. It is a little over 200 years since the birth of Owen Jones, and it therefore seems a suitable moment to embark on the rehabilitation of the career and legacy of one of the often forgotten heroes of Victorian design. In the obituary in *The Builder* Jones was described as 'the most potent apostle of colour' and the Britain of Jones's early career was described as 'a land where colour was as much feared as the small-pox'.[1]

Jones grew up in a world dominated by the austere 'whiteness' of neo-classicism, and the notion of studying examples of architectural polychromy would have been a most tempting and exciting prospect for such a young, ambitious architect as Jones; although certainly a controversial one for early nineteenth-century Britain. Jones would have received early exposure to the idea of colour within architecture by the architect Lewis Vulliamy, to whom he was articled as an apprentice. Vulliamy had received the Royal Academy's travelling scholarship in 1818 and was one of the first British architects to visit the Middle East, most notably studying the polychrome Islamic architecture of the mosques of Constantinople.[2] Having completed his apprenticeship with

Fig. 1.   Preparatory study for mosaic portrait of Owen Jones, by Reuben Townroe, 1876
(P.14-1934). © V&A Images

Vulliamy and his studies at the RA schools, Jones immediately embarked on his own Grand Tour, beginning with Italy, Sicily and Greece. There had of course been earlier observations of colour within classical architecture, for example the late eighteenth-century travels of James Stuart and Nicholas Revett, from which they returned with reports of traces of pigment on Greek ruins – published as their four-volume Antiquities of Athens. These theories of classical polychromy continued with Jacques-Ignace Hittorf's restoration drawings of ancient temples in Sicily, in which he lavishly applied intense primary colours to entire façades. These bold re-imaginings of classical architecture were exhibited at the Paris Salon in 1831 and sparked considerable controversy and criticism. It was this same year that Jones arrived in Greece, *en route* from Italy and Sicily, and it was in Athens that he met the young French architect, Jules Goury. Goury had been assisting the architect and theorist Gottfried Semper, who was himself currently engaged in researching the possibility of colouring in Ancient Greek buildings. It was in this context of an exciting new appraisal of the history of architecture that Jones and Goury decided to head further south and explore the classical and medieval sites of Egypt.

Having seen the potency of coloured decoration in the Islamic mosques and tombs of Cairo, they then proceeded to Turkey where they spent much time exploring the architecture of Constantinople, before obtaining rides on French military ships and making their way to southern Spain. It was here, in Granada, where the splendour of the Spanish Islamic Alhambra Palace was to offer Jones and Goury the inspiration and sources required to provide a paradigm shift in the current thinking on design and decoration. Jones and Goury spent a full six months studying the decoration of the Alhambra in great detail, making meticulous paper impressions and plaster casts of virtually every surface of the palace complex. Some of these plaster casts still exist in the collections of the V&A today. Jones was fascinated with what he described as the 'infinite possibilities for invention of designs' that he saw in the Alhambra tilework. He and Goury made numerous drawings, to analyse the remarkable intricacy of the Islamic systems of flat-patterning and tessellation (Fig. 2). Jones realized that understanding such designs lay at the heart of the Alhambra's magical qualities. It was an unprecedented survey in terms of the sustained attention to architectural detail, and the ambition to present the Alhambra as a masterpiece of Islamic design, rather than as a romanticized, semi-fictionalised relic of a fallen Islamic empire. In 1832, while Jones and Goury were still in Egypt and two years before their arrival at Granada, Washington Irving published

Fig. 2.   Drawings of tilework at the Alhambra Palace, by Owen Jones and Jules Goury, 1834 (9156N). © V&A Images. (See Plate V.)

his *Tales of the Alhambra*. This collection of essays and short fiction was a record of Irving's stay at the Alhambra in 1828, and certainly contributed to the continuing mythology surrounding the semi-ruined medieval palace. At first sight of Granada, Irving described it as 'a most picturesque and beautiful city, situated in one of the loveliest land-scapes I have ever seen'. Filling his notebook with descriptions and observations, Irving nevertheless felt that his writing would not do justice to the building, stating 'how unworthy is my scribbling of this place'. It is fair to assume that Jones and Goury experienced the same feeling of awe and aesthetic paralysis when confronted with the intoxicating system of decoration and polychromy on first entering the Alhambra. This perhaps explains why the two young architects felt that it was their duty to persevere with their detailed observations and to return to Europe with what would be the first ever comprehensive account of the architectural structure and design of the Alhambra Palace. Tragically, Goury died of cholera towards the end of their stay at the Alhambra. Jones brought his body back to France and returned to London determined to publish their work. The Owen Jones scholar, Kathryn Ferry, has discovered unpublished letters in the British Library which describe the beginning of Jones's mission to disseminate their Alhambra studies.[3] The letters were written to the Egyptologist Robert Hay in February 1835, by the architect Frederick Catherwood who had known Jones and Goury in Egypt:

I forgot to mention that Mr Jones has returned. He had the misfortune to lose poor Goury at Granada of the cholera which attacked him one evening at 7 and by 4 the next day he was a corpse. No less than 10,000 persons died in the town for no one was allowed to leave. They were 6 months prisoners in the Alhambra and have made without exception the most beautiful drawings of that palace I ever saw in my life. They will probably be bought and published by the French Government which is in treaty for them. Jones will have them in his possession for 4 or 5 months and they are then to go back to France. Coste's work is nearly out and I understand from Mr Jones that it is very beautiful. The French Government are publishing for him.

The work which Catherwood refers to at the end of this quotation is Pascal Coste's *Architecture Arabe ou Monuments Du Kaire* which was published in Paris in 1839.[4] Coste was an architect employed by the governor of Egypt, Muhammad Ali, between 1817 and 1827, to design and oversee various constructions (Fig. 3). Coste had exhibited his Cairo drawings at the 1831 Paris Salon – the same year that Hittorf had exhibited his controversial restorations of polychrome Ancient Greek temples. As was also the case with Jones and Goury, Coste failed to get

Fig. 3.   Drawing for *Architecture Arabe ou Monuments du Kaire*, by Pascal Coste, *c.*1820
(SD.272:32). © V&A Images. (See Plate VI.)

support from the French Government to publish these important architectural drawings, and after a lengthy series of complex negotiations
ended up publishing them himself. The trials and tribulations experienced by Coste would prove to be similar to those experienced by Jones
during his prolonged, and costly, campaign to publish his Alhambra
drawings. James Cavanagh Murphy's *The Arabian Antiquities of Spain*,
published in 1815, is considered the first important study of Islamic
architecture to have appeared in Britain. It was, however, criticized by
contemporary reviewers for its inaccuracies and for its liberal treatment
of some of the finer details of the Islamic decoration. In contrast, Jones
and Goury's publication of their Alhambra studies was intended to be
a faithful reproduction of the splendour and beauty of the Nasrid
Empire's most important built legacy. It is a testament to Jones and
Goury's dedication to the project that their two-volume publication,
published more than 150 years ago, still represents the most accurate
record of the Alhambra's decoration ever created, and is still used by
architects, structural engineers, conservators and restorers who are
involved with the significant refurbishment works at the Alhambra
Palace even today. It is probably no overstatement to say that their

Alhambra publication remains one of the most important books ever published on Islamic architecture and design. As an indication of his passion for the project – in the preface Jones included an excerpt from Victor Hugo's *Les Orientales*, describing the Alhambra as a 'palace that genius has gilded like a dream and filled with harmony'. Following Goury's premature demise, Jones understandably felt a specially zealous determination to do justice to the decoration at the Alhambra, and was soon investigating various methods of printing their extensive studies.

Jones's monumental publication, *Plans, Elevations, Sections and Details of the Alhambra*, was eventually published in two volumes and twelve parts between 1836 and 1845, and revolutionized colour printing. It represented a landmark in publishing, being the first book fully to exploit the potential of printing using the relatively new technique of chromolithography on a sustained level. Not only was this project significant in the history of colour printing but it was also a milestone in the history of architectural books, setting new standards in terms of communication and accuracy of details (Fig. 4). It is also important to keep sight of the fact that Jones was embarking on his great printing experiment at a time of revolution and reform in the world of design and architectural education. The Architectural Society and the Institute of British Architects (later to become the RIBA) had recently been founded, Sir John Soane's house and collections had recently been given to the nation, and various Acts of Parliament had contributed to the debate on issues of manufacturing standards and industry competitiveness with other nations – most notably leading to the establishment of the Government Schools of Design. It was against this background of renewal that Jones set himself the task of producing a book which looked to the Islamic world for inspiration and would provide a source of new models and principles for students of architecture and design. Sotheby's sale catalogue of Jones's library the year after his death, in 1875, shows that he owned a copy of Alois Senefelder's *A Complete Course of Lithography*, 1819.[5] In his text, Senefelder admitted that he had not yet perfected the technique of mixing coloured inks, indicating a particular problem with mixing greens and yellows. The artist Charles Hullmandel (1789–1850), who later developed a reputation for his tinted lithographs, was the first to pioneer chromolithography in Britain, and had visited Senefelder in Munich. Hullmandel's obituary in *The Builder* dates to 1822 his first attempt at printing in colour which, the obituary goes on to state, 'he carried to considerable perfection'. Kathryn Ferry has suggested that this may refer to George Hoskins's *Travels in Ethiopia*, published by Longman & Co. in 1835, and which included four

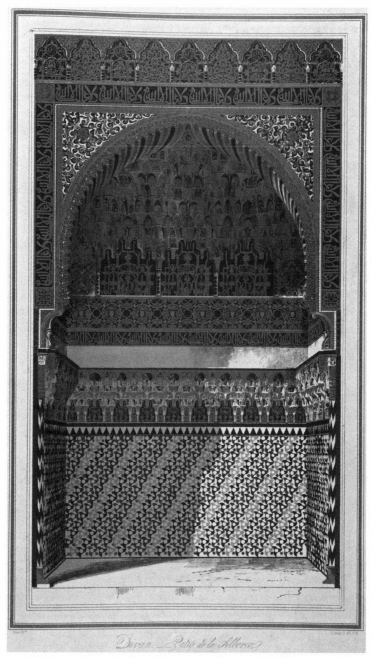

Fig. 4.   Plate from *Plans, Elevations, Sections and Details of the Alhambra*, by Owen Jones,
1845 (NAL: 110.P.36). © V&A Images. (See Plate VIII.)

chromolithographed plates by Hullmandel, reproducing a frieze from the royal tombs at Thebes.

The various technical issues surrounding chromolithography appear to have been overcome by 1832 by the printing firm Thomas De La Rue & Company, as indicated by their patent for the 'Manufacture of Ornamental Playing Cards', describes the process of 'printing the colours of playing cards from lithographic stones when the said colours used for that purpose are mixed with oil'.[6] It goes on to describe various techniques of printing with gold, silver and other metals. It was around the early 1830s that Owen Jones began working as a designer for De La Rue & Company. He spent 30 years working for three generations of the printing firm and designed an astonishing variety of products including playing cards, postage stamps, menu cards, scrap books and chess-boards. It is likely that this early exposure to the process of chromo-lithography provided the impetus Jones needed to pursue the various routes of experimentation required to undertake the publication of his *Alhambra* drawings.

It has long been known that Henry Vizetelly's printing firm was responsible for producing the letterpress and woodblocks for Jones's *Alhambra*, but what has not been quite so clear is the attribution of the crucial coloured plates. Kathryn Ferry's extensive research has done much to clarify some of the questions surrounding the genesis of the publication. As already explained, *Plans, Elevations, Sections and Details of the Alhambra* came out in two volumes over a period of almost ten years, from 1836 to 1845. Volume 1 consists predominantly of plans of the building complex, elevation views of key architectural features, structural details, depictions of the painted stucco decoration and some topographical views. Volume 2 consists of large-scale details of architec-tural elements such as arches, spandrels, beams, cornices, windows, porticoes and doors. Volume 1 was issued in ten parts, each consisting of five individual plates. Owing to notices of publication which appeared in periodicals such as the *United Service Journal*, we know that the initial five plates were issued in April 1836, the first two of which were black and white engravings. The remaining three plates however were chromolithographed, and therefore are the earliest coloured plates produced by Jones. However, as Kathryn Ferry has pointed out, the inscriptions on these three coloured plates differ between various copies of the *Alhambra*, showing that different printers using different tech-niques were employed. The evidence seems to indicate that two distinct print runs were being issued at the same time. The copies in the British Library and the British Architectural Library at the RIBA include inscriptions for these plates which state that they were drawn on zinc by Owen Jones and printed by Day and Haghe. Copies of the *Alhambra* in the Cambridge University Library and the Bodleian Library Oxford have inscriptions which state that these same plates were 'Drawn, Lithographed, Printed in Colours and Published by Owen Jones, London, 1836'. These inscriptions would seem to indicate an end to the exploratory collaboration between Jones and the printers Day and Haghe, and might also show that Jones was right in thinking there was no printing firm capable of producing chromolithographed plates to the standard befitting his Alhambra studies. It is also significant that these inscriptions do not mention the use of zinc plates – perhaps suggesting that that particular experiment with printing surfaces was a failure. These two assumptions are supported by a previously unpublished letter identified by Kathryn Ferry in the Cambridge University Library, written in June 1836 by Jones to his friend Joseph Bonomi, another colleague from his days travelling in Egypt.[7] In the letter, Jones relates that 'when my work was printed at the printers a most horrid waste of time, paper, and consequently money, took place'.

In response to an earlier enquiry from Bonomi regarding Robert Hay's intention to publish the drawings from his expedition to Egypt, Jones goes on to say that 'should Mr Hay have any intention of engaging in a similar undertaking then I should advise him to have no connexion with printers from the beginning . . . no printer will give his undivided attention to a single work and in this case it is absolutely necessary'. This was clearly an indication of Jones's intention to take on the research and printing of the *Alhambra* volumes himself. As to the matter of the technique used, Jones informed Bonomi that 'with regard to the employment of zinc in lithography I believe it is at all times but an indifferent material, but for printing in colours it is a total failure . . . It appears that the colours have a chemical operation upon the zinc'. Jones goes on to inform Bonomi that he had visited Paris to consult with the leading French chemists Michel Chevreul and Leonor Merimée, to seek their advice on the use of zinc, apparently to no avail. He also says that he has consulted Michael Faraday but these enquiries also came to naught. In Henry Vizetelly's memoirs, he describes how Jones boldly set out on his own to continue publishing his epic *Alhambra* volumes: 'Nothing daunted, Owen Jones took a suite of rooms in the Adelphi, engaged the best ornamental draughtsmen and printers he could secure and set up printing presses.'[8] Jones described to Bonomi how this improved system also meant redrawing his 'unfortunate' zinc plates on to stone. The significant effort involved in producing this majestic work was a true labour of love. Jones's personal financial outlay was also considerable. Denbighshire county records show that in 1837, while printing the *Alhambra*, Jones mortgaged the Welsh estates that he had inherited from his father for £1,142.[9] As one contemporary press cutting put it, 'the loss had been fully anticipated, and served only to give a zest to his future labour. It was in itself an education, and it gave him that supreme advantage in all vocations, a distinct speciality of his own'.[10] When he died Jones was still in possession of the stones, plates and blocks used during the nine years of printing the *Alhambra* – an indication of how involved he was in his great printing project. Sotheby's records for the sale of his library include 288 lithographic stones, 31 copper plates, 23 zinc plates and 26 wood blocks which were bought by Bernard Quaritch, who published a further edition of the *Alhambra* in 1877, three years after Jones's death.[11] Jones could rest easy in the knowledge that he had finally achieved his dream of publishing his drawings of the Alhambra – a tribute to his late friend and travelling companion, Jules Goury, as well as being a record of the six months they spent completing a pioneer survey of one of the most important examples of Islamic architecture in the world. The volumes were issued by subscription, which allowed Jones to earn money during the publishing process, and also helped to make it affordable for practitioners and students: those who might not have been able to find the money for the entire work in one payment. This was an important factor in securing the *Alhambra*'s potential as an educational resource. For those who could afford the volumes in one go, the first volume was sold for £21 and the second volume for £10. The price may have been high for some architects, but was modest compared to the 144 aquatints in Thomas Daniell's *Oriental Scenery* which sold for £210. In reviewing Jones's *Alhambra*, the Athenaeum stated that 'there has hardly, if ever, appeared a more magnificent work for the benefit of the architect or of the decorator', and went on to declare that 'the engravings can scarcely be surpassed, nor have any been before attempted on so large a scale, and of so laborious a character. The details, which are numerous, are drawn on stone, and printed in gold and colours by Mr O. Jones himself, and we need no further warrant for their truth and perfection.' It is interesting to note that despite the single-mindedness that Jones and Goury demonstrated in providing a faithful exploration of the nuanced and complex principles of Spanish Islamic decoration, many of the contemporary accounts of the publication seem to focus on its achievements as a landmark in colour printing and publishing rather than as a new source of inspiration for practising architects and designers.

As was revealed by his meticulous attention to the detail of the tilework at the Alhambra, contemporary developments in tile and mosaic design in Britain held a particular fascination for Jones. There had been recent experiments in the use of architectural tiles in France and Germany, mainly due to their appeal as a replacement for painted decoration, and for their durability against the dirt that often blackened urban buildings. Architects such as Pugin were interested in exploring the use of tiles in buildings as a way to replicate the aesthetic of medieval churches – a strategy loaded with various nineteenth-century social and religious agendas propagated by contemporaries such as John Ruskin. In contrast, Jones was interested in contemporary tile and mosaic designs in order to adopt models of tessellation and geometry observed first-hand in Cairo and Granada, thereby provoking a sense of modernity and potentially a new style for Victorian Britain – one which was not associated with historicized styles such as neoclassicism and the Gothic Revival, each with their own issues regarding nationhood and perceived cultural heritage. Jones collaborated with a number of tile manufacturers, and along with the architect Matthew Digby Wyatt, an expert on Byzantine mosaics, contributed to the promotion of Britain's emerging tile industry in the 1840s. Jones also provided tile designs for the industrialist John Marriott Blashfield, a pioneer in tile production. Blashfield had been a subscriber to Jones's *Alhambra*, and must have been sufficiently impressed with his accomplishments in that publication, as he then went on to commission Jones to design two houses for him at Kensington Palace Gardens in 1843, two years before the final volume of Jones's *Alhambra* had been released.[12] The year previously, Jones submitted a number of patterns which were chromolithographed for a book entitled *Designs for Mosaic and Tessellated Pavements* published by Blashfield in 1842 (Fig. 5). The book aimed to explore new possibilities for polychromy within tile design, but also included in the preface a summary of the latest techniques to be employed in tile-cutting and ceramic manufacture. It is worth bearing in mind that during the long gestation period for the Alhambra, it is likely that Jones would have put his printing presses into use for other publications for which he supplied chromolithographic plates during the 1840s. This would not only have made financial sense, but would also have allowed Jones to pursue a parallel printing practice contributing to the burgeoning gift book trade. This would have allowed Jones to expand on his theories on polychromy and flat-patterning by providing a design education by stealth to the rapidly-growing, discerning Victorian middle class.

As Rowan Watson has described, there were two opposing strategies

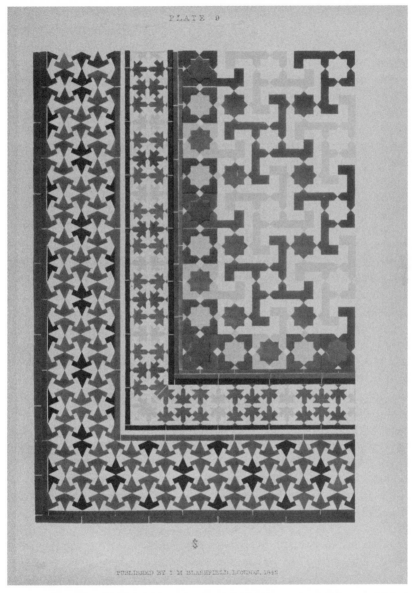

Fig. 5.   Plate 9 from *Designs for Mosaic and Tessellated Pavements*, by Owen Jones, published
by J. M. Blashfield, 1842 (NAL: 89.G.8). © V&A Images. (See Plate VII.)

when it came to the promotion of medieval illumination in nineteenth century Britain.[13] In one corner were reformers such as Pugin and Ruskin who promoted illumination as part of a campaign to combat prevailing attitudes and social evils; and in the other resided passionate design educators such as Owen Jones, Noel Humphreys and Matthew Digby Wyatt who looked to the technology of chromolithography as a way to lift illumination out of the hands of the connoisseur collector and into the living rooms and libraries of the middle classes, in an attempt to raise the standards of design and taste. Jones himself owned a number of illuminated manuscripts, including an early fifteenth-century Sarum Psalter, which passed into the possession of George Reid, a linen manufacturer from Dunfermline who amassed a large collection of illuminated manuscripts. Eighty-three of these, including Jones's Sarum Psalter, he donated to the Victoria and Albert Museum in 1902, where it now resides in the National Art Library (Fig. 6). Jones supplied chromolithographed illuminations for a number of gift books during the 1840s, 1850s and 1860s, collaborating with publishers such as Day and Son, John Murray and Longman & Co. These books ranged from religious books such as *The Song of Songs* and *The Preacher*, both published in 1849 and *The Victoria Psalter*, published in 1861, through to secular texts such as Thomas Moore's *Paradise and the Peri*, published in 1860, and based on a traditional Persian folk tale (Fig. 7). Jones was also keen to expand his designs beyond the limits of the book's pages, engaging himself actively with designing appropriate covers for his illuminated books. He developed innovative binding techniques using papier-mâché and plaster to, as he put it, 'enshrine the book like a casket'. He especially felt that the bindings of modern religious books failed to reflect the quality and sacred nature of their contents. This notion of appropriateness, fitness and utility within design was something he was to further explore with his later architectural work, especially that of his decoration at the Great Exhibition. The stunning bindings for *The Preacher* were made using deeply-reliefed metal plates to incise and heat-stamp the pattern into the wood, whereby the burned effect managed to emphasize the resemblance to weathered, medieval wooden bindings. Similarly, his relievo-leather binding for *Winged Thoughts*, published in 1851, suggested a carved wood aesthetic, but the delicacy of the technique also allowed him to emboss elements of his illuminations from the main text. A similar approach was being undertaken by Henry Noel Humphreys, a protagonist within the design reform circle around Owen Jones, and an expert in medieval manuscripts. His *Miracles of Our Lord*, published by Longman & Co. in 1848,

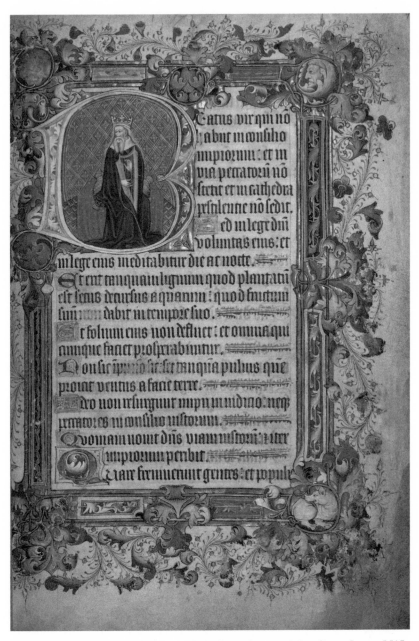

Fig. 6.   Leaf from Sarum Psalter, *c.*1410, formerly owned by Owen Jones (NAL:
MSL/1902/1683). © V&A Images

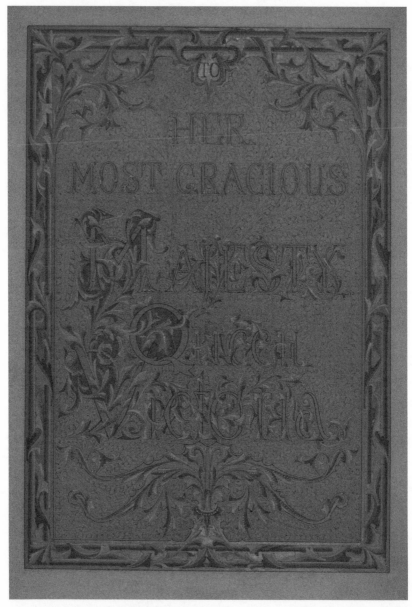

Fig. 7.   Plate from *The Psalms of David* (*The Victoria Psalter*), by Owen Jones, 1861 (NAL: SH.97.0004). © V&A Images

featured a papier-mâché binding which was based on a carved ivory cover executed in the twelfth century. Jones supplied the chromolithographed plates for Humphreys' *The Illuminated Books of the Middle Ages*, also published in 1848. As Rowan Watson has pointed out, when reading these books one is taken aback by the defensive tone in the prefatory texts which insists that illumination is not exclusively a Catholic art. Jones and Humphreys were keen to revive the art of illumination as a device which could be used to inspire higher ambitions within fellow practitioners. This desire to decontextualize decoration is a theme that we see Jones return to in his seminal treatise on design education, *The Grammar of Ornament*, where hundreds of samples of pattern and colour are taken out of their real-world contexts and applied to the flat page to inspire something brand new.[14] The architectural historian John Britton, together with Augustus Charles Pugin, father of the famed Gothic Revival architect, A. W. N. Pugin, had published his *Specimens of Gothic Architecture* in 1821. In a lecture given at the Society of Arts in April 1852, Jones stated that although he had little sympathy with the contemporary British craze for Gothic buildings, he did however respect the attention to detail and research into medieval craftsmanship which was involved.[15] Although the result of very different motivations and agendas, as described earlier, Jones would have appreciated the mutual single-mindedness in their respective ambitions to unlock the secrets of a great bygone age of design and decoration, and above all to maintain a resolute faithfulness to the original. Jones was not interested in explicit references to past decoration simply as a means of contributing to the revival of a historical style – he felt instead that the focus should be on identifying the principles held within these objects and buildings in order to learn crucial lessons which would allow contemporary designers to create a style unique and appropriate for the times they lived in.

Some of Jones's book illuminations may have also offered a space for exploration and experimentation in his wider design work, especially when concerned with his designs for wallpapers and textiles. This can be seen when comparing his illuminations for *Paradise and the Peri* with certain wallpaper designs that he completed for the manufacturers Jackson & Graham from the same period. Jones also produced a large number of furniture designs throughout his career for Jackson & Graham, and it is interesting to speculate on the parallel strategies that may have formed in his mind when designing the interior of a room and when designing the illumination for a book. When engaged in interior decoration, Jones would place the bold colours and ornament high in a room, in order not to clash with the furnishings, textiles, works of art on walls, and most importantly the inhabitants of that particular space. This might be compared to the strategy Jones employed when illuminating the borders of the printed page, ensuring that his chromolithographed plates worked to support and enhance the all-important text, but did not detract from it, or compete with it for visual punch. While studying the decoration of the Alhambra, Jones had been captivated by the epigraphs and sacred Qur'anic texts which adorned almost every architectural surface of the palace complex. These texts were often written in the first person, and so could be read as if the building itself was speaking. Owing to Islam's prohibition of images of human and divine forms, calligraphy provided a vital role in manifesting the voice and physical presence of prophets and God within buildings such as the Alhambra. Much of this text would be abstracted and rationalized within an architectural context to such an extent that it would sometimes be difficult to read and therefore could be experienced through the simple pleasure of following the sinuous curves of the Arabic text. Jones's close observations of this type of text as pure, constructed ornament is very likely to have had an influence on how he developed his strategies for book illumination upon returning to London.

The unification and synthesis of ornament which Jones explored and developed through his designs for gift books and other printing endeavours would have represented an important prologue to what was to become his most significant architectural project, the Great Exhibition of 1851. Jones had earned a worthy reputation during the 1840s through a number of projects: the exhibition of his unexecuted designs for the interiors for the new Houses of Parliament had received glowing reviews from the Athenaeum, and above all, his contributions to contemporary developments in tile manufacture and design had brought him to the attention of leading design reformers such as Henry Cole, who subsequently asked Jones to contribute articles to his fledgling *Journal of Design and Manufactures*. The landmark publication of the *Alhambra* was also a significant factor in elevating Jones's profile. The subscribers to the *Alhambra* had included prominent British architects, engineers and builders such as Thomas Henry Wyatt and Thomas Minton, but notably it also included a number of figures who went on to become members of the Great Exhibition Building Committee, including Isambard Kingdom Brunel, Charles Barry, William Cubitt, Charles Cockerell and Pugin.[16] Having witnessed Jones's immense talent for colour and decoration, through his observations at the Alhambra – it would certainly have seemed tempting to invite him to take part in this

Fig. 8.   Original design for Great Exhibition interior decoration scheme, by Owen Jones, 1850 (546-1897). © V&A Images. (See Plate IX.)

great project. Jones was appointed Director of Decoration for Joseph Paxton's vast iron and glass palace and was also responsible for the arrangement of exhibits, which had been drawn from nations far and wide in an attempt to showcase the world's best examples of decorative design and to inspire creativity and raise standards in contemporary manufacture. During his early travels Jones had been fascinated by the use of simple primary colours in the monuments of Ancient Greece and Egypt, the Islamic architecture of Cairo, and most significantly, the presence of similar colour schemes in the stucco plasterwork at the Alhambra. Jones had relished using bold, primary gouache-like blocks of colours when printing his chromolithographed *Alhambra* plates, and he would have welcomed the opportunity to create an 'illumination' on a much grander, architectural scale (Fig. 8). His paint scheme utilised only the primary colours: red, blue and yellow – and was carefully applied in strict proportions and with specific applications. For example, blue was applied to concave surfaces, yellow to convex surfaces, and red to the horizontal planes. Jones's intention was to use the contrasting colours in order to clarify the form of the building and to distinguish between the dizzying sequences of iron columns. Although initially receiving much criticism in the periodicals of the time, Jones's controversial paint scheme eventually opened to great acclaim, and was seen by six million people over just five months. Jones felt passionately that architectural decoration should be there to enhance a building's design, and should not exist as a surface layer of pattern on top of the structure. He felt that ornament should always derive from, and be founded upon, the principles of architecture. This principled stance can also be seen in much of his book design and illumination, where his applied ornament seems only to serve the text, and enhance its meaning – creating a unified, collaborative ecosystem of design on the printed page.

Soon after the Great Exhibition closed, the Government School of Design was re-located to new premises at Marlborough House, and Henry Cole was appointed Director. Cole, Jones, Pugin and others were asked to select key objects from the Great Exhibition – objects which they felt best represented principles of good design. These selections were then purchased and became the core teaching collections at Marlborough House – a collection which was also available to the public as the Museum of Ornamental Art. It was eventually transferred across London to become the founding collection for the South Kensington Museum in 1857, later to be known as the V&A. Jones delivered a number of lectures at the School of Design at Marlborough House but never joined as a fully signed-up member of the faculty. This is most probably due to his preoccupation with his next major project – the reerection of the Crystal Palace at Sydenham. Reconfiguring the building in south London gave Jones and others the opportunity to shift the focus away from examples of contemporary manufacture and towards showcasing the best examples of historical ornament and design, while still maintaining an international outlook. A number of Fine Arts Courts were conceived, allowing visitors to take a conceptual journey through time and geographical space, visiting courts dedicated to examples such as Ancient Egypt and Greece, medieval England, Renaissance Italy and, of course, the Alhambra.[17] In addition to recreating key examples of architecture, the courts also offered the opportunity to exhibit plaster casts of important examples of sculpture, friezes and other decorative fragments.

Rowan Watson singled out David Laurent de Lara as a leading figure in the popularization of illumination as a domestic leisure activity.[18] He has also identified an advertisement in the *Athenaeum* for 18 November 1854 which declared 'A limited number of ladies wanted immediately, to pursue the fashionable and lucrative arts of "illumination on vellum" and "Lithography" for objects at the Crystal Palace, intended for publication'. The Crystal Palace had opened just five months previously, and this advertisement was indicative of an ambition to produce a comprehensive colour-illustrated catalogue of the exhibits. The project came to nothing, but it is interesting to note that the vacuum created by the failure of this commercial printing endeavour may have contributed to the momentum required for Owen Jones's next great printing project: *The Grammar of Ornament*. Day & Son – the royal lithographers, and also the firm involved in the early attempts to print Jones's *Alhambra* – had previously published a highlights catalogue of the Great Exhibition.[19] The catalogue was released to the public in 40 parts, each part consisting of four plates, in fortnightly instalments, between October 1851 and March 1853. The postscript states that 'Shortly after the opening of the Great Exhibition the publisher called upon the author . . . stating his desire to demonstrate, upon a great scale, the capabilities of colour-printing as an auxiliary to industrial education. . . .' It was illustrated with 158 chromolithographs, 109 of which were produced by Francis Bedford – who went on to great acclaim as a photographer of British landscapes.[20] The other illustrators involved included Philip Henry Delamotte, who a few years later completed a photographic survey of the Sydenham Crystal Palace Fine Arts Courts, and Noel Humphreys – Owen Jones's collaborator in the revival of medieval ornament as a source for design education. In the years leading up to the Great Exhibition and immediately after it, Jones had been refining his theories on design, colour and ornament through various articles, and lectures at institutions such as the Society of Arts, the Royal Institute of British Architects and the Government School of Design at Marlborough House. Many of the design principles that Jones had expounded upon had become assimilated as part of the teaching frameworks at the School of Design, and had even been included as an educational appendix to the catalogue for the Museum of Ornamental Art.[21] It is likely that Jones felt there was a need somehow to make the exhibits at the Sydenham Crystal Palace accessible to a wider audience – to assist those design students and practitioners who could not visit London. Similarly, Cole, being the great self-promoter that he was, would have thought it advantageous to create something in book form which could act as a mobile design aid, in support of the objects at Marlborough House, to aid those students not able to attend lectures or visit the teaching collections. We know from Cole's diaries that as early as February 1852 Jones was visiting him armed with materials for *The Grammar of Ornament*.[22] These diary entries may very well refer to a sketchbook for the *Grammar* held in the RIBA collections which maps out an indicative chapter list and includes some samples of ornament in watercolour.[23] The intention was to produce a comprehensive account of the best examples of ornament from various periods of history, and from diverse geographical sources. The book was very much a parallel project to the Sydenham Crystal Palace: instead of walking through different Fine Arts Courts, readers of the book would educate themselves by leafing through various chapters, each dedicated to a different culture or period. The book was published by Day & Son in December 1856, and consisted of a preface summarizing Jones's 37 design propositions, followed by 20 chapters of ornament which offered a total of 100 chromolithographed plates.[24] Francis Bedford was again responsible for the drawings on stone. Jones's desire was that these samples of ornament would not encourage copying but instead would make the reader analyse the principles held within them, acting as a signpost to new design sources which might inspire originality. The material represented within the *Grammar* was drawn from previously published examples but also from collections that Jones had consulted in at institutions such as the British Museum, the Louvre, and the South Kensington Museum and elsewhere – and of course much was based on his own primary research during his early travels (Fig. 9). It is to Jones's credit that he took a sustained approach to showcase and was continually emphasizing the importance of Moorish, Islamic and Far Eastern ornament from outside Western Europe, and particularly from the Islamic world. In addition to chapters examining, for example, Renaissance, Celtic and Byzantine decoration, Jones features chapters dedicated to those on Maori, Chinese and Indian ornament; a further four chapters (one fifth of the entire book) focussed on Turkish, Arabic, Moorish and Persian design. Jones displayed a great sense of 'design democracy' in his studies for the *Grammar*. To illustrate his principles for decoration fully, he drew upon a wide range of material, including examples of architecture, sculpture, metalwork, textiles, ceramics, manuscripts, mosaics, woodwork and even leaves and flowers from nature. Jones demonstrated a skilful ability to reconfigure decoration and ornament from the three-dimensional real world to the confines of the flattened, printed page. By freeing these physical objects from their original contexts, and from the straightjacket of representation, Jones was undoubtedly contributing to the nineteenth century's 'reorganisation of vision'. Through the capacity of chromolithography for rationalization – texture, relief and shadow were distilled down to individual blocks of flat colour – the *Grammar* transformed objects rather than replicating them. Further to this, the actual technical processes of chromolithography seemed to specifically support one of Jones's design principles, described in the preface of the *Grammar*.

Fig. 9. Plate XLIII ('Moresque Ornament') from *The Grammar of Ornament*, by Owen Jones, 1856 (NAL: 49.G.53). © V&A Images

Proposition 29 states that 'When ornaments in a colour are on a ground of a contrasting colour, the ornament should be separated from the ground by an edging of lighter colour'. Nicholas Frankel has previously singled out this particular design principle as tailor-made for the inherent inconsistencies that can occur when faced with issues of registration in chromolithography.[25] Due to accidental gaps in the print created when the lithography stones are not quite aligned correctly, white edging may often result as a rather fortuitous Jonesian by-product. This happy accident in the printing process only serves to accentuate Proposition 29, and may very well not have been noticed had the printing been more perfect. Jones's achievements in adapting ornament for the printed page seem to have resonance decades later when Walter Benjamin stated that 'certain art forms aspire to effects which could only be fully obtained with a changed technical standard'.[26]

It is interesting to note how Jones's rationalization of decoration may have had an impact on the art of photographing architectural sites and examples of ornament. Audiences in the 1860s had been accustomed to the familiar topographical views of the Alhambra produced by photographers such as Francis Frith and Charles Clifford – romanticized images which were still hanging on the coat-tails of a mythology perpetuated by writers such as the afore-mentioned Washington Irving. However, in the 1870s, through photographers such as Jean Laurent, we see a shift towards a much more sterile, fragmented interpretation of architectural decoration: a view perhaps indebted to Jones's samples of decoration in the lusciously chromolithographed plates of his *Alhambra* volumes.

The year after *The Grammar of Ornament* was published, Jones was awarded the RIBA Gold Medal. The *Athenaeum* described Jones's design sourcebook as 'beautiful enough to be the hornbook of angels . . . the book is bright enough to serve a London family in summer instead of flowers and to warm a London room in winter as well as a fire'. Owen Jones considered himself first and foremost a designer of buildings and was proudest of his work as an architect, yet because so many of his buildings never got beyond the presentation drawing or have been demolished, he is now almost forgotten in this field. It is ironic, and rather sad, that his posthumous reputation therefore rests almost entirely on his innovative achievements in publishing and the use of chromolithography, his best known work being *The Grammar of Ornament.*

As his obituary in *The Building News* put it: 'Although he erected few buildings of magnitude, the influence of Mr Owen Jones's life as a teacher of the philosophy of Art has greatly changed the national taste, and his examples and writings have done more to implant a knowledge of true Art than if he had left us a magnitude of buildings.'[27]

References

1. *The Builder*, 9 May 1874, XXXII, p. 384.
2. A number of Vulliamy's drawings of Constantinople are in the V&A's Searight Collection of Middle Eastern drawings (see refs SD1158 to SD1166).
3. Dr Kathryn Ferry has published a thorough account of the history of the printing of Jones's seminal Alhambra volumes in her article 'Printing The Alhambra', *Architectural History*, vol. 46 (2003), pp. 175–88.
4. The V&A's Searight Collection of Middle Eastern drawings includes all the original watercolours and drawings for Coste's *Architecture Arabe ou Monuments Du Kaire*.
5. 'Catalogue of the Valuable Library of the Late Owen Jones Esq. Sold by Sotheby, Wilkinson and Hodge, Saturday 10 April 1875', lot number 167 (British Library, S.C.S.717).
6. Specification of Thomas De la Rue, Manufacture of Ornamental Playing Cards, Patent number 6231, awarded 23 February 1832; as cited in Ferry, *Architectural History*, vol. 46 (2003), p. 178.
7. Letter from Owen Jones to Joseph Bonomi, London, 17 June 1836, Cambridge University Library, Add. MS 9389/2/J/18; as cited in Ferry, *Architectural History*, vol. 46 (2003), p. 177.
8. H. Vizetelly, 'Glances Back Through Seventy Years', 1893.
9. 'Mortgage of a Farm in the County of Denbigh', 27 September 1837, Denbighshire Record Office, Ruthin, papers of Mainwaring of Galltfaenan, DD/GA/683; as cited in Ferry, *Architectural History*, vol. 46 (2003), p. 182.
10. Press cutting in Owen Jones Box, John Johnson Collection, Bodleian Library. This source was identified in Ferry, *Architectural History*, vol. 46 (2003), pp. 175–88.
11. 'Catalogue of the Valuable Library of the Late Owen Jones Esq. Sold by Sotheby, Wilkinson and Hodge, Saturday 10 April 1875', lot number 167 (British Library, S.C.S.717).
12. Kensington Palace Gardens extends north to south from Bayswater Road to Kensington High Street. Following on from an Act of Parliament and responding to the recommendations of a Treasury-appointed committee in 1838, these 28 acres of royal kitchen gardens were detached from the grounds of Kensington Palace and handed over to the Commissioners of Woods and Forests, to be laid out for building in the 1840s. The houses designed by Jones for J. M. Blashfield were one of the first building projects on this new building site.
13. R. Watson, 'Publishing for the Leisure Industry: Illuminating Manuals and the Reception of Medieval Art in Victorian Britain'; chapter in *The Revival of Medieval Illumination*, eds T. Coomans and J. De Maeyer (Leuven, 2007).
14. O. Jones, 'The Grammar of Ornament'; first published by Day & Son, London, 1856. The folio plates were drawn on lithographic stone by Francis Bedford.
15. O. Jones, 'An Attempt to Define the Principles Which Should Regulate the Employment of Colour in the Decorative Arts'; lecture read before the Society of Arts, 28 April 1852.
16. A full list of subscribers can be found in the early pages of the combined volume editions of Jones's *Alhambra*.
17. Jones was responsible for the Egyptian, Greek, Roman and Alhambra Courts at

Sydenham. Other notable contributors included Matthew Digby Wyatt who designed the Byzantine and Romanesque Court (and was also a key contributor to the Byzantine chapter of Jones's *Grammar of Ornament*) and A. W. N. Pugin who designed the Medieval Court.

18. R. Watson, 'Publishing for the Leisure Industry: Illuminating Manuals and the Reception of Medieval Art in Victorian Britain'.

19. Matthew Digby Wyatt, *The Industrial Arts of the Nineteenth Century: A Series of Illustrations of the Choicest Specimens Produced by Every Nation at the Great Exhibition of the Works of Industry, 1851*; published by Day & Son, London, 1851 to 1853.

20. The V&A's collections include a number of photographs of selected Great Exhibition objects, made by Bedford as preparatory studies for his lithographic stone drawings for this publication (see refs E.427 to 439-1995).

21. J. C. Robinson, *A Catalogue of the Museum of Ornamental Art, at Marlborough House, Pall Mall*, published by Chapman & Hall, London, 1855.

22. Cole Collection, National Art Library, Victoria & Albert Museum. The collection comprises diaries, notebooks, correspondence and books owned by Sir Henry Cole, first director of the V&A.

23. A volume of watercolour studies for *The Grammar of Ornament* is held in the RIBA collections (ref. VOL/19); donated by Jones's two sisters in 1880.

24. The V&A collections include 100 original drawings made for *The Grammar of Ornament* plates (see refs 1574 to 1673).

25. N. Frankel, 'The Ecstasy of Decoration: *The Grammar of Ornament* as Embodied Experience', *Nineteenth Century Art Worldwide*, Winter 2003, pp. 1–32.

26. W. Benjamin, 'The work of art in the age of mechanical reproduction' (1935), in *Illuminations*, transl. H. Zohn (London, 1970).

27. *The Building News*, 8 May 1874.

Art Publishing and the Leisure Market, from the 1840s to the 1870s

ROWAN WATSON

THE NATURE OF ACCESS to what society agreed to call 'works of art' changed rather dramatically in the nineteenth century. Governments encouraged the emergence of something we take for granted today: galleries and museums financed by the public purse (even if charging for admission). The basis of these new institutions was the ready-made collection, brought together by individual connoisseurs or amassed over generations by patrician families, supplemented by programmes of acquisition that required systematic support from the Treasury. The aim was to train the public to approach art in the way dictated by traditional connoisseurship (and indeed to exclude undesirable art), to absorb the moral values thought to be inherent in art, to develop the ability to discern excellence in consumer goods, and to celebrate national traditions of collecting and producing art. Arguments about the nature of art and the kind of art best suited to a new role became prominent in the public arena. What was comprehended by the term 'art' has changed over the centuries, and it is clear that with nineteenth-century developments came a widening range of works that were dealt with under the rubric of art. At the same time, the virulent disagreements inherent in defining roles and values in art were aired in ways that reached wider publics than ever before.[1]

This paper will consider publications that served as introductions to art and that enabled new audiences to gain access to works of art, to evaluate them and to develop the practice of art. The publishing programmes considered were generated both by institutions and by commercial enterprises. The aim is to compare major publications with those that were almost ephemeral in character, the latter often barely described in library catalogues but which we can assume, on account of their cheapness, to have had the widest circulation. Works discussed constitute a selection, but they may help to identify some general trends.

Interest in and enjoyment of art as defined by generations of critics and connoisseurs has always signified an element of leisure and sufficient wealth to acquire originals or reproductions, or at least the ability to devote time to an activity not directly related to keeping alive. In the eighteenth century, an educated gentleman was expected to have opinions about painting, sculpture and architecture. The Grand Tour, centred always on Italy and Rome, was an accepted rite of passage for the sons of the aristocratic and gentry classes; apart from tutors, guides and chaperones to direct them to monuments and galleries and to steer them away from places of ill repute, there was an enormous literature to ensure that proper lessons were absorbed – the sisters of those making the Grand Tour doubtless had to be satisfied with such publications. At the highest level of society, 'taste' could be developed without a Grand Tour: Lord Burlington could discover a passion for Italian architecture *after* his trip to Italy in 1712 and returned there in 1719 to indulge it, whereas Robert Walpole (1676–1745) could rival him as a patron without stepping beyond the Alps. Collectors such as these made their palaces in England the focus of attention where art was concerned. By the 1830s, there was a general awareness beyond the confines of collectors and connoisseurs that rich art collections were located in stately homes around Britain. It can probably be said that the collections in question were dominated by 'Old Masters' or works that emulated their classical ideals; Joshua Reynolds's key work on the theory of art, *The Discourses* (1769), could only serve to enhance their significance

Though in private hands, these collections were much visited by those with leisure. John Harris has traced the publishing history of 'Country house guides' up to the 1830s.[2] Among the most visited was Stowe. Guides between the 1740s and 1790s could be had for prices ranging from 6*d.* to 2 guineas, available from the gatekeeper, local inns, or bookshops. Harris sees the second decade of the nineteenth century as the high point for country house guides of this sort.

The cult of the country house as the guardian of an artistic culture that defined national values was supported by an astonishingly success-ful publication, *The mansions of England in olden times*, published by Joseph Nash between 1839 and 1849 and sold at £4 4*s.* for each of the four volumes (£10 10*s.* if coloured); the plates could be acquired individually. Famous stately homes were shown in romantic scenes peopled with contented families in Elizabethan or Jacobean dress. Such images satisfied the one-nation conservatism of the Young England movement in which Disraeli was so prominent, a movement which cherished the idea of a genial Baron entertaining his neighbours, tenants and servants of all classes united in a mutually-supportive, wholesome society, untroubled by class difference. Images from the work were re-used in the popular literature of the 1840s, for example in the *Sunday Magazine* that sold each week for 1*d.*

As a corrective to the overwhelming prestige of foreign masters, popular works of the 1830s insist on the genius of indigenous artists. Allan Cunningham's *Lives of British painters, sculptors and architects* (1830–3), sold at £1 1s. for six volumes, was unashamedly chauvinistic, lamenting Henry VIII's patronage of foreign artists, only portraiture 'surviving the general wreck' of British art; the first glimmerings of renewal came with Hilliard and Isaac Oliver; Rubens and van Dyck 'improved nature' under Charles I and there was guarded acceptance of Lely and Kneller but these gave way to the splendours of native genius represented by Hogarth and Reynolds (the merging here of conflicting philosophies). Sarsfield Taylor's history of the fine arts in Great Britain, which was published in 1841 at £1 1s. for two volumes, was more blatantly xenophobic: the Romans had debauched the native Britons, Tudor patronage of foreigners ushered in decadence which led to the degenerate Baroque. Implicit in works such as these was the idea that government support for the arts was essential.[3]

More authoritative was the approach of Gustav Waagen. His *Works of art and artists in England* published notes of a tour of private collections in the kinds of mansions depicted by Nash. Waagen relayed the judgments of the international connoisseur. His work celebrated and gave judicious opinions about works of 'Old Masters' from Italy and France. Published in German in 1837, it appeared in English in 1838 at £1 16s. for three volumes, and was re-published in 1854. The work reinforced the notion that patrician collections were guardians of the nation's artistic heritage, one that linked British culture to the wider European environment – the idea that private collectors held the essence of the nation's cultural capital was to be promoted by the 'Loan exhibition of works of art' in South Kensington in 1862.

Readers of Waagen were doubtless among those with leisure to undertake their own Grand Tour with the help of the celebrated guides published by John Murray, the first in 1836 and by the early 1850s covering most of Europe and beyond. From the early 1850s Murray's guides were available as well for the counties of England, now accessible by railway.[4] Then, as now, art and architecture (and from 1851 great exhibitions) were major prompts to travel.

Murray was the publisher of what had been the standard guide for the British abroad, Mariana Starke's *Travels on the Continent written for the use and particular information of travellers*, which appeared in various forms between 1820 and 1832 at 15s., part travelogue, part guide and part manual with instruction on the degree of elation one should feel before this painting or that monument. The new Murray guides were cheaper than Starke, at prices between 6s. and 12s. They differed from Starke in being pocket-sized – in fact the format of a prayerbook. Cardinal Newman relished the anecdote about the Milanese cleric ecstatic at the piety of the British, who toured his church with their noses in small red volumes as they paid their devotions to art-works installed there.[5] By 1860, Abel Heywood, the radical politician and printer who was twice mayor of Manchester (in 1862–3 and 1876–7), was providing an equivalent for 1d. The *Guide to Coniston and Furness Abbey* (1867) not only presented one of the glories of Cistercian architecture but also recommended the Lake District as a place for sketching, walking and fishing (Fig. 1).[6]

Such works were among materials effectively marshalled by Peter Mandler to identify an effort in the early Victorian period to promote a popular and national history that was the 'common property of all classes' and marked by 'symbols of a shared past'. By the 1870s, the argument for cultural solidarity between the owners of stately homes and the rest of the population was less convincing: Mandler contrasts the intervention of a working-men's committee to save Aston Hall in 1857 with the lack of a popular response when the owners of Warwick Castle appealed for help after it had burnt down in 1871.[7]

By this date, the landscape had been radically changed. There were now government-funded galleries and museums with a mission to make art available to the public. That their collections included works from celebrated historic, private and aristocratic collections was an added attraction for an audience unsure of being able to discern good from bad, distinguished provenance being a guarantee of value – guide books were liable to give as much weight to provenance as to the artist.

The debates that surrounded the establishment of the National Gallery in 1824 (first at no. 100 Pall Mall, moving to Trafalgar Square in 1838, and losing the Royal Academy to Piccadilly in 1868), the South Kensington Museum after 1851 and the National Portrait Gallery in 1859 have been much discussed. What is striking is the directness with which Sir Robert Peel, for instance, could proclaim the view that encouraging the masses to visit art galleries would create a bond between classes and minimize the danger of social unrest, or that Henry Cole, organizer of the Great Exhibition of 1851 and director of the museum set up in its wake, first in Marlborough House and then in South Kensington (today known as the V&A), could announce that attracting the 'artisan classes' to late evening and week-end opening of galleries instilled civic values and kept them away from drink. Anxiety about the defiling of public galleries by those using the space 'merely to lounge'

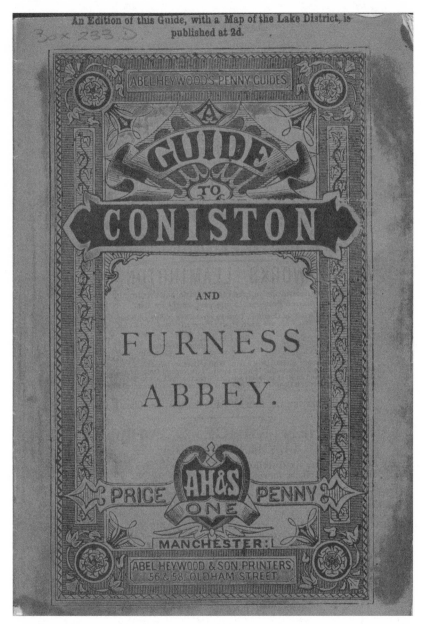

Fig. 1.   A guide to Coniston and Furness Abbey (Manchester: Abel Heywood, 1867). NAL pressmark 233.D.Box. Trips to the 1867 Paris Great Exhibition were advertised, as well as some 33 'Popular Penny Guides' for places including Alton Towers, York, Ilkley with Bolton Abbey, Kenilworth and Warwick. A testimonial for the series was dated 1865.

and without the mental equipment to appreciate art in the correct manner was expressed by people as various as Waagen, Lord Russell, Sir Charles Eastlake and Sir Michael Faraday.[8] The linking of social stability with access to art united radicals like Joseph Hume and Tories like William McKinnon in parliamentary debates in 1841. The Society for Obtaining Free Admission to National Monuments (Patron: Prince Albert; Chairman: Joseph Hume; active from 1839) could report in 1842 that 'the principle may be said to be now fully approved . . . that the character of the working classes becomes established for orderly and peaceable conduct and improved taste'. But it was the success of the 1851 Great Exhibition that gave full justification to their view.[9] What kinds of publishing enterprises were prompted by this new environment?

The first major work that enabled access to these public collections came from a commercial quarter. In 1842, the firm of John Murray published Anna Jameson's *Handbook to the Public Galleries of Art in and near London* at 10s.; a second edition came out in 1845. The work covered the National Gallery, Windsor Castle, Hampton Court, Dulwich Picture Gallery, 'Barry's Pictures' (that is to say the paintings depicting the 'Progress of Civilisation' by James Barry at the Royal Society of Arts) and Sir John Soane's Museum. In an extended introduction, one that was to set a pattern for guide books thereafter, Jameson gave lengthy advice on how to evaluate paintings, how to describe them and what qualities to look for. An analytical framework was provided, with headings under which any work could be interrogated and judged. Jameson evidently preferred Old Masters. Titian and Velasquez were discussed in reverent tones, while *Village Festival* painted by David Wilkie (1785–1841) before his Italian trip of 1825 was deemed 'a scattered composition', though it was 'perfectly genuine and national'. This was the language of the traditional connoisseur, and the long introduction was clearly intended to bring the aspirant reader into such a realm.

Jameson's work ante-dated two major publications of texts long treasured by art collectors but unavailable in modern editions. Horace Walpole's *Anecdotes of painting in England* (1762–71), based on the notebooks of George Vertue, was republished by Bohn in 1849 in three volumes.[10] The same publisher produced Vasari's great work, *Lives of the painters of the most eminent painters, sculptors and architects,* for the first time in a complete English translation, in 1850–52. Walpole's work, which had sustained a series of books by authors celebrating British artists, had followed Vasari's model (while regretting that lack of native talent forced him to adopt the title *Anecdotes* rather than *Lives of English painters*). Familiarity with Vasari was the sign of the connoisseur. Proof of the discernment of the great collector and critic William Ottley (1771–1836) lay in his mastery of Vasari: it was said that he could recognize paintings by Italian Masters instantaneously on the basis of his knowledge of Vasari's descriptions.[11] Writings on art that appeared after 1850 make clear that both the Walpole and Bohn's translation of Vasari's *Vite de' più eccellenti pittori, scultori e architettori* (Florence, 1550 and 1568) by Mrs Jonathan Foster were read intensely by art critics and journalists. These were expensive books: the Walpole sold at £2 2*s*., and the Vasari at 3*s*. 6*d*. for each of the five volumes, prices hardly designed for a mass audience.

The Walpole and the Vasari publications suited a reading public that savoured the burlesque and caricature found in such writers as Dickens: each painter was attached to an anecdote that served to characterize his art and give him a distinct personality. Characterization of artists and their work by anecdotes drawn from their private lives suited popular journalism.[12] The *Art Journal* in 1856 declared it inevitable when discussing the work of a contemporary artist, James Clark Hook (1819–1907), that the private lives of artists was the best way to understand their art, and the great rise in the coverage of art, both in periodicals devoted to the subject and in journals such as the Whig *Edinburgh Review* or the Tory *Quarterly Review*, was to reinforce the biographical approach, with what today would be called its 'human interest' philosophy.[13]

Hugely significant for publishing and for the marketing of art was the series of exhibitions that began with the Great Exhibition of 1851 and continued with the Manchester Art Treasures Exhibition of 1857, the 1862 Great Exhibition and its associated Loan Exhibition of Works of Art, and the three National Portrait Exhibitions of 1866, 1867 and 1868. Ephemeral publications, often so ephemeral as to escape cataloguing in libraries, rather than the expensive official catalogues, are likely to give the best guide to the experience – or the intended experience – of the mass of visitors.

These 'blockbuster' exhibitions, made possible by the advent of railway travel, accelerated the visiting of museums and galleries as leisure pursuits. The 1851 Great Exhibition appears almost as a learning experience for entrepreneurs, one that was to widen the market for publications on art generally. In 1851, some 6¾ million paying visitors visited the capital in five and a half months for the exhibition and needed guidance, entertainment, nourishment and souvenirs. The full official catalogue was a weighty volume of over 800 pages but, in a manner totally traditional for the publishing industry, sections of the large catalogue were recycled so that they could be published in one shilling formats, a price which became a standard for subsequent exhibitions. The one shilling guides were also accompanied by official pamphlets at 2*d.* – the pages of the latter look more like the appendix of an official administrative report than a souvenir, but the decision to produce them reflects a very definite effort to reach a new public.

It should be stressed that a price of 1*s.* was hardly affordable for anyone earning less than what we might loosely call a 'middle-class' wage.[14] Given that entry to the 1851 Exhibition (which ran from 1 May to 15 October) was 5*s.* from 5 May and 1*s.* from 26 May (2*s.* 6*d.* on Fridays, 5*s.* on Saturdays, for those fearful of crowds attracted by the lower price), one imagines a brisk trade in publications that cost only a few pence. The organizers of the exhibition could select what was available for sale at the exhibition, and could thus control to some degree the profitability of any given publication. Guides to London that mention the exhibition are more prominent than exhibition guides produced by independent commercial publishers who had no link with the organization of the exhibition. The full title of the booklet produced by Henry Beal & Son for 4*d.* indicates the market: *A visit to London during the Great Exhibition, showing the visitor at a glance what to see and how to see it, at small expense in six days . . . to which are appended excursions around London* (1851). This, remarkably, had no advertisements other than a list of Beal's publications; it provided a brief description of what was to be on display and a picture of the Crystal Palace. A similar publication by a consortium of booksellers, *The strangers' guide to London and its environs for 1851* by Hugh C. Gray (London: Allen, Collins, Vickers, Winn, Wood, Dipple, Pattie, Purkis, Clements 'and all booksellers', 1851), was more typical in including copious advertisements.

It is worth looking at the earlier history of these cheaper publications, since they ante-date the experience of 1851 and thus the period when it was demonstrated that mass gatherings of people unused to London and genteel ways created an entrepreneurial opportunity rather than social disorder. The parliamentary committee on national monuments and works of art in 1841 had taken a consistent interest in published guides, and its interrogations of witnesses contain useful information about prices and sales. On 27 May 1841, Samuel Parson, 'Boatswain of the Painted Hall' at Greenwich, declared that he sold about 100 copies of the 6*d.* guide a week, but reflected that 6*d.* was more than a sailor could afford and agreed that a guide at 1*d.* would have had more success. John Grundy, in charge of the apartments and pictures at Hampton Court, explained to the committee that he had produced a catalogue at 6*d.*, and that a guide by John Jesse at 5*s.* was also available;[15] he suggested that he sold 10,000 catalogues a year with the implication that most were of the 6*d.* article. The Keeper of the National Gallery, William Seguier, gave details of sales of his one shilling catalogue (6,821 copies in the year ending 31 March 1841) but doubted, despite being pressed, that anything useful could be produced at 6*d.* a copy and claimed that no objections had been made to the current price.[16]

The radical Joseph Hume (1777–1855) was not the only MP whose desire for guides at low prices was countered by officials giving evidence in 1841. He had a history of arguing for easier access to national monuments. In the 1839 report of the Society for Obtaining Free Admission to National Monuments, of which he was chairman, Hume celebrated the fact that the Queen had opened Hampton Court to all without payment except on Saturdays and had 'commanded that . . . its collections . . . be increased by many pictures from other palaces'. In the Society's report of 1842, Hume could claim that the official catalogue of the National Gallery had, 'on the recommendation of your committee, been reduced in price from a shilling to four-pence'; Hume went on to note 'with much pleasure the liberality of the trustees in permitting catalogues, prepared by individuals, to be sold at the entrance to the Gallery, at the prices of one penny and of three-pence, to the great accommodation of all classes of visitors'.[17] Hume in fact seems to have begun to produce these pamphlets himself with a cavalier attitude to the origin of the texts. Henry Cole, in an account dated 1 June 1843, described how he had in August 1841 produced three guides to the National Gallery priced at 6*d.*, 3*d.* and 1*d.*, part of a series that covered Dulwich Gallery, the pictures in the Soane Museum, 'Barry's Pictures' at the Royal Society of Arts and pictures at the British Museum (about 110 portraits, 'hung above the Ornithological presses'), all at these prices. Cole had sent copies of his National Gallery pamphlets to the trustees, keeper and secretary of the National Gallery, but their receipt had not been acknowledged. These publications all had the title 'Handbook'; Cole noted that Anna Jameson had adopted the word for her own substantial guide of 1842 and he insisted that his guide had appeared nine months before Jameson's book: the 'hand-book' idea was his. Cole then described how he had discovered that his texts were being plagiarised in pirate editions. With other parties who had similarly suffered ('Mr Murray, Miss Lambert, Mr Grundy'), Cole initiated proceedings against the culprits. Cole declared that he had recently obtained an injunction against the rogue publisher for piracy of his handbook for Hampton Court. The account goes on to describe Cole's dealing with Joseph

Hume, MP, who 'continues to identify himself so closely with the plagiarisms on my National Gallery [pamphlet], that it is doubtful whether he himself is not responsible for them' – subsequent paragraphs make quite clear that Hume was indeed responsible. The actual publishers of these pirated texts were named as 'Talboys, Clarke & Co', and 'Clarke & Wilson'; by 1843, they were being called 'Hume's catalogues'.[18]

Appearing under the pseudonym Felix Summerly, Cole's guides were all published by George Bell. The places covered were Westminster Abbey, Sir John Soane's Museum, the Temple Church, London Sights, Hampton Court, Dulwich and Canterbury, as well as *Felix Summerly's day's excursions out of London to Erith, Rochester and Cobham in Kent*.[19] Cole's six-penny guide to the National Gallery had 36 pages and nine plates each with a single woodcut image; the cover included two woodcuts, on pink paper.[20] The handbooks for Dulwich Gallery, and for the Soane Museum, British Museum and Society of Arts, of 1842 had 32 and 48 pages respectively, with cover designs based on Greek vases printed on attractive pink and brown paper, but no indication of price – they probably represent the 6*d*. editions (Fig. 2).[21]

Cole's introduction in his 6*d*. 1841 guide to the National Gallery commented that only one in 76 visitors had bought the one-shilling guide, and that his cheaper catalogue was prompted by the institution's unwillingness to provide a less expensive version. He gave an account of the institution's history and advice on what to look for in the pictures. Cole assumed that the Old Masters would be difficult to appreciate, so he recommended starting with English paintings by Constable and Hogarth, before moving gently on to Rubens, Murillo and Correggio. The former were easy to enjoy, considered Cole, but he asked readers to 'exercise a little modest forbearance towards works [he singled out the work of Sebastiano del Piombo (1485/6–1547)] which some parts of the world have looked upon with reverence and emotion for three hundred years . . . Above all, whenever you visit these works of creative genius which make their authors more divine than mortal, come in a spirit of lowliness and reverence, and you will assuredly depart all the wiser and better for doing so'.[22] Each picture had some kind of commentary; there were ten plates plates of illustrations (the one shilling version had 50 plates) and a chronological list of painters. Included were appendices in which Cole revealed his interest in administrative matters by setting out tables with details of visitor numbers and parliamentary grants for acquisitions. The pamphlet does indeed seem to have provided a model from which Anna Jameson developed her own book.

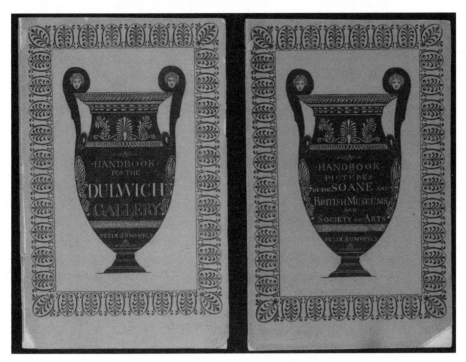

Fig. 2. Covers of Felix Summerly, *Hand-book for the Dulwich Gallery* (London: Bell and Wood, 1842) and *Hand-book for the pictures in the Soane Museum, the Society of Arts, and British Museum* (London: Bell and Wood, 1842)

Cole's Felix Summerly guides were overtaken in the 1850s by the publications of Henry Green Clarke, the very publisher who had worked with Joseph Hume. He is recorded as publisher between 1842 and 1865. His guides worked to a standard formula and from the mid-1840s covered every art institution in the capital. Clarke's earliest guides had covers of coloured paper decorated with woodcut scenes of the places described, and a series title, *Clarke's hand book guides to free galleries of art* (Fig. 3). The 6*d.* edition for Hampton Court, dated 1843, had 32 pages, publicity for Clarke's publications being confined to the orange-coloured covers; the 3*d.* version for Hampton Court had the green covers with the same cuts and 16 pages.[23] The larger version, presumably that for 1*s.*, had prefatory essays on pages numbered 1–54 with integrated woodcuts and 30 unnumbered pages for the catalogue of pictures and tapestries.[24] By 1843, Clarke's pamphlets were including on their titlepages the fact that they were officially allowed to be sold at the entrance to the institution in question. *The National Gallery; its pictures*

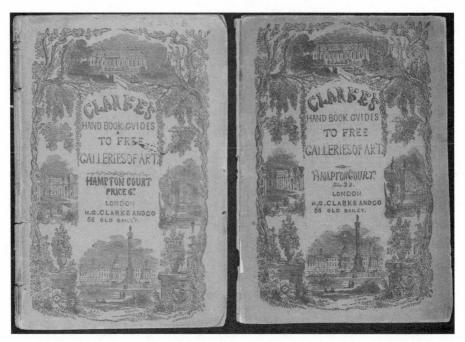

Fig. 3.   Covers of the 6*d*. and 3*d*. versions of *The Royal Gallery, Hampton Court Palace* (London: H. G. Clarke & Co., 1843). (See Plate X.)

and their painters. A hand-book guide for visiters (sic) by Henry Green Clark of 1843 was 'sold (by permission of the Trustees) at the entrance to the National Gallery' and cited a passage from the Parliamentary report on National Monuments and Works of Art of 1841 which recommended the production of cheap catalogues. The accompanying list of publications referred to a collected edition of Clarke's guides priced at 2*s*. 6*d*., and guides for each separately priced at either 1*s*. or 6*d*., with 'abridged editions, 3*d*. and 1*d*.' – the prices echo those achieved by Cole in 1841.[25] The texts of these pamphlets appear as an abbreviation of Cole's text, with the lists of paintings by school and a chronological account of gifts, both features that Cole had developed. From 1844, Clarke's guide to the National Gallery had a text by the history painter George Foggo (1793–1869), conceivably commissioned as a result of Cole's law suit.[26] By the 1850s, Clarke's 'Hand-Books' had very different covers that were either typographical or which imitated binding designs, usually an arabesque cartouche with a central graphic motif. Clarke evidently came to an agreement with most museum directors. His South Kensington guides were available at the museum, and, for example, his 1860 six-penny guide to the British Museum, *The British Museum; its Antiquities and Natural history*, with its elegant light blue cover and frontispiece of the Portland Vase, proclaimed on its cover that it was 'Sold by permission at the entrance to the Museum', giving the work an official endorsement.

After the Great Exhibition of 1851, Clarke was in a position to exploit an expanding market. He produced cheap guides to art galleries and cultural institutions on a common model, at prices between 1*d*. and 1*s*. As the national collections were augmented, notably with the foundation of the South Kensington Museum after 1851, and the gifts of the Robert Vernon and Turner collections in 1845 and 1856, Clarke's guides became immediately available. The 32-page guide for South Kensington, *The Museum of Ornamental Art. A hand-book for visitors* (H. G. Clarke, 1853), sold for 3*d*. It was not illustrated and gave merely a list of objects often with prices paid under the 'Divisions' into which the objects were divided; it had several pages of advertisements. Clarke's 1855 edition of the *National Gallery of painting and sculpture* included a *Catalogue of the Turner Collection now on view at Marlborough House*, and a section on the Vernon Collection of British pictures; sold at 1*s*., it had sixteen plates of illustrations. The guide for the Vernon Collection alone cost 6*d*. When, in 1857, the South Kensington Museum acquired the Sheepshanks collection, intended to be the core of a collection of British Art, Clarke immediately had a 6*d*. guide available (Fig. 4). These publications were all issued with pages of advertisements before and after the main text and illustrations.

The Great Art Treasures Exhibition in 1857 was Manchester's reply to London's exhibition of 1851. It had a mere 1.3 million visitors and included over 16,000 works of art (among them 1,123 Old Masters, 689 'Modern masters' and 386 British portraits). The official catalogue was available for 1*s*., something of a triumph for this price: there were 232 pages, biographical notices for ancient masters (none for modern masters), lengthy texts for works from the new Museum of Ornamental Art (the South Kensington Museum) and a list of lenders. However, publications of the same or a lower price were more glamorous in having illustrations, brightly coloured covers and the added diversion of illustrated advertisements. There was a veritable boom in cheaper publications by commercial printers and publishers. William Blanchard Jerrold produced his *Jerrold's guide to the exhibition. How to see the Art Treaures Exhibition* (Manchester, 1857), some 64 pages, unillustrated, at 6*d*. Handbooks consisting of reprints of 'critical notices' from the *Manchester Guardian* sold at the same price, unillustrated but consisting

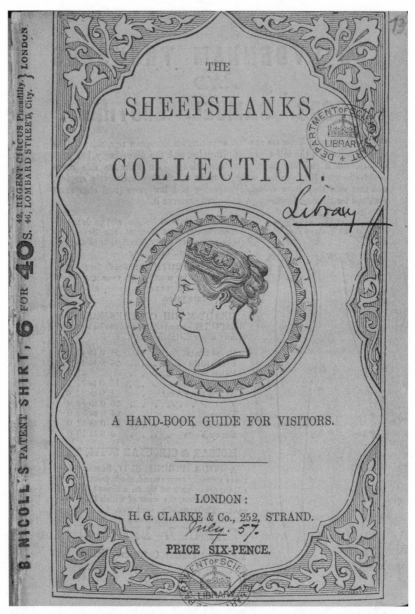

Fig. 4.   Cover of *The Sheepshanks Collection. A descriptive catalogue of the Gallery of British Art in the South Kensington Museum* (London: H. G. Clarke & Co., 1857)

of between 84 and 128 pages. Abel Heywood's *What to see and where to see it, or the Operatives' guide to the art treasures exhibition*, 'Dedicated to the working classes of Lancashire and Yorkshire' (Fig. 5), contained 20 pages of dense text for 1*d*. For 1*s*., those disposed to sneer at modern art – works by Pre-Raphaelite painters – could acquire *Poems inspired by certain pictures at the Art Treasures Exhibition* with eight full-page caricatures of offending works (Fig. 6). *A yewud chap's trip to Manchester to see the Queen, Prince Albert, an' th'Art Treasures Eggshibishun* (Manchester: Abel Heywood, 1857) at 4*d*. flattered local patriotism and included integrated woodcuts.

This industry of cheap publication created a challenge for Henry Cole as director of the South Kensington Museum. Its first catalogues sold at 6*d*., and from its inception, the museum issued as well lists of materials at one or two pence. Thus it produced for 1*d*. an inventory of the gift of British paintings made by John Sheepshanks in 1857, a pamphlet of 24 pages, of which thirteen were taken up by an essay by Richard Redgrave. As part of the 1862 Great Exhibition, an event planned since 1857 as a sequel to the 1851 exhibition, the South Kensington Museum hosted the 'Loan exhibition of works of art', and with it was published a major catalogue: the whole cost 5*s*., but there were individual parts that could be acquired for 1*s*. In response to the Clarke guide, and to match its price, the museum produced in 1857 the six-penny *Catalogue of the British Fine Art Collections at South Kensington*, published by the museum's official publisher, Chapman & Hall. It had readable texts for each catalogue entry, and its success is indicated by the statement in the 1862 edition which declared it to be the 21st thousandth re-printing. The exhibitions of national portraits of 1866, 1867 and 1868 were accompanied by lists of exhibits sold for a few pence, but the opportunity here was taken to use photography: nearly 3,000 works were displayed and photographed, each individual photograph available for sale. The undertaking was organized by the Arundel Society for Promoting the Knowledge of Art as part of their campaigns for distributing images of works of art, here acting as the agent for the Department of Science and Art.[27]

If an institution like the South Kensington Museum emulated the publishing idea of H. G. Clarke, the format was restrictive for some aspects of public collections. The catalogue of Italian sculpture produced by J. C. Robinson in 1862 was aimed at a different market: it was illustrated with 20 plates as well as some integrated images, and sold at 7*s*. 6*d*. Robinson described it as 'the first of a series of detailed divisional catalogues'.[28] Acknowledged today as a major landmark in the study of

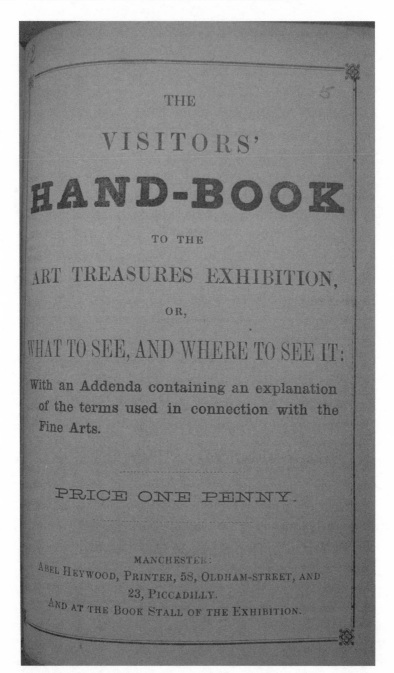

THE

VISITORS'

HAND-BOOK

TO THE

ART TREASURES EXHIBITION,

OR,

WHAT TO SEE, AND WHERE TO SEE IT:

With an Addenda containing an explanation
of the terms used in connection with the
Fine Arts.

PRICE ONE PENNY.

MANCHESTER:
ABEL HEYWOOD, PRINTER, 58, OLDHAM-STREET, AND
23, PICCADILLY.
AND AT THE BOOK STALL OF THE EXHIBITION.

Fig. 5.   Cover of *What to see, and where to see it! or the Operatives Guide to the Art Treasures Exhibition* (Manchester: Abel Heywood, 1857)

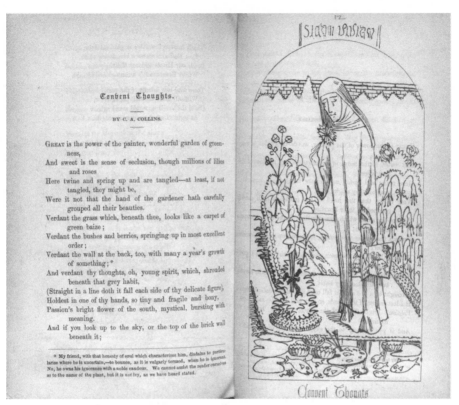

Fig. 6. The section on 'Convent Thoughts', a painting by Charles Allston Collins today
at the Ashmolean Museum, Oxford, from *Poems inspired by certain pictures at the Art
Treasures Exhibition, Manchester, by Tennyson Longfellow Smith, of Cripplegate Within,
edited by his friend, the Author of 'Thorns & Thistles', illustrated by the Hon. Botibol
Bareacres, and dedicated with profound admiration and awe to that greatest of modern
poets, philosophers, artists, art-critics, and authors, the immortal Buskin* (Manchester:
'Sold at the book-stall of the Exhibition, and by all respectable booksellers', 1857)

the subject, it appears not to have been widely distributed or sold; many
copies were sent to interested parties in the UK and abroad as gifts.
The *Art Journal* found it 'too delicate and costly'. But by the 1870s,
this format and price became the basis of the museum's publishing.
The catalogues produced by John Pullen, who had been specifically
appointed Keeper in 1864 to oversee such publications, were more
relevant to scholarly research than to attracting mass audiences to the
collections.[29] The museum's Divisional Catalogues', most of them entitled *Descriptive Catalogue,* followed the model of Robinson's catalogue:

between 1872 and 1878, collections of ivories, miniatures, furniture and woodwork, musical instruments, bronzes and 'fictile ivories' (casts of ivories) were published in this format, at prices between 12s. and £2; the catalogue of bronzes announced the price of 30s. on its titlepage.[30]

Texts of these catalogues were the basis of a series aimed at a less specialized audience, the *Science and Art Handbooks,* which, published from the mid-1870s, gave general introductions to the subjects documented by the museum's collections. Like Robinson's catalogue, they were published by Chapman and Hall for the Committee of Council on Education, and were designed to a very similar standard. The HMSO objected to the price, which did not recover costs, but the museum insisted that it retail at 2s. 6d., and succeeded in establishing the principle that paper-bound copies could be acquired at the museum itself for 1s., a price that reflected the museum's concern to reach as broad an audience as possible.[31] But the works themselves reflect a movement towards the more expensive scholarly monograph as the basis for understanding art, discussed below.

The publications just discussed were paralleled by another kind of work, one which reflected a similar popular interest in art from a different perspective. The foundation of South Kensington Museum was part of a huge enthusiasm for art education – indeed, one of its divisions managed a national system of art and design education with art schools all over Britain and Ireland that followed a prescriptive programme of instruction. From the 1850s, works that enabled people to develop their own art practice were having an enormous commercial success. Manuals and guides on drawing, sketching and a variety of forms of painting, as well as embroidery, needlework and illumination, were published in huge numbers. They indicate a student and amateur practice of unprecedented proportions, and it is worth considering this as another aspect of the promotion of art, one parallel to that of the institutions and businesses just discussed.

The practice of art was a significant part of the leisure activities of the wealthier classes. Victoria and Albert provided a model: in the 1850s and 1860s their children were taught to draw, paint and illuminate. For those who did not have tutors, cheap manuals became available and experienced exponential growth, to judge by the re-printings and appearance of new editions, between about 1850 and 1870. Traditionally, drawing was taught by copying the works of celebrated artists, and this approach was supported by works such as that of John Syer, *Selection of studies from the portfolios of various artists* (London: George Rowney, 1854), with six plates, 'Each plate 1s. 6d.'. A system of teaching drawing at South Kensington was different in being vocational and aimed at the 'artisan classes': it was intended for students who would become designers for industry. An example of such books was *Drawing lessons as given at Marlborough House* (London: George John Stevenson, 1857), sold for a matter of pence and marketed for schools and aspirant students. Its prescriptive programme, based on progression through geometric exercises and perspective, was replicated in schools throughout the country. In this vein were A. A. Clapin's *Perspective for schools* (London: George Bell, 1879), F. M. Black's *National First Grade Elementary Drawing Book* (1875), sold at 4*d.*, and the *Drawing Copy Book* published by Marcus Ward in about 1870 at 3*d.*

Very different in intention – and intended as an express attack on the 'South Kensington system' – was the drawing book of John Ruskin. He had taught drawing at the Working Man's College since 1854. His *Elements of Drawing*, published by Smith, Elder & Co, first appeared in 1857 at 7*s.* 6*d.* The third edition in 1861 had '8000th' on its titlepage; the author thereafter refused to allow further editions. Ruskin's method was to make drawing the means of understanding art. In seeking to train the eye to look, he advocated studying shadows cast by natural forms, and insisted, for example, on examining the play of light on near and distant objects without imposing mathematical and geometrical patterns on any composition. The manual was greeted with some vituperative reviews.[32] Drawing for Ruskin was to be a way of enabling the thought processes, indeed the moral character, of great artists to be followed and understood, not to prepare for a career as a clerk in a drawing office.

Ruskin's philosophy could appeal to those for whom drawing was a leisure activity not undertaken for career advancement. It was for the amateur, and that this was a market of enormous proportions is made clear by the sheer quantity of guides that appeared in the 1850s and 1860s. A precursor may have been a publication of 1843 by Henry Clarke,[33] but almost all were published after this date by the stationers who specialized in artists' materials and who can be taken to have acted as wholesalers supplying a range of outlets. The design format appears to have been established by 1849. Usually measuring 175–180 × 110–120 mm, they had yellow covers, a varying number of integrated illustrations and plates, and advertisements on leaves or a booklet bound at the end. Rowney & Co, a company that had sold artists materials since the 1780s, were early players in the market. George Harley's *A guide to pencil and chalk drawing for landscape* (1849) was priced at 'one shilling stitched, one shilling and six pence bound in cloth' and had 44 pages, eight inserted plates and integrated woodcuts, with sixteen pages of advertisements and testimonials. Of the same date was Henry O'Neill's *Guide to pictorial art*, priced at 1*s*. 6*d*. stitched, and 2*s*. bound in cloth, the rear cover with a list of titles; it contained 94 pages, eighteen pages of advertisements and some integrated diagrams. Richard Pratchett Noble's *Guide to water colour painting*, in its 4th edition by 1850, had 60 pages, yellow covers with a list of titles, and 44 pages of advertisements; significantly, it had a colour frontispiece which, at 1*s*. 6*d*. stitched or 2*s*. bound in cloth, suggests a large print-run.

Rivals soon appeared. The commercial success of Winsor & Newton went back to the 1830s when they produced improved water- and oil-based pigments for artists. Their *Art of landscape painting in watercolours* by Thomas Rowbotham and Thomas L. Rowbotham came out at 1*s*. in 1850 and was reviewed in the *Art Journal* (1850, p. 132). The eighth edition (48 pages, 24 pages of advertisements) appeared in 1852. William Day's *Art of miniature painting comprising instructions necessary for the acquirement of the art*, had numerous illustrations and appeared in 1852 at 1*s*. with 58 pages, a frontispiece, integrated images and 20 pages of advertisements; on the rear cover was a list of nine other works at a shilling on aspects of painting and drawing (Fig. 7). The *Art Journal* (1852, p. 324) commented that Day's book 'may be consulted advantageously by the learner'. Of a similar format and the same price was Aaron Penley's *System of water-colour painting, being a complete exhibition of the present advanced state of the art, as exhibited in the works of the modern water-colour school*, the sixth edition (64 pages with 24 pages of advertisements), published in 1852.

The firm of Reeves had pioneered improved colours for painters from the late eighteenth century. By the 1850s, they had also become involved in publishing. Their successful manual by Henry Warren, *Painting in water colour*, appeared in two parts in 1856, presumably to keep each part priced at 1*s*.; the first had a coloured frontispiece, the second three colour pictures, in both cases to accompany integrated woodcuts.

Another supplier of artists' materials was the firm of Jabez Barnard. In 1855, the company published A. N. Rintoul's *Guide to painting photographic portraits, draperies and backgrounds in water colours with numerous coloured diagrams* at 2*s*. (Fig. 8). By 1861, Barnard's could publish *A practical treatise on landscape painting and sketching from nature* by John Chase and James Harris for 1*s*., illustrated with a series of drawings in colour; the rear covers had a list of titles of related works, most related to sketching and illuminating. Among its 58 pages was a chapter on 'Art Education' (which recommended painting as 'useful in every walk

WORKS PUBLISHED BY WINSOR AND NEWTON.

Eighth Edition, Price 1s.
THE ART OF
LANDSCAPE PAINTING IN WATER-COLOURS.
BY THOMAS ROWBOTHAM,
AND THOMAS L. ROWBOTHAM, JUN.

Eighth Edition, Price 1s.
A SYSTEM OF WATER-COLOUR PAINTING.
BY AARON PENLEY,
BEING A SEQUEL TO MR. ROWBOTHAM'S BOOK AS ABOVE.

Eleventh Edition, Price 1s.
THE ART OF SKETCHING FROM NATURE.
BY THOMAS ROWBOTHAM.
With Twenty-Six Illustrations,
BY THOMAS L. ROWBOTHAM, JUN.,
Engraved on Wood by Dalziel.

Third Edition, Price 1s.
THE ART OF
PORTRAIT PAINTING IN WATER-COLOURS.
BY MRS. MERRIFIELD.

Seventh Edition, Price 1s.
INSTRUCTIONS IN THE ART OF
LANDSCAPE PAINTING IN OIL-COLOURS.

Third Edition, Price 1s.
THE ELEMENTS OF PERSPECTIVE.
ILLUSTRATED BY NUMEROUS EXAMPLES AND DIAGRAMS.
BY AARON PENLEY.

Fourth Edition, Price 1s.
THE ART OF
PORTRAIT PAINTING IN OIL-COLOURS.
BY HENRY MURRAY.

Fourth Edition, Price 1s.
INSTRUCTIONS IN
THE ART OF FIGURE DRAWING.
BY C. H. WEIGALL.
Containing Sixteen Illustrations,
DRAWN ON WOOD BY THE AUTHOR, AND ENGRAVED BY WALTER G. MASON.

Third Edition, Price 1s.
ARTISTIC ANATOMY OF THE HUMAN FIGURE.
BY HENRY WARREN.
With Twenty-Three Illustrations,
Drawn on Wood by the Author, and Engraved by Walter G. Mason.

WINSOR AND NEWTON, 38, RATHBONE PLACE,
And Sold by all Booksellers and Artists' Colourmen.

Fig. 7. Rear cover of Charles William Day, *The art of miniature painting, instructions necessary for the acquirement of that art*, 2nd edition (London: Winsor & Newton, 1852)

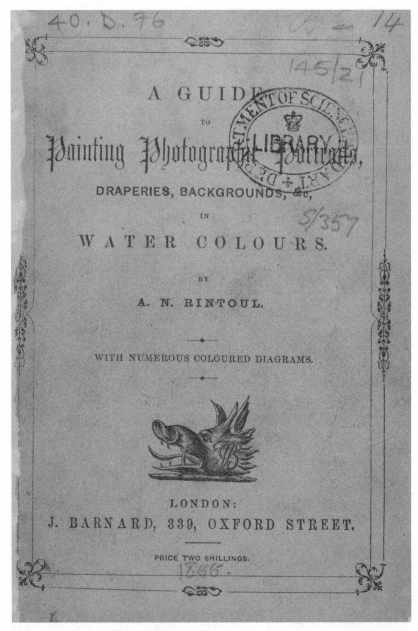

Fig. 8. Cover of Alexander Nelson Rintoul, *A guide to painting photographic portraits, draperies, backgrounds, &c, in water colours . . . with numerous coloured diagrams* (London: Jabez Barnard, 1855)

of life – rather than music, girls should learn sketching . . .'), and the book included 42 pages of advertisements.

Such was the success of these books that the publishers began to market them as a series, with each work priced at 1s. Already in 1852, Winsor & Newton's *Art of miniature painting* by Charles William Day had listed nine aids to painting, each for a shilling.[34] Subjects covered included water-colour, miniature, landscape and flower painting, drawing, colouring of photographs and illumination.[35] By 1863, Winsor & Newton were marketing 23 titles as their 'One Shilling Hand-Books on Art' (Fig. 9).[36] The rear cover of Rowney's *Water colour painting* by R. P. Noble, published in 1850, listed fifteen works of which three were at 1s. and three at 1s. 6d. – the range proposed included traditional portfolios of images to act as models.[37] Rowney's *Guide to oil painting,* published in 1855 in two parts, listed fourteen works, of which eleven were priced at 1s.[38] The marketing language makes clear that the amateur artist was a major target. Art as an amateur practice received significant validation by royal gestures such as Queen Victoria's visit to the exhibition of water-colours by amateur artists in 1860.[39]

The women's market was particularly significant. Training in drawing and colouring had been advocated in the 1850s as an activity for which women had a natural proclivity, and an activity by which respectable women could earn a living. In a pioneering spirit, the South Kensington Museum after its foundation recruited women to assist in producing illustrated works.[40] The Illuminating Art Society in 1857 had the enthusiastic backing of a number of noble ladies, from Viscountess Dungarvan to Baroness de Rothschild, and its work was favourably reviewed by the *Art Journal*.[41] The Female School of Design, had been set up in 1837 for 'Middle-Class but needy women who required employment'. When Henry Cole managed to incorporate the school into the art education empire of the South Kensington Museum in 1852, he sought to change its nature from a school that trained indigent women to an institution that could become financially self-supporting. Day-time classes and fees meant that classes became increasingly monopolized by women seeking skill in art as an accomplishment rather than a means of employment. When the school needed new premises in 1860, the Princess of Wales led the fund-raising. In 1862, Queen Victoria allowed the school to become the Royal Female School of Art, and in 1866 she attended the opening of the new building.[42] *The Graphic* for 4 April 1885, with its typical diet of military heroism in Britain's colonial wars, had no doubt that art was for women. On its cover was a picture of a ladies' sketching club at work on Hampstead Heath: in the

ONE SHILLING HAND-BOOKS ON ART

With Illustrations, &c.

A MANUAL OF ILLUMINATION.

A COMPANION TO MANUAL OF
ILLUMINATION.

THE ART OF MARINE PAINTING
IN WATER-COLOURS.

THE ART OF LANDSCAPE
PAINTING IN WATER-COLOURS.

A SYSTEM OF WATER-COLOUR
PAINTING.

THE ART OF PORTRAIT PAINTING
IN WATER-COLOURS.

ARTISTIC ANATOMY OF THE
HUMAN FIGURE.

TRANSPARENCY PAINTING ON
LINEN.

THE ART OF TRANSPARENT
PAINTING ON GLASS.

THE PRINCIPLES OF COLOURING
IN PAINTING.

DRAWING MODELS AND THEIR
USES.

THE ART OF SKETCHING FROM
NATURE.

ART OF LANDSCAPE PAINTING IN
OIL-COLOURS.

THE ART OF PORTRAIT PAINTING
IN OIL-COLOURS.

THE ELEMENTS OF PERSPECTIVE.

THE ART OF FIGURE DRAWING.

HINTS FOR SKETCHING IN WATER-
COLOURS FROM NATURE.

THE PRINCIPLES OF FORM IN
ORNAMENTAL ART.

THE ART OF FLOWER PAINTING.

ART OF MINIATURE PAINTING.

INSTRUCTIONS FOR
CLEANING, REPAIRING, LINING
AND RESTORING OIL PAINTINGS

THE ART
OF PAINTING AND DRAWING IN
COLOURED CRAYONS.

In the Press.
THE ART OF MARINE PAINTING
IN OIL COLOURS.

Second Edition, Revised and Enlarged, 1 *vol. with* 870 *Illustrations,* 10s. 6d.

HERALDRY,

HISTORICAL AND POPULAR.

By Charles Boutell, M.A.

London : Winsor and Newton, and Sold by all Booksellers and Artists' Colourmen.

Fig. 9.   Rear cover of Thomas Hatton, *Hints for sketching in water-colour* (Winsor & Newton, 1862)

accompanying texts, the editor expresses surprise at their youth and beauty, the assumption being that old men and un-lovely ladies (old ladies) were more commonly met with. It is difficult not to imagine that these were the groups at which the one-shilling manuals were aimed.

The chronological range over which these one-shilling manuals were published is difficult to establish. As ephemeral publications, they have not survived well. Libraries tend to hold one or two copies of early editions, so that their holdings do not allow the rate of publication to be followed. They evidently were produced up to the end of the nineteenth century, but it seems that they had their greatest success in the 1860s. Begun just before 1850, by the mid-1870s they have a distinctly out-of-date feel. One might have expected these entrepreneurial publishers to update their design, but it seems that the market itself began to dry up. There were specific reasons why one variety of manual flourished in the last three decades of the nineteenth century, and its success was due to more than the undoubted novelty of its design. Marcus Ward of Belfast produced a hugely successful series of manuals, carefully marketed as sets. They were initially funded by the wealthy Anglo-Irish philan-thropist Vere Foster (1819–1900), who recruited the firm of Marcus Ward, with its great experience of colour printing, for the writing, painting and drawing manuals that he designed (Fig. 10). Foster and Ward achieved secure contracts with the Irish Education system (and also subsequently with English Schools and the New York Depart-ment of Public Instruction) to provide textbooks – some four million were produced before the end of the century.[43] The series was sold to Blackie after 1876, but the format and design remained unchanged. Consisting of an introductory text and plates, often all coloured, the Vere Foster books sold for between 18*d*. and 2*s*.; while each item was patently part of a series, copies were proudly marked 'Each part complete in itself'.

As regards the one-shilling manuals of Winsor & Newton, Rowney, and their competitors, it may be that the market was saturated, that these humble works had satisfied one generation but had less relevance to another, or that new technologies could produce more attractive works in different formats. One might hazard a guess that culturally they were out of date by the end of the 1870s. They corresponded to a period when the practice of art was taken to be a path to moral improvement. The marketing language associated with the one-shilling manuals proposed the practice of art, on the one hand, as morally edifying, and on the other as supporting a tradition of Britishness, watercolours in particular being seen as an expression of national genius. By the 1870s, the artist was less

Fig. 10.   Vere Foster's Complete Course of Painting in Water-Colors, Part II (London, Dublin, Edinburgh, Glasgow: Blackie & Son [1879?]), with plates printed by Marcus Ward, Belfast

a philosopher guiding the viewer towards truth and morality than a professional who could execute works of brilliance.

This was certainly the polarity that separated, for instance, that apostle of morality, John Ruskin, from the mondaine Whistler or Lord Leighton. For the latter, art was to be explained by the expert and consumed by the public, rather than engaged in as a morally edifying educational activity. Cole and Robinson had based art education on the display of series of carefully chosen historical works; by the 1870s art was assumed to require lengthy scholarly catalogues to be fully understood. Ruskin saw the practice of art as the basis of moral reform. Alma-Tadema, Whistler, Lord Leighton and their like saw themselves as professionals whose works required admiration not imitation. Theirs was a world of the weighty, de luxe and expensive monograph with superb reproductions, rather than the mass-circulated handbook or guide priced at a mere shilling. Perhaps more symptomatic of the times was Mrs Charles Heaton's *History of the life of Albrecht Durer* (London: Macmillan, 1870), 31*s*. 6*d*., based on a more sustained kind of research, or Moriz Thausing's book on Albrecht Dürer, 42s., translated into English by Fred A. Eaton and published by John Murray in 1882, which brought solid German scholarship into debates about art. A publishing success that perhaps characterized the new environment was Sampson's series entitled *Illustrated biographies of the great artists*, issued from 1879 at 3s. 6d. a volume with as many as 20 illustrations; most artists were hallowed names of the past, but by 1881 the series was suggesting a modern tradition dominated by English artists, with the inclusion of David Wilkie (d.1841), Turner (d.1851) and Landseer (d.1873). By 1891, William Mulready (d.1863) and George Cruikshank (d.1878) had been added, while new biographies of Hogarth and Tintoretto were said to be based on 'new research'. A canon was established which largely excluded modern German and French painting, the latter with the exception of the Barbizon School whose landscapes had a particular interest for a British public rather obsessed with the genre.[44] Taken as a whole, art publishing in Britain in the period discussed here sustained an environment hostile to the reception of modernity, so that Symbolist painting, Impressionism and Post-Impressionism, for example, became domiciled only with difficulty and at the expense of prolonged combat.

References

The works reproduced are all from the V&A's National Art Library (NAL), and are published by kind permission of the Board of Trustees of the Victoria & Albert Museum.

1. Paul Oskar Kristeller, *Renaissance thought and the arts* (Princeton University Press, 1990); Paul Greenhalgh, 'The history of craft', *The Culture of Craft*, ed. Peter Dormer (Manchester University Press, 1997), pp. 20–52.

2. John Harris, 'English Country House Guides, 1740–1840', *Concerning architecture: essays on architectural writers and writing presented to Nikolaus Pevsner*, ed. John Summerson (London: Penguin Press, 1968), pp. 58–74.

3. The earlier history of this idea is discussed in Jonathan Conlin, *The nation's mantelpiece: a history of the National Gallery* (London: Pallas Athene, 2006), chapter I.

4. W. B. C. Lister, *A bibliography of Murray's handbooks for travellers* (Dereham, 1993); Victoria Cooper and Dave Russell, 'Publishing for leisure', *Cambridge History of the Book in Britain*, vol. VI, 1830–1914, ed. David McKitterick (Cambridge University Press, 2009), pp. 491–9.

5. John Pemble, *Mediterranean Passion. Victorians and Edwardians in the South* (Oxford University Press, 1988), pp. 71–2.

6. NAL pressmark: 233.D Box; a *Guide to Liverpool* (1874) was 2d. (NAL pressmark: 233.D Box).

7. Peter Mandler, *The rise and fall of the stately home* (Yale University Press, 1997).

8. Colin Trodd, 'The paths to the National Gallery', *Governing cutures: art institutions in Victorian London*, ed. Paul Barlow and Colin Trodd (Aldershot: Ashgate, 2000), pp. 31, 39–40.

9. Colin Trodd, 'Culture, Class, City: the National Gallery, London, and the sources of

education, 1822–1857', *Art apart: institutions and ideology across England and north America*, ed. Marcia Pointon (Manchester University Press, 1994), p. 33 et seq.; *Society for Obtaining Free Admission to National Monuments and public edifices containing works of art: Report* (1842), from the Joseph Hume Pamphlet Collection, Library, University College London, URL: http://www.jstor.org/stable/60206273.

10. See Nigel Llewellyn, 'The *Anecdotes of painting* and continental European art history', *Horace Walpole's Strawberry Hill*, ed. Michael Snodin (V&A and Yale University Press, 2009), pp. 137–53.

11. A.A., 'William Young Ottley, artist and collector', *Notes & Queries*, 2 April 1938.

12. For the flood of works taking a biographical approach to art, see Julie F. Codell, 'Serialised artists' biographies. A culture industry in late Victorian Britain', *Book History*, vol. 3 (2000), pp. 94–125.

13. Tom Devonshire Jones, 'Art in the *Edinburgh Review*', *The British Art Journal*, vol. IX. no. 3 (2008); and 'Art in the *Quarterly Review*', ibid., vol. X, no. 1 (2009).

14. For the market implied by the 1*s.* price, see Simon Eliot, 'Never mind the value, what about the price? Or, How much did Marmion cost St John Rivers?', *Nineteenth Century Literature*, vol. 56, no. 2 (September 2001).

15. John Grundy, *The stranger's guide to Hampton-Court Palace and Gardens*: the earliest edition I have found is that of 1843 in the British Library (shelfmark 796.c.53); the 6th edition, 're-written and enlarged', was dated 1844. For an edition of 1857, see NAL, pressmark: 243.D.26. Edward Jesse, *A summer's day at Hampton Court, being a guide to the palace and gardens with an illustrative catalogue of the pictures according to the new arrangements recently opened to the public* (London: John Murray, 1839), NAL pressmark Forster 12° 4619, with ten inserted plates, bound in green cloth with a design blocked in gold on the front cover.

16. See the *Report from the select Committee on National Monuments and Works of Art*, 16 June 1841, pp. 105, 123, 129, 134. Grundy's guide, *The Stranger's guide to Hampton Court Palace and Gardens* (London: G. Bell, 1829 and later editions), had 36 pages and covers of pink paper with woodcuts; Jesse's guide, *A summer's day at Hampton Court*, had 136 pages, nine inserted illustrations and a frontispiece.

17. See note 9, and for the 1839 report, Joseph Hume Pamphlet Collection, Library, University College London, URL: http://www.jstor.org/stable/60212049.

18. Cole's account appears in a prefatory unpaginated 'Advertisement', dated Notting Hill Square, 1 June 1843, in *Felix Summerly's Hand Book for the National Gallery, with reminiscences of the most celebrated pictures drawn from the originals by John, James, and William Linnell* (London: George Bell, 1843). Copies consulted were those in the NAL (pressmark: S 900141) and British Library (shelfmark: C.129.a.26). The comments on Anna Jameson dated 13 June 1842 appear in Cole's *Hand-Book for Free Picture Galleries, namely the National Gallery and the Dulwich Gallery . . . by Felix Summerly* (London: Bell and Wood, 1842), BL shelfmark: 1402.b.54. See also Elizabeth Bonython and Anthony Burton, *The Great Exhibitor. The Life and Work of Henry Cole* (V&A Publications, 2003), p. 84, where reviews of Cole's pamphlets are mentioned.

19. Susanna Avery-Quash, '"Creating a taste for beauty": Henry Cole's book ventures', 2 vols, Cambridge University PhD, 1997, deals almost entirely with the design aspect of Cole's publications.

20. NAL, pressmark 55.CC.6. The pamphlet actually bears no date, but the account of attendance includes the year 1843.

21. NAL, pressmarks 55.CC.4 and 5.

22. NAL, pressmark 55.CC.6. Part of this text is cited in Jonathan Conlin, *The Nation's*

mantelpiece. A history of the National Gallery (London: Pallas Athene, 2006), p. 219.

23. NAL, pressmarks 243 B Box; 607.AH.0019.

24. NAL, pressmark 243 B Box.

25. NAL, pressmark 601.AG.0002; the handbooks are of sixteen pages, of which three are taken up with advertisements for Clarke's other publications. Their price is not given, but they are likely to have cost 1*d*. The Parliamentary Report of the Select Committee is that ordered on 16 June 1841.

26. British Library, shelfmark: 155.c.1(9).

27. See Anthony J. Hamber, *'A higher branch of the art'. Photographing the Fine Arts in England, 1839–1880* (Amsterdam: Gordon and Breach, 1996), pp. 303–14.

28. *Ninth Report of the Science and Art Department of the Committee of Council on Education* (London: Eyre & Spottiswoode for HMSO, 1862), p. 112.

29. Anthony Burton, *Vision and Accident. The story of the Victoria and Albert Museum* (V&A Publications, 1999), pp. 82–3.

30. For the titles, see Elisabeth James, *The Victoria and Albert Museum. A bibliography and exhibition chronology, 1852–1996* (London: Fitzroy Dearborn with the V&A, 1998). Prices of the catalogues appear in a leaflet of 1873, *A list of publications issued by the Science and Art Department for the use of Schools of Art, for prizes, and generally for public instruction* (London: printed by Eyre & Spottiswoode, sold by Chapman & Hall, 'agents to the Department for the sale of examples', 1873).

31. Very useful information on the politics of publishing at the South Kensington Museum can be found in Elizabeth James, 'Reaching Readers? The South Kensington Museum Art Handbooks', MA thesis, MA in the History of the Book, Institute of English Studies, School of Advanced Study, University of London, 2003, *passim*. See p. 14 for the statement that only 422 copies of the print-run of 2,000 of Robinson's catalogue had been sold by July 1863.

32. See, for instance, *Blackwoods Magazine*, January 1860, pp. 32–44.

33. In 1843, H. G. Clarke & Co. advertised in his guide to the National Gallery (NAL pressmark 601.AG.0002) a book titled *The hand-book of painting in water colors. Imp. 32°, gilt edges, price 1s.* The only copy I have located of this work is in the Yale University Library, callmark: ND2130 H36 1843, which I have not seen.

34. NAL, pressmark 40.D.148.

35. Illuminating manuals are listed in Rowan Watson, 'Publishing for the leisure industry: illuminating manuals and the reception of a medieval art in Victorian Britain', *Nineteenth-century Belgium Manuscripts and Illuminations from a European Perspective. The Revival of Medieval Illumination*, ed. Thomas Coomans and Jan De Maeyer, KADOC Artes 8 (Leuven: Leuven University Press, 2007), pp. 102–06.

36. See the rear cover of Thomas Hatton, *Hints for sketching in water-colour* (Winsor & Newton, 1862), NAL pressmark 39.P.22.

37. NAL, pressmark 39.P.19.

38. NAL, pressmark 40.D.84.

39. *Art Journal*, 1860, p. 182.

40. From 1852, the museum had classes in chromolithography 'for female students only'; the students were to provide illustrations for a catalogue of the Museum's collections 'thus aiding the production of a useful work . . . acquiring the knowledge of an art peculiarly suitable to them, and for which there is an increasing public demand'; *First Report of the Department of Practical Art* (HMSO, 1853), p. 382; Board of Trade, Department of Science and Art, *A catalogue of the Museum of Ornamental Art at Marlborough House* (HMSO, 1854), Appendix A, p. 88.

41. Rowan Watson, 'Publishing for the leisure industry' (2007), pp. 91–2.

42. Anthea Callen, *The angel in the studio: women in the Arts and Crafts Movement, 1870–1914* (London: Astragal Books, 1979), especially pp. 27 et seq.

43. See D. Roger Dixon, *Marcus Ward and Company of Belfast* (Belfast Education and Library Board, 2004). The company was sold to Blackie & Co. after 1876. Ward's speciality was colour printing, for packaging and memorabilia as much as books. Kate Greenaway was among those supplying designs for Valentine cards and other work.

44. Further volumes from 1882 were called a 'New Series' and sold at 2*s*. 6*d*. If these books are taken as a barometer, it is apparent while Mulready and Cruikshank had joined the ranks of the 'Great Artists' by 1891, the only nineteenth-century German painter so honoured was Overbeck (d.1869). No English Pre-Raphaelite painter was included. The French Barbizon painters were Millet (d.1879), Rousseau (d.1867) and Diaz (d.1876), and also Corot (d.1875), Daubigny (d.1878) and Dupré (d.1889), subjects of a collective biography in two volumes in 1890. Horace Vernet (d.1863), Delaroche (d.1856) and Meissonier (d.1891) were other French painters in the series, their historical and anecdotal works being in much the same vein as the products of prestigious English artists.

The Art Collector and the Catalogue
from the early 1620s to the early 2000s

CHARLES SEBAG-MONTEFIORE

THE EXTRAORDINARY GROWTH of private art collection catalogues in the second half of the nineteenth century reflected a combination of a growing interest in provenance and the history of art collecting, the scholarship of some collectors and the vanity of others. Frank Herrmann suggested – tongue in cheek – that their value and interest were in inverse proportion to their size.[1] But, considered as a class from the seventeenth century onwards, private art collection and sale catalogues tell us of the successive formation and dispersal of collections of pictures, drawings and other works of art by providing firm evidence of ownership at a fixed date. A study of such catalogues is in effect a study of the history of collecting. In nearly four centuries, the best of their kind have meta-morphosed from a simple inventory or hand-list into informative and well-illustrated works of scholarship, frequently handsomely printed at a private press. The eighteenth century practice of visiting country houses, which created the need for guidebooks, stimulated the process. This essay examines the development of the private collection and sale catalogue from the early 1620s to the early 2000s.[2]

Printed catalogues differ from manuscript inventories in that their inherent purpose is to convey information to a wider readership, whereas manuscript inventories tend to be compiled for the use of the owner, his family or advisers, often being produced following a marriage or death. Hence manuscript catalogues can be viewed as a discrete subject in themselves and, with a handful of exceptions, they remain firmly outside the scope of this article.

The first 40 years of the seventeenth century saw a period of an unprecedented importation and accumulation of great works of art under the auspices of Charles I and a group of his courtiers, only to be reversed after the outbreak of the Civil War. The rapid formation and dispersal of the collections of the King and the members of his circle (chiefly Lord Arundel and the Dukes of Buckingham and Hamilton) represented a seismic shift in European taste. Seldom had pictures travelled so extensively or changed hands in such swift succession. Despite his numerous failures as monarch, Charles I was the most discerning and successful English royal collector of all time. Shy as a man and opinionated as a ruler, his passion for classical and renaissance works of art, his discriminating taste, his awareness of leading contemporary painters and sculptors and the works he commissioned from them, enriched the royal collection in a manner never subsequently matched.

Abraham Van der Doort, who in 1625 was appointed Keeper of the King's Pictures for life, compiled the first manuscript inventory of the royal collection. Oliver Millar[3] described the entries in Van der Doort's catalogue as 'written in greater detail and providing more information on provenance, size, condition and frames than can be found in any known inventory of the royal collection before the great inventory, begun at Prince Albert's instigation, by Richard Redgrave'. Over a hundred years later, Van der Doort's manuscript was edited by George Vertue and prepared for publication by Horace Walpole: the book was published in 1757.[4]

By the exacting standards of the twentieth century, the inaccuracies and omissions of the 1757 edition became more evident, and a definitive edition of the Van der Doort catalogue was prepared in 1960 by Sir Oliver Millar,[5] who wrote in the foreword that the catalogue was 'perhaps the finest inventory of its kind ever compiled in England. It is certainly the most important single source for our knowledge of the growth, arrangement and quality of a collection unrivalled in the history of English taste. The care and restraint with which it is drawn up bear witness to the connoisseurship in Charles I's circle and parts of the catalogue are presented in such detail that they help us to envisage the appearance of some of the royal apartments in the age of Inigo Jones.'

The antiquarian publication of Charles I's catalogue in 1757 prompts an obvious question: what is a catalogue for? Horace Walpole, as so often, put his finger on it in his anonymous introduction to that book.[6] 'Catalogues of this sort are deservedly grown into esteem: while a collection remains entire, the use of the catalogue is obvious; when dispersed, it often serves to authenticate a picture, adds to its imaginary value, and bestows a sort of history on it. It is to be wished that the practice of composing catalogues of conspicuous collections was universal: and perhaps even this, so coarsely executed, may tend to incite more elegant imitations.' He was entirely right. Apart from their contribution to art history and scholarship, catalogues are essential for the study of provenance.

George Villiers (1592–1628), eight years older than the King, was created 1st Duke of Buckingham in 1623. He kept his pictures in York

House, a palace on the Thames which he bought in 1624. His most famous masterpiece was Titian's *Ecce Homo* (Vienna), which he bought in Venice in 1621. Two manuscript inventories of Buckingham's collection were made, in 1635[7] (listing 330 pictures) and 1648[8] (200 pictures only). Out of the 330 pictures in the earlier list, there were (either originals or copies) 22 Titians, 21 Bassanos (father and son), 17 Tintorettos, 16 Veroneses, 10 Palmas, 3 Bonifazios, 2 Correggios, and 1 Giorgione. Eleven pictures by Andrea del Sarto made him the best represented Florentine painter. The inventory listed three Leonardos, two Raphaels, and one Michelangelo. Of contemporary painters, there were sixteen pictures listed by Domenico Feti. The influence of Caravaggio was a major theme at York House with pictures by Baglione, Manfredi, Honthorst and Gentileschi and several works listed as by Caravaggio himself. A surprising entry is an early version of El Greco's *Christ Driving the Traders from the Temple* (Minneapolis), an artist generally overlooked by British collectors until the nineteenth century. Northern pictures included portraits by Mor and Pourbus the Younger, Mabuse, Elsheimer and, of course, Rubens.

The earliest printed inventory known to me of a British art collection is Selden's *Marmora Arundelliana*, published in 1628 with a second edition in 1629. The titlepage is printed in red and black and the text of this handsome work is mostly in Latin and Greek, with some Hebrew. Arundel, who was fifteen years older than King Charles I and certainly encouraged the King to collect, bought pictures, especially by Holbein and Venetian painters, drawings and sculpture. William Petty travelled all over the Ottoman Empire for Arundel and Buckingham and he secured many of Arundel's classical inscriptions subsequently catalogued by Selden.

The result of the brilliant burst of collecting by the Stuarts and the Whitehall Circle was that a visitor to London on the eve of the Civil War would have seen some of the finest pictures in the world located in London within a mile of the present National Gallery in Trafalgar Square. The mansions of the Strand included Suffolk House (shortly to be bought by Lord Northumberland and to be rebuilt as Northumberland House); York House (which still contained the Duke of Buckingham's collections fifteen years after his assassination); Durham House (leased to the 4th Earl of Pembroke), Somerset House (which Charles I had given to Henrietta Maria); and Arundel House. St James's Palace contained some of the King's most magnificent pictures. On the other side of St James's Park was Wallingford House (near the site of the present Admiralty in Whitehall), home to the 1st Duke of Hamilton.

Whitehall Palace, filled with great and famous pictures, stood opposite. Downstream at Blackfriars, Van Dyck's collection of important pictures by Titian remained untouched after his death in 1641. On the fringes of London, the royal palaces of Greenwich, Richmond, Hampton Court, Nonsuch and Windsor Castle contained further treasures. It is to be regretted that, apart from Selden's catalogue of Arundel Marbles, no inventories were printed to record these riches.

An anonymous pamphlet, printed in 1642, is the opposite of a catalogue and is entitled *A Deep Sigh Breath'd Through the Lodgings at White-Hall, Deploring the absence of the Court, and the Miseries of the Pallace*. The anonymous author passed gloomily through the deserted rooms of Whitehall Palace, bemoaning the absence of furnishings, smells, sounds and crowds. The author described Whitehall as 'A Pallace without a Presence' and added that 'his Majesties great Beef-eaters [who] had wont to sit in attendance' in the Guard Chamber were 'now all vanisht, nothing left but bare Walls and a cold Harth, from whence the Fire-Irones are removed too'.

In 1649, commissioners were given extensive powers to draw up full inventories of the King's collections and to put valuations on the individual items. These included not just paintings and statues but tapestries, which were frequently looked upon as most valuable, and furniture of all kinds including chairs, cushions and stools.[9] This *Inventory of the Late King's Goods* spawned many copies, even into the eighteenth century, but even the later copies are useful as they group the pictures in the palaces where they were hung, including Greenwich, Wimbledon, Nonsuch, Hampton Court as well as the two palaces where the greatest pictures were displayed – St James's Palace and Whitehall Palace.

It was not until the early eighteenth century that the next printed catalogue of a private collection was published. Although not a full catalogue, reference should be made to the undated sequence of 20 plates, engraved by Hamlet Winstanley, reproducing Italian and Dutch pictures collected by James Stanley, 10th Earl of Derby (1664–1736).[10] Lord Derby sent Winstanley, who was born near Knowsley Hall, to Rome to look out for pictures: he was abroad between 1723 and 1725. This folio work was begun in 1727 and may have been published circa 1730.[11]

The first proper catalogues were compiled at the instigation of Thomas Herbert 8th Earl of Pembroke (1656–1733). The third son of the 5th Earl, he succeeded his brother in 1683, holding the earldom for 50 years. Serious-minded, learned and industrious, he held many offices of state, including that of Lord High Admiral in 1702. He made good the family fortunes and was a collector on a large scale, adding pictures, coins and medals and sculpture from the Mazarin, Arundel and Giustiniani collections.

Towards the end of his life, it appears that this methodical man wanted to commission catalogues of his collections. He chose Count Carlo Gambarini to compile that of the pictures. The book, *A Description of the Earl of Pembroke's Pictures, now Published by C. Gambarini of Lucca*, was published in 1731. It has the distinction of being the earliest printed catalogue of a British collection of pictures: this statement excludes auction catalogues, which are considered later in this article. The catalogue gives the name of the artist and title of the work, with occasional dimensions and provenance. Francis Russell has observed that the Earl's approach to collecting pictures was akin to his systematic and methodical pursuit of coins and medals, with one example from every painter, and suggested that Pembroke owned a copy of Padre Orlandi's *Abecedario pittorico*, first published in 1704.[12] The names of a number of earlier artists appear in his catalogue, including Masaccio, Fra Angelico, Signorelli and Bellini, but Pembroke's purchases of works by Cambiaso, Luca Giordano and Panini show that more contemporary artists also appealed to him.

Gambarini, who came from Lucca, wanted to obtain commissions to write catalogues of other collections: the introduction to his Wilton catalogue contained a useful list of contemporary collectors with whom Gambarini hoped to curry favour. This list includes the Dukes of Somerset, Devonshire, Kingston, Buckingham, Argyll and Kent, Lord Cholmondeley, Lord Tyrconnel, Sir Robert Walpole, Sir Paul Methuen, Sir James Thornhill and Richard Mead. Gambarini's blandishments did not succeed and it is our loss that the Wilton catalogue remains his only published work.

Lord Pembroke's coins and medals were catalogued by Nicola Francesco Haym, who was born in Rome of German parents *c*.1678. In 1704 he came to London, where he died in 1729. Musicologists know him as a cellist and composer, who took a leading part in the establishment of Italian opera in London and as the man who wrote the libretto for many of Handel's operas, including *Giulio Cesare* and *Tamerlano*. Haym was also a connoisseur of medals. In 1719 he wrote and etched the plates for *Del Tesoro Britannico*, an ambitious attempt to publish a corpus of Greek and Roman coins in British collections. Among the collections mentioned are those of the Duke of Devonshire, the Earl of Winchilsea, Sir Robert Abdy, Sir Andrew Fountaine and Sir Hans

Sloane. Pembroke too is mentioned but with the explanation that few of Pembroke's coins were included in *Del Tesoro Britannico* as 'His Lordship designs to publish his own collection apart'.

Haym's catalogue *The Earl of Pembroke's Medals in V. Parts* is undated but must have been written before March 1729, when Haym's library was sold in a posthumous auction.[13] My copy is one of only two copies of the original printing in Haym's lifetime. According to a letter from Roger Gale to William Stukeley dated 2 December 1732[14] which refers to this book, an almost insuperable problem arose to prevent publication: according to Gale '100 of the engraved plates were irretrievably lost' having been sold or pawned by Haym's widow, of which Gale traced many to the 'brazier's furnace'. Gale continued: 'by good fortune, my lord has recovered two intire impressions of the whole and I left him under a resolution of having the 100 plates wanting to be re-engraved from their draughts in his hands'. This catalogue is normally found with a new titlepage, engraved in 1746, distributed after the death of Lord Pembroke. I have compared my copy with the 1746 edition: all the pages with manuscript amendments in my copy have been re-engraved to appear correctly in the later edition. It remains to say that the Pembroke collection of coins and medals was sold at auction by Sotheby's in July and August 1848 in a twelve-day sale of 1,500 lots.

For his sculpture, Lord Pembroke chose Cary Creed, an engraver completely unknown save for this one work. The titlepage, like that of Haym's work, was engraved in a cursive script: *The Marble Antiquities, the Right Hon*^{ble} *the Earl of Pembroke's at Wilton*. To say that the attributions in this catalogue are optimistic is an understatement: the text at the foot of the first engraved plate in this catalogue reads 'Cupid breaking his Bow when he married Psyche, big as life. By Cleomenes. E of Pembroke's'. How did Creed know that the sculptor was Cleomenes? The attribution is likely to have been imposed by Lord Pembroke, with Creed meekly engraving the words Lord Pembroke instructed. This catalogue exists in four states: a first edition of *c*.1729 with 16 plates and a different titlepage; a second edition with 40 plates of 1729 or 1730; a third edition of 1731 with 70 plates and a second version of the 1731 edition, identical save for the addition of four further plates to make 74 in all.

The sequence of eighteenth century catalogues of Wilton stands with Stowe as the most remarkable continuous record of any British collection. This collection included the great *Group Portrait of Philip, 4th Earl of Pembroke and his Family* painted by Van Dyck in 1634–5, which hung in Durham House off the Strand until it was moved to Wilton in

Fig. 1. A page from the rare first edition of Haym's catalogue of coins and medals at Wilton. The illustration shows an example of manuscript amendments, in this instance the names of the Roman Emperors Tiberius, Domitian and Titus.

about 1652. The earliest catalogue was written by Richard Cowdry, *Description of the Pictures, Statues, Busto's, Basso-relievo's and other Curiosities at Wilton House* and appeared in two octavo editions of 1751 and 1752. The text is laid out as a guide book for visitors: dimensions and provenance information are not provided. Six years later, in 1758, James Kennedy issued his *New Description of the Pictures, Statues, Busto's, Basso-relievo's and other Curiosities at Wilton House.* As the collection of pictures and works of art was gradually expanded, a regular demand arose for updated versions: Kennedy's octavo *Description* extended to nine octavo editions between 1758 and 1779. In 1769, Kennedy published his guidebook in a new quarto format as *A Description of the Antiquities and Curiosities in Wilton-House.*[15] Two subsequent editions were published, in 1781 and 1786. This was again cast as guidebook, but as a quarto to keep on the shelf rather than in the pocket while touring the house.

George Richardson commenced a rival sequence of octavo Wilton guidebooks in 1774 in competition with Kennedy. His *Aedes Pembrochianae* ran to thirteen editions between 1774 and 1798, ultimately outlasting Kennedy's final octavo edition of 1779. Before leaving Wilton, I cannot resist quoting from a letter by Horace Walpole to Lord Strafford dated 13 September 1759: 'I have lately been at Wilton, and was astonished at the heaps of rubbish. The house is grand and the place glorious; but I should shovel three parts of the marbles and the pictures into the river.'[16]

The sequence of guidebooks to Stowe was the longest of any house in Great Britain. Whereas the span of Wilton guidebooks was approximately 70 years, that of Stowe exceeded a century. The earliest book, on the gardens only, was published in 1732. The latest, a description of both the house and the gardens, appeared as late as 1838. During these 106 years, no fewer than 38 descriptions were published, an astonishing rate of one new version every 33 months. This frequency is largely explained by the number of visitors to the celebrated gardens. The information given about the pictures is somewhat sparse and its style resembles a handlist rather than a catalogue.

As with Wilton, there was competition between rival authors. Benton Seeley (1716–95) produced the earliest guidebook in 1744, *A Description of the Gardens of the Lord Viscount Cobham at Stow in Buckinghamshire.* The book was well received and further editions were produced to keep pace with the expansion of the gardens. George Bickham the younger (1706?–71) published a rival octavo guidebook *The Beauties of Stow* in 1750, which ran to three editions. The Seeley family comprehensively saw off Bickham: between 1744 and 1832, they published no fewer than 26 editions of their Stowe guidebook.

Generations of Grenville extravagance and unsustainable mortgages led to the well-known sale of Stowe in 1848, six years after that of Strawberry Hill. So great was the interest in this sale that a priced and annotated copy of the sale catalogue was produced afterwards, showing the prices achieved and the buyers' names.[17]

Turning to auction sales, the first sale as we know it today, with lot numbers and a printed catalogue, originated in Holland. The first known British book sale was held in London in 1676,[18] and the earliest recorded picture sale in 1686.[19] In the early years, sale catalogues amounted to little more than an inventory, listing in numerical sequence the name of the artist and title of the picture.

By the 1740s, auctioneering had become more sophisticated. One of the leading auctioneers, Christopher Cock of the Great Piazza, Covent Garden, was engaged to sell the pictures, antiquities, busts, bronzes, coins and medals belonging to Edward Harley, 2nd Earl of Oxford (1689–1741). The sale, which began on 8 March 1742, took twelve days to complete.

Robert Harley, 1st Earl of Oxford (1661–1724), and his son favoured portraits of eminent contemporaries (by Kneller, Dahl and Richardson) and the heads of well-known historical figures such as King Henry VIII, Sir Walter Raleigh, Shakespeare, Edmund Spenser and Charles I. Their taste in old masters included pictures by Bassano, Carlo Dolci, Salvator Rosa and Sebastiano Ricci, Roman views by Locatelli and Panini, northern landscapes and seascapes by Ferg and Willem van der Velde, still-lives by Bogdani and Verelst, and works attributed to Rubens, van Dyck and Rembrandt, Claude and Poussin. The dispersal of the Harley collection created opportunities for the next generation of collectors. My copy is priced and annotated with buyers' names, including the Dukes of Bedford, Leeds and Richmond, Lords Ancaster, Bristol, Essex, Halifax and Hervey, Lord James Cavendish, James West of Alscot, George Knapton, Mr Lethieullier and Horace Walpole.

This leads me to make the obvious but crucial point that annotated copies are far more interesting than unmarked ones, particularly for provenance research. One sad consequence of a library passing into institutional hands is that the practice of scholarly annotation, so helpful to later generations, generally ceases.

Lord Oxford and his father are best remembered as the creators of the Harleian Library, which was housed at Wimpole Hall in Cambridgeshire. The printed books were estimated at more than 50,000

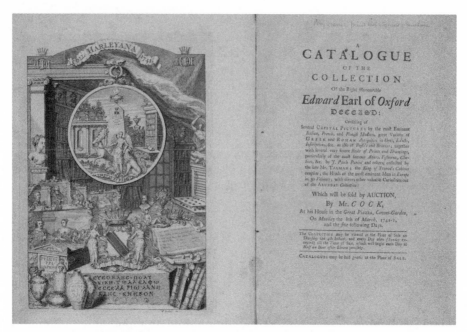

Fig. 2.   The frontispiece to the Harley sale was engraved by Vertue and depicted a collection of antiquities, books and paintings grouped around a block of stone bearing a Greek inscription on which is balanced Harley's coronetted coat of arms.

volumes, 400,000 pamphlets and 41,000 prints, and were dispersed by auction after the 2nd Earl's death in 1741. The manuscript collection eventually amounted to 7,000 manuscripts in European, Hebrew and various oriental languages, 14,000 charters and 700 rolls. The manuscripts included the Harley Golden Gospels (possibly made in Aachen *c.*800), some fine Anglo-Saxon manuscripts (for example, the Ramsey Psalter and the Bury St Edmunds Gospels), medical and alchemical treatises and works of classical literature. Humfrey Wanley (1672–1726), whose diary is such an important source of information about the growth of the collection, was appointed librarian to the Harleys in 1708. This manuscript library was sold to Parliament in 1753, as the second foundation purchase (after Sloane's collections) for the British Museum, by the widow of the 2nd Earl of Oxford (Henrietta Cavendish Holles) and their daughter and heiress, Margaret Cavendish-Bentinck, Duchess of Portland.

Collecting was not confined to the aristocracy with large estates: the mania had spread to the professions. Dr Richard Mead (1673–1754) was famous throughout Europe as a physician, scholar and collector.

His sympathetic full-length portrait by Allan Ramsay belongs to the Foundling Museum. Mead's pictures were sold after his death, on 20, 21 and 22 March 1754, by Abraham Langford, the partner and successor to Cock after the latter's death in 1748. The copy which belonged to the 4th Duke of Bedford[20] is annotated with the word 'myself' beside several pictures to indicate his purchases. One was Sebastiano Ricci's *Christ Healing the Blind Man*, which left Woburn early in the nineteenth century and was acquired by the National Gallery of Scotland in 1994.

Sir Luke Schaub (1690–1758) was a Swiss-born diplomat who attracted the notice of George II and whose daughter Frederica Augusta married William Lock of Norbury Park. Schaub's pictures were sold in a posthumous sale between 26 and 28 April 1758, by Langford. The most active purchaser at the sale was Margaret Harley, Duchess of Portland, who paid £2,208 8s. 0d. for fourteen lots in the sale which, as a whole, fetched £7,774 14s. 6d. The Duchess thus accounted for over 28% of the aggregate hammer price. Her purchases can be readily identified in later catalogues of the Portland collection of paintings.[21]

Horace Walpole described the sale in a letter to Sir Horace Mann dated 10 May 1758:

You would have been amazed, had you been here at Sir Luke Schaub's auction of pictures. He had picked up some good old copies cheap when he was in Spain . . . With these he had some fine small ones, and a parcel of Flemish, good in their way. The late Prince [Frederick, Prince of Wales] offered him £12,000 for the whole, leaving him the enjoyment for his life. As he knew £12,000 would not be forthcoming, he artfully excused himself by saying that he loved pictures so much that he knew he should fling away the money. Indeed, could he have touched it, it had been well; the collection was indubitably not worth £4,000. It has sold for near eight! A copy of the King of France's Raphael went for £700. A Sigismonda, called by Correggio, but certainly by Furini, his scholar, was bought in at upwards of £400. In short, there is Sir James Lowther, Mr Spencer, Sir Richard Grosvenor, boys with 20 and £30,000 a year, and the Duchess of Portland, Lord Ashburnham, Lord Egremont and others with near as much, who care not what they give.[22]

The Duchess of Portland's Museum was dispersed in a huge sale, conducted by Skinner, which lasted 38 days from 24 April 1786. The majority of the lots comprised shells, corals and petrifactions, crystals, spars and ores and what were described as 'British and exotic insects'. The sale also included coins and medals, china, gold and silver, prints and drawings, miniatures and missals. Shown prominently on the engraved titlepage is the Portland Vase, sold by the Barberini family in 1778 to Sir William Hamilton and by him to the Duchess in 1784. The

A

CATALOGUE

Of the GRAND and CAPITAL

COLLECTION

OF

Italian, *Flemiſh*, and *Dutch*

PAINTINGS,

OF THE

Hon. Sir LUKE SCHAUB,

𝕷𝖆𝖙𝖊𝖑𝖞 𝕯𝖊𝖈𝖊𝖆𝖘𝖊𝖉;

Amongſt which are the choiceſt W O R K S of

RAPHAEL,	ALBANO,	LUCA GIORDANO,	VANDYCK,
A. and L. CARRACCI,	CORREGIO,	C. LORRAINE,	JORDAENS,
M. ANGELO,	GUIDO,	POUSSIN,	WOVERMANS,
GUERCINO,	P. DA CORTONA,	MURILLO,	TENEIRS,
TINTORETTO,	P. VERONESE,	REMBRANDT,	P. BRILL,
TITIAN,	P. LAURA,	RUBENS,	OSTADE,

And ſeveral other M A S T E R S of great Eminence.

Which, (by O R D E R of the A D M I N I S T R A T R I X)
Will be ſold by A U C T I O N,

By Mr. *LANGFORD*,

At his *Houſe* in the *Great Piazza*, *Covent Garden*,

On *Wedneſday* the 26th, *Thurſday* the 27th, and *Friday* the 28th
of this Inſtant *April* 1758.

The ſaid Collection may be viewed on *Monday* the 24th, and every Day after till
the Time of Sale, which will begin *punctually* each Day *at Twelve o'Clock.*

CATALOGUES of which may be had at Mr. LANGFORD's, in the *Great Piazza* aforeſaid,
Price SIX-PENCE, *which ſhall be returned to all ſuch as become Purchaſers.*

CONDITIONS of SALE as uſual.

N. B. *At the End of the* firſt Day's Sale *will be ſold* Sir Luke's LANDAU, *with a neat* Crane Neck, *hung
on Springs, and lined with light Cloth.*

Fig. 3.   The titlepage of the sale catalogue of Sir Luke Schaub's pictures, held on
26–28 April 1758, sold by Langford, priced and with buyers' names throughout

vase fetched 980 guineas to a Mr Tomlinson, probably acting for her son the third Duke. In 1810 the fourth Duke lent it to the British Museum, which acquired the Vase in 1945.

Horace Walpole catalogued the famous collection of pictures at Houghton formed by his father Sir Robert Walpole, who was in 1742 created 1st Earl of Orford. This work, *Aedes Walpolianae*, was his first published art criticism.[23] In the introduction, Horace Walpole wrote that his account was meant as a *Catalogue* rather than a *Description* of the pictures, adding that 'the Mention of Cabinets in which they have formerly been, with the Addition of Measures will contribute to ascertain their Originality, and be a kind of Pedigree to them'. Horace Walpole made plain his real affection for the house his father had built and the collection which embellished it: 'There are not a great many Collections left in Italy more worth seeing than this at Houghton: In the Preservation of the Pictures, it certainly excells most of them.'

The frontispieces of both editions were engraved by George Vertue from miniatures by Zinke. The 1747 edition had that of Sir Robert only with a distant view of Houghton Hall, whereas the 1752 edition contained images of both his parents. The catalogue also contained a plan of the ground and principal floors and a very detailed description of all the principal rooms and their contents. One room on the principal floor was then known as the Carlo Maratta Room: Sir Robert owned six works by this artist, including a large *Judgement of Paris* and *Acis and Galatea* as well as the superb *Portrait of Pope Clement IX Rospigliosi*. The Houghton collection was sold in 1779 to the Empress Catherine of Russia, and the papal portrait, with the other Houghton masterpieces, is now a vital part of the collections of the Hermitage Museum in St Petersburg.

Over 20 years later, Horace Walpole turned his attention to his own house at Strawberry Hill. In 1774 he printed *The Description of the Villa* in an edition of 100 octavo copies, with six on large paper. The work began with a brief history of the houses on the site preceding Strawberry Hill and quickly moved onto a description of the individual rooms and their contents. The book continued thus for 116 pages by which time, Horace Walpole was afflicted by the problem which strikes all collectors who compile catalogues. Additions soon make the work incomplete and give rise to the need for an appendix. This resulted in another 25 pages. The Appendix was followed by a *List of the Books Printed at Strawberry Hill*, which interestingly refers to books printed as late as 1781. Further purchases necessitated a further section (of four pages) entitled '*Additions since the Appendix*', the first of which was the well-known

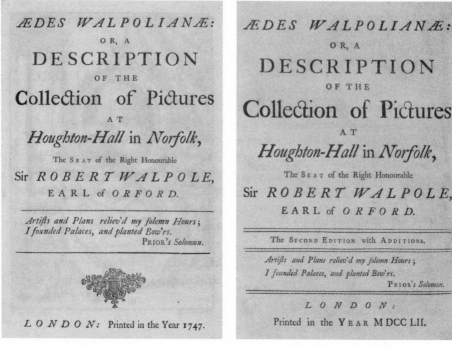

Fig. 4.   Horace Walpole wrote that 'in 1747 I printed my account of the collection of
pictures at Houghton under the title Aedes Walpolianae. It had been drawn up in
1743. I printed but 200 copies, to give away. It was very incorrectly printed:
another edition, more accurate and enlarged, was published 10 March 1752'.

portrait by Reynolds of his three Waldegrave nieces (National Gallery of
Scotland), to be followed by yet another section (of six pages) entitled
'*More Additions*', on the final page of which Walpole referred to an event
which took place in 1784.

The 1774 *Description* had taken ten years to evolve and in 1784
Horace Walpole decided to reprint the entire book again, this time in
quarto with the information re-arranged to show the objects in the
rooms where they were then placed. It constitutes as detailed an
inventory as one could wish for, but as Wyndham Ketton-Cremer
implied, it seems peculiar that equal attention appears to be given to a
Sèvres cup and saucer as to the Reynolds portrait of his nieces.[24]
Whereas the 1774 edition was unillustrated, the 1784 edition contained
many images of which the evocative views of the Library, Tribune and
Gallery at Strawberry Hill are familiar examples.

Walpole's remark in *Aedes Walpolianae* that catalogues served to confer a provenance on works of art was to prove prophetically personal. The contents of Strawberry Hill were themselves dispersed in a sale conducted by George Robins in 1842.[25] The sale catalogue ran into a number of editions.

By the turn of the century, the great aristocratic collections became the subject of catalogues, particularly as the houses were open to recommended visitors on certain days in the season. Cleveland House in St James's, which then belonged to Lord Stafford (1758–1833), was open every Wednesday for four months, from May 1806. Stafford was the nephew and heir of the 3rd and last Duke of Bridgewater, who had vastly increased his family wealth by developing canals for the transport of coal from his mines for sale in Manchester and Liverpool, thus playing a significant, if unlikely, role in the Industrial Revolution. Bridgewater bequeathed to Lord Stafford a life interest in the vast Bridgewater estates and collections. Taken together with his wife's Sutherland estates in Scotland, he became enormously rich and was described by Charles Greville as 'the Leviathan of Wealth' and 'the richest man who ever died'. On his father's death in 1803, he succeeded as 2nd Marquess of Stafford and was created 1st Duke of Sutherland in 1833.

In 1808 John Britton published his *Catalogue Raisonné of the Pictures belonging to the Most Honourable the Marquis of Stafford, in the Gallery of Cleveland House.* The New Gallery at Cleveland House contained not only three paintings by Raphael from the Orléans collection, but also Titian's *Three Ages of Man,* Tintoretto's *Entombment of Christ,* and works by Annibale Carracci, Domenichino, Guercino, Francesco Mola and Salvator Rosa. Britton's text is somewhat verbose, but at least contains information on the provenance of those pictures which derived from the Orléans collection. A guest being entertained in the Dining Room of Cleveland House must have found it a heady experience in the company of exceptionally fine Venetian pictures including three by Titian – *Diana and Actaeon, Diana and Callisto* and *Venus Anadyomene.*

The splendour and renown of the collection led to the appearance of several catalogues, but the finest of them was produced in 1818 by William Young Ottley and Peltro William Tomkins.[26] It was produced as a heavy folio of letterpress and plates in four parts, but a limited number of coloured copies were produced and offered for sale for the enormous sum of £171 4s. According to one website which calculates the purchasing power of the pound, the cost of a coloured copy would now be equivalent to over £10,000. Such a calculation depends critically on the assumptions employed, but it is not surprising that Tomkins sold only a few copies and was subsequently declared bankrupt.

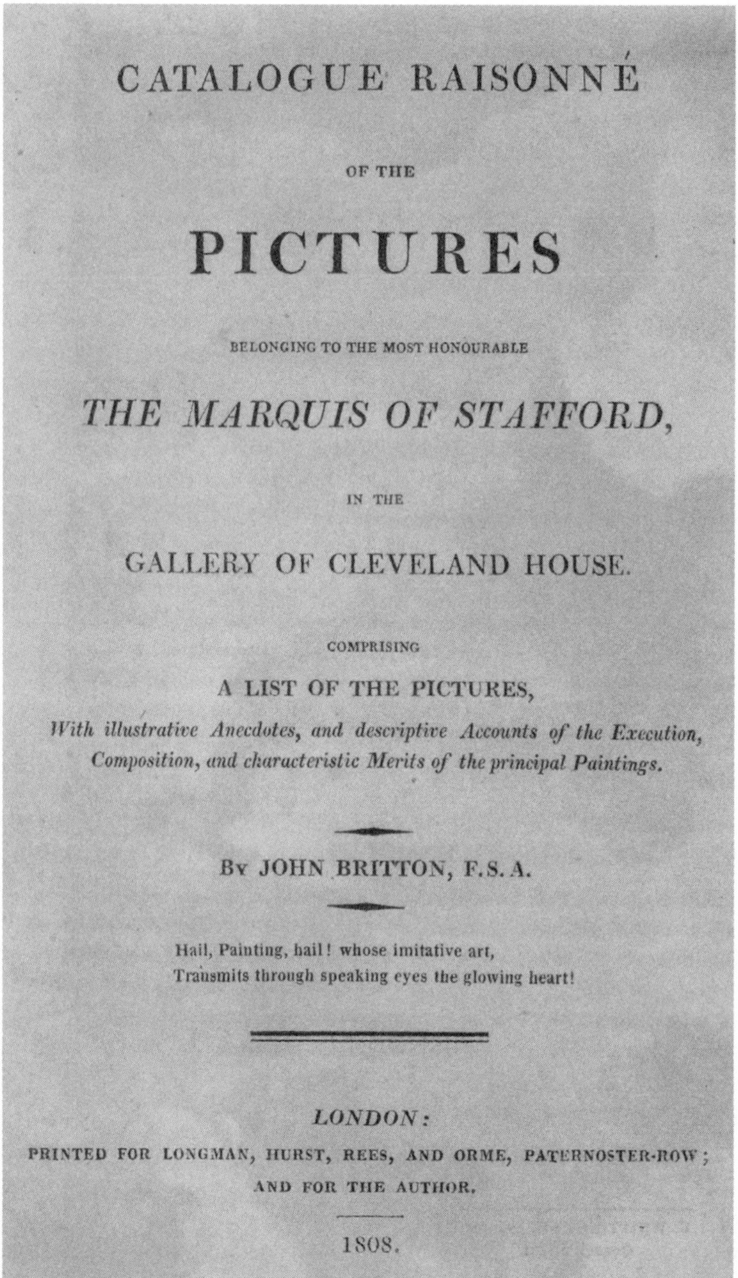

CATALOGUE RAISONNÉ

OF THE

PICTURES

BELONGING TO THE MOST HONOURABLE

THE MARQUIS OF STAFFORD,

IN THE

GALLERY OF CLEVELAND HOUSE.

COMPRISING

A LIST OF THE PICTURES,

*With illustrative Anecdotes, and descriptive Accounts of the Execution,
Composition, and characteristic Merits of the principal Paintings.*

By JOHN BRITTON, F.S.A.

Hail, Painting, hail! whose imitative art,
Transmits through speaking eyes the glowing heart!

LONDON:

PRINTED FOR LONGMAN, HURST, REES, AND ORME, PATERNOSTER-ROW;

AND FOR THE AUTHOR.

1808.

Fig. 5.   The titlepage of John Britton's catalogue of Lord Stafford's pictures at Cleveland
House

Fig. 6.   View of the New Gallery at Cleveland House. Raphael's 'Holy Family with a Palm Tree' is visible in the centre of the left wall below Annibale Carracci's 'Danae on a couch with a Cupid' (see Fig. 8).

The coloured copy of Ottley and Tomkins is an exceptional catalogue. One remarkable feature of the publication is the series of plates depicting the hanging arrangements of the pictures in every room. The Regency furniture is also depicted and the windows looking through to Green Park. Each picture is described *in extenso*, all with dimensions and provenance information, wherever possible. The engraving of the New Gallery (1818) can readily be compared with that of John Britton (1808). Ottley and Tomkins's work gives us a very clear idea of the interiors, with their pictures and furnishings and the general arrangement of the rooms.

John Young was Engraver in Mezzotinto to the King and Keeper of the British Institution. In 1820 he compiled the catalogue of the pictures at Grosvenor House[27] belonging to Robert Grosvenor, 2nd Earl Grosvenor, who was created 1st Marquess of Westminster in 1831. Young's style was to provide a description of each picture, its measurements, provenance and an engraved image. These pictures remained *in situ* until 1924, when Grosvenor House was given up and many pictures sold. John Young also catalogued the collections of John Julius

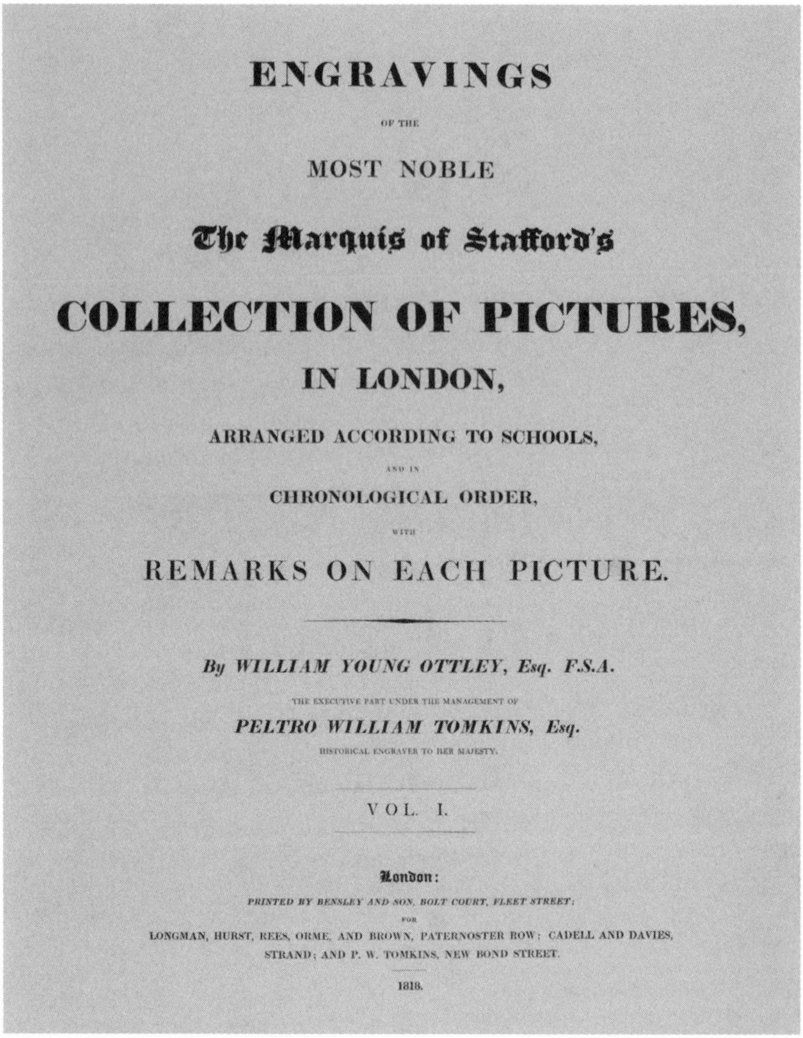

ENGRAVINGS

OF THE

MOST NOBLE

𝕿𝖍𝖊 𝕸𝖆𝖗𝖖𝖚𝖎𝖘 𝖔𝖋 𝕾𝖙𝖆𝖋𝖋𝖔𝖗𝖉'𝖘

COLLECTION OF PICTURES,

IN LONDON,

ARRANGED ACCORDING TO SCHOOLS,

AND IN

CHRONOLOGICAL ORDER,

WITH

REMARKS ON EACH PICTURE.

By WILLIAM YOUNG OTTLEY, Esq. F.S.A.

THE EXECUTIVE PART UNDER THE MANAGEMENT OF

PELTRO WILLIAM TOMKINS, Esq.

HISTORICAL ENGRAVER TO HER MAJESTY.

VOL. I.

London:

PRINTED BY BENSLEY AND SON, BOLT COURT, FLEET STREET;

FOR

LONGMAN, HURST, REES, ORME, AND BROWN, PATERNOSTER ROW; CADELL AND DAVIES,
STRAND; AND P. W. TOMKINS, NEW BOND STREET.

1818.

Fig. 7.   Titlepage of 'The Stafford Gallery', by Ottley and Tomkins, 1818, the finest and
most elaborate of the catalogues of Lord Stafford's pictures

Angerstein,[28] whose collection was bought by Parliament in 1824 as
the foundation of the National Gallery, as well as those of Sir John
Fleming Leicester[29] and Lord Stafford.[30]

Sir John Fleming Leicester was untypical as a collector as he
eschewed pictures by continental artists and became a leading patron
of contemporary British artists. His collection of exclusively British

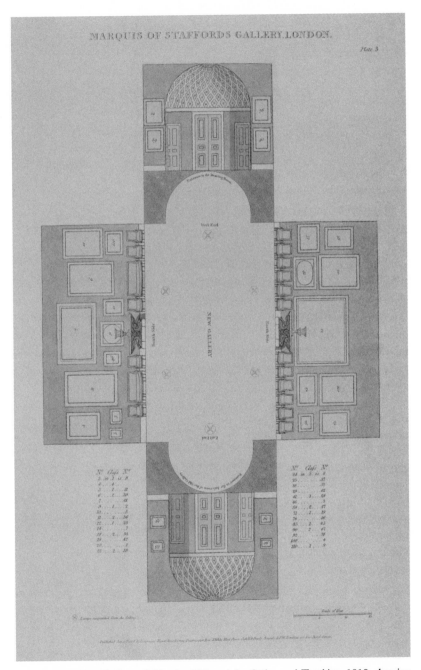

Fig. 8.   'The New Gallery of Cleveland House', by Ottley and Tomkins, 1818, showing the hanging arrangement of the pictures. (See Fig. 6 and Plate XI.)

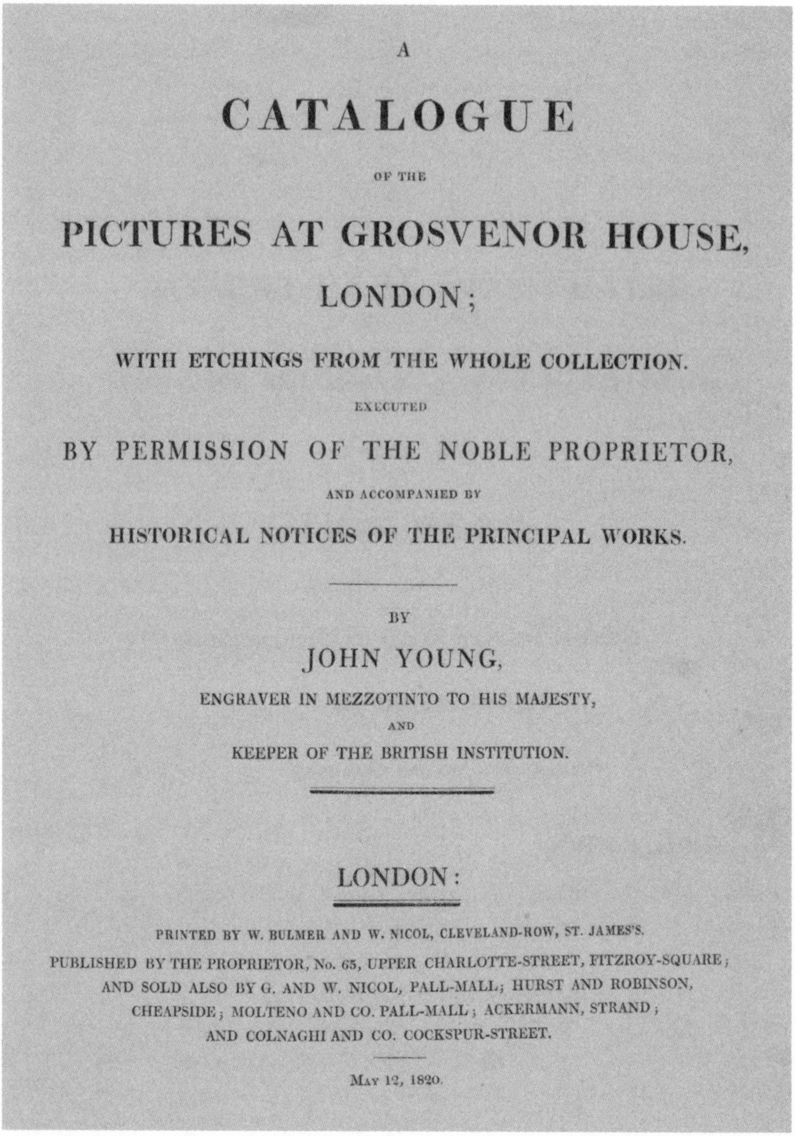

A

CATALOGUE

OF THE

PICTURES AT GROSVENOR HOUSE,

LONDON;

WITH ETCHINGS FROM THE WHOLE COLLECTION.

EXECUTED

BY PERMISSION OF THE NOBLE PROPRIETOR,

AND ACCOMPANIED BY

HISTORICAL NOTICES OF THE PRINCIPAL WORKS.

BY

JOHN YOUNG,

ENGRAVER IN MEZZOTINTO TO HIS MAJESTY,

AND

KEEPER OF THE BRITISH INSTITUTION.

LONDON:

PRINTED BY W. BULMER AND W. NICOL, CLEVELAND-ROW, ST. JAMES'S.

PUBLISHED BY THE PROPRIETOR, No. 65, UPPER CHARLOTTE-STREET, FITZROY-SQUARE;

AND SOLD ALSO BY G. AND W. NICOL, PALL-MALL; HURST AND ROBINSON,

CHEAPSIDE; MOLTENO AND CO. PALL-MALL; ACKERMANN, STRAND;

AND COLNAGHI AND CO. COCKSPUR-STREET.

MAY 12, 1820.

Fig. 9. Titlepage of the *Catalogue of the Pictures at Grosvenor House* by John Young, 1820

paintings was displayed in galleries in Tabley House in Cheshire and in his London house, 24 Hill Street, to which he admitted the public. Pre-dating John Young's catalogue of 1825, William Carey catalogued Leicester's collection in 1819.[31] Carey was a passionate advocate of British artists and his definition of a 'lover of the fine arts' was that of 'patron of the British school'. His text is wordy, but an engraved frontispiece depicts the London Gallery evocatively and shows prominently Turner's *View of Tabley Lake and Tower, Calm Morning* (Petworth, National Trust).

Understandably the standard of provincial cataloguing and printing in the early nineteenth century did not match that of the capital. Lord Bagot's pictures at Blithfield in Staffordshire were the subject of a catalogue, privately printed in Uttoxeter in 1801.[32] It is a simple handlist, detailing only the title of the picture and the name of the artist to whom it was attributed. No attempt was made to describe the pictures, or to give measurements or provenance. The 1814 Marbury Hall catalogue is also no more than a handlist.[33] This was a significant collection formed by John Smith Barry, later Lord Barrymore. Such scant detail appears parsimonious to today's students of provenance.

An idiosyncratic collector, Thomas Lister Parker of Browsholme Hall (1779–1858), went on the Grand Tour in 1800, visiting France, Italy and Russia, returning home in 1801 with a collection of paintings, drawings and prints. His early interest in pictures was for the old masters: his earliest recorded purchase, of 1799, was a landscape by Claude. He bought his most remarkable picture at Sir William Hamilton's sale in 1801, the *Portrait of Juan de Pareja* by Velasquez (Metropolitan Museum, New York). In 1807 the Browsholme gallery contained over 50 paintings, chiefly Dutch and Italian. Parker catalogued his collection of pictures in both 1807 and 1808.[34] More than a handlist, Lister also gave intermittent information on provenance. In 1808 he sold most of his old masters (partly due to financial pressures) and thereafter concentrated on patronage of contemporary British artists, especially Turner and Northcote, but the printed list provides firm evidence of the fine pictures which once hung at Browsholme in Lancashire.[35]

Sir George Scharf (1820–95) was an inspired choice as the first Director of the National Portrait Gallery, which he served with brilliant success from 1857 to 1895. A talented artist, he visited country houses all over Britain to catalogue and sketch paintings, identify portraits and search out pictures for the Gallery to acquire. He was commissioned by three aristocratic owners to catalogue their collections of pictures:

all three owned fine sequences of historical portraits, which played to Scharf's strength. First, in 1860 came the catalogue of the pictures in Blenheim Palace.[36] He brought a high degree of professionalism to the task of describing the pictures, but it seems odd that such a methodical author should not also have provided the dimensions and provenance of the pictures, as was occasionally provided as early as the 1731 Wilton catalogue: perhaps this category of information interested him less than the images of the sitter. For Lord Derby Scharf compiled a catalogue of pictures at Knowsley, published in 1875,[37] and in about 1877 he began work on the extensive collections belonging to the Duke of Bedford. The Bedford project was a protracted one: volumes were privately printed in draft form at irregular intervals between 1877 and 1890, when the definitive works were printed in three parts.[38] The first, devoted to portraits at Woburn Abbey, and the second, titled 'imaginary subjects, landscapes, drawings and tapestries' at Woburn Abbey, are usually bound together. The third part, which covered the Duke's London collection at 81 Eaton Square, was privately printed in a separate volume.

One of the most attractive catalogues of the early nineteenth century was privately printed at Lee Priory in 1817.[39] Horace Walpole deemed the owner, Thomas Brydges Barrett, to be the man to carry the Gothic tradition into the nineteenth century and, in his will, Walpole bequeathed to Barrett a copy of every book printed at the Strawberry Hill Press. Barrett chose James Wyatt as the architect to convert his Elizabethan house into Gothic style. The vignette on the attractive titlepage shows the result. Inside, the design was briefly to list the pictures on the left-hand side and to set out on the facing page biographical notes about the artists. Although perfectly produced, its use as a catalogue is limited, with no description of the pictures, dimensions or information on provenance.

An early Victorian private press, whose remarkably high standard of work contrasts oddly with how little it is known, was the Duncairn Press. This was set up by Edmund MacRory, a Bencher of the Middle Temple. He used to print during the long holidays at his father's house near Belfast and in 1856 printed the *Catalogue of a Collection of Pictures at Duncairn*. The very attractive titlepage is printed in red and black, with a vignette of the house and the whole page is contained in a red border. Inside, the stylish sense of design was maintained, with reasonably professional notes on the pictures and their dimensions.

An entirely different privately printed catalogue, *The Handbook of Raby Castle*, was written by the Duchess of Cleveland, the wife of the 4th and last Duke of that title. They lived at Raby Castle in the north of

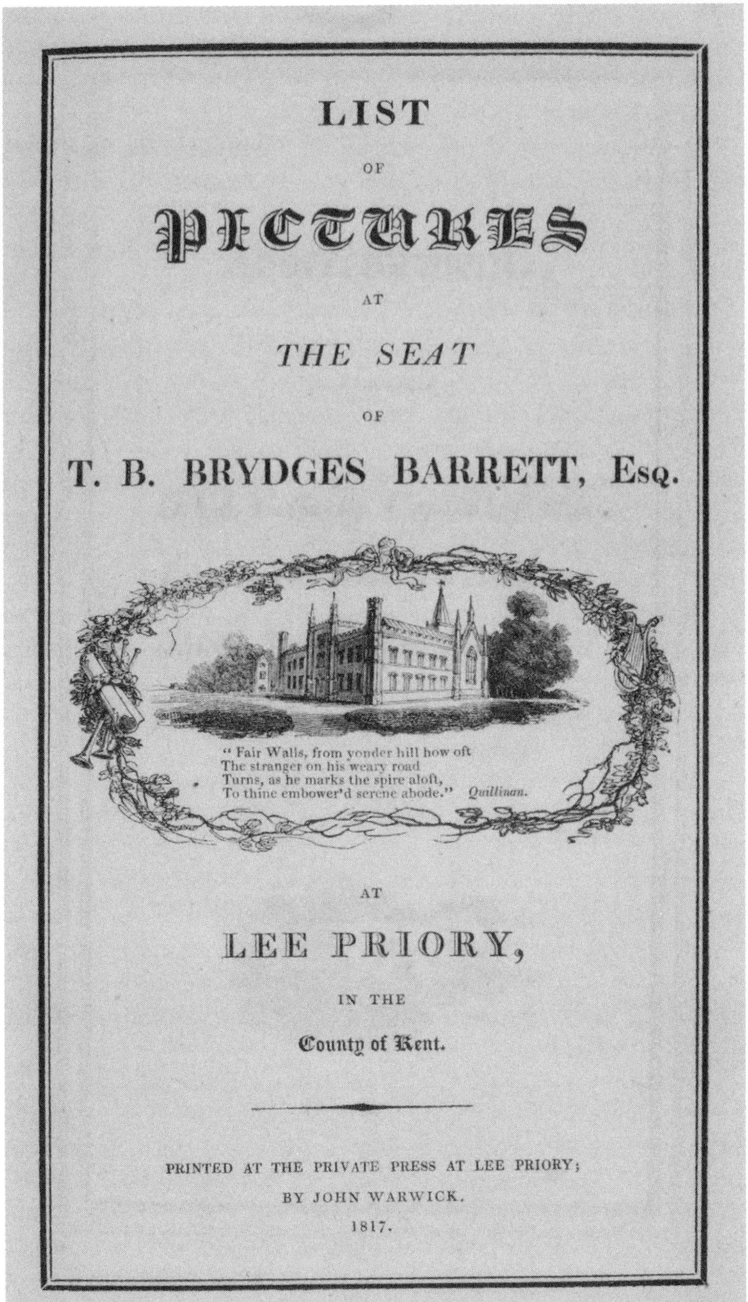

LIST

OF

𝕻𝕴𝕮𝕿𝖀𝕽𝕰𝕾

AT

THE SEAT

OF

T. B. BRYDGES BARRETT, Esq.

" Fair Walls, from yonder hill how oft
The stranger on his weary road
Turns, as he marks the spire aloft,
To thine embower'd serene abode."   *Quillinan.*

AT

LEE PRIORY,

IN THE

County of Kent.

PRINTED AT THE PRIVATE PRESS AT LEE PRIORY;
BY JOHN WARWICK.
1817.

Fig. 10.   Titlepage of the *List of Pictures at . . . Lee Priory*, privately printed at the house

England and Battle Abbey in the south. The Duchess wrote scholarly books about both houses and included remarkably complete details of the pictures, chiefly Dutch and Flemish, bought by her husband Duke Henry. The Duchess's own copy of her book on Raby (privately printed in 1870) is extensively annotated: the inscription shows that it must have been kept at Battle Abbey.[40] Both her books were modelled on the bachelor 6th Duke of Devonshire's *Handbook of Chatsworth and Hardwick*, privately printed in 1844 in a very limited edition, which could have been as small as 25 copies.

The first Superintendent of the South Kensington Museum, which was to evolve into the V&A, was Sir John Charles Robinson (1824–1913). He purchased a vast number of works in marble, bronze, maiolica and terracotta and used his connoisseurship to benefit the young museum by buying at the low prices then available. He also advised some private collectors, including John Malcolm of Poltalloch (whose superb collection of drawings was bought by the British Museum);[41] Sir Francis Cook and Robert Napier, a pioneering Clydeside ship-builder. In 1865 Robinson prepared a privately printed catalogue of Napier's vast collections of pictures, sculpture and works of art of all kinds,[42] which he displayed at his house, West Shandon in Dumbartonshire. Christie's made much use of Robinson's catalogue when Napier's collection was sold in a posthumous auction in 1877.

The earliest known catalogue of a private collection illustrated by photography appeared in 1858 and was devoted to the collection of drawings formed by Henry Reveley at Brynygwyn, North Wales.[43] The folio volume contained 60 large photographs, mounted on stiff cards, of drawings attributed to artists as varied as Leonardo da Vinci, Raphael, Titian, Guercino, Durer, Van Dyck, Rembrandt, Canaletto and Rowlandson. Six years later, Christie's used photography for the first time in an auction sale catalogue: the vendor was John Watkins Brett deceased of Hanover Square, and his extensive collection was sold on 5 April 1864 and the nine following days.

Sir Francis Cook (1817–1901) inherited a textile trading business and vastly increased its scale. He lived at Doughty House in Richmond and at Monserrate, near Sintra in Portugal, a house which had belonged to Beckford in the eighteenth century. He was also a most successful collector, whose private collection was, like the National Gallery, designed to show the progress of European painting from the Italian quattrocento onwards. By the time of his death, he left over 500 paintings including works by Fra Filippo Lippi and Titian, Antonello da Messina, Clouet, Claude and Poussin, Van Eyck, Metsu, Rembrandt

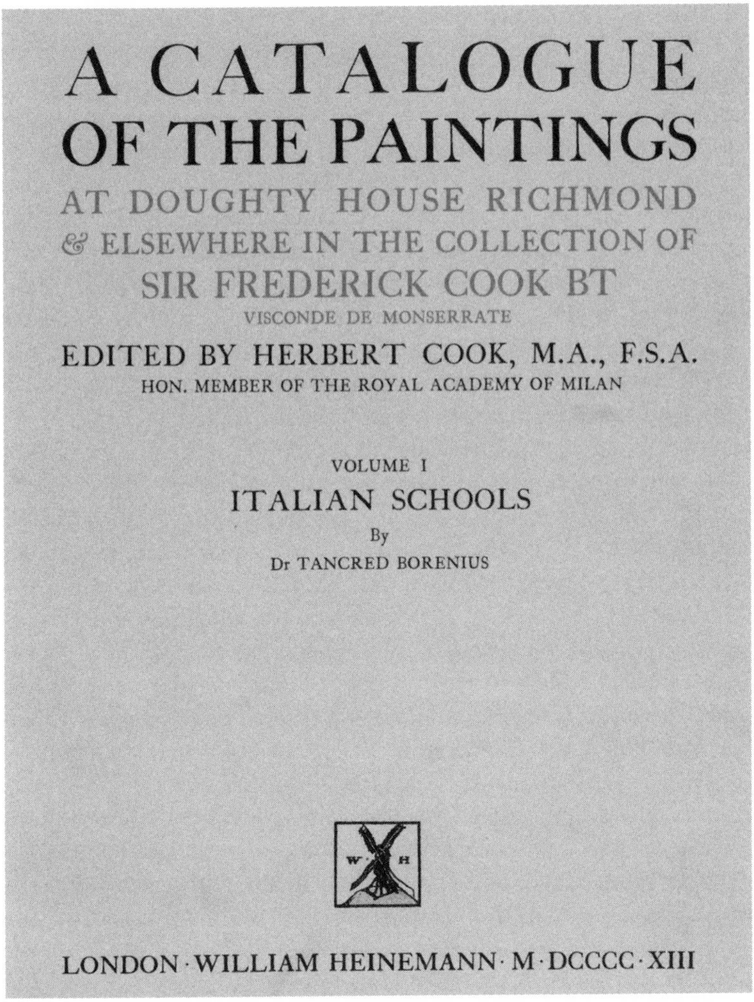

A CATALOGUE
OF THE PAINTINGS

AT DOUGHTY HOUSE RICHMOND
& ELSEWHERE IN THE COLLECTION OF
SIR FREDERICK COOK BT

VISCONDE DE MONSERRATE

EDITED BY HERBERT COOK, M.A., F.S.A.

HON. MEMBER OF THE ROYAL ACADEMY OF MILAN

VOLUME I

ITALIAN SCHOOLS

By

Dr TANCRED BORENIUS

LONDON · WILLIAM HEINEMANN · M · DCCCC · XIII

Fig. 11.   Titlepage of Volume I of the catalogue of paintings in the Cook collection at
Doughty House and elsewhere. Many of the 500 numbered and signed copies
were destroyed in a firestorm caused by a zeppelin during the First World War.

and Velazquez. He also collected classical sculpture and gems, medieval
jewellery, renaissance bronzes, maiolica, silver, ivories, Elizabethan
miniatures and much else. An *Abridged Catalogue of the Pictures at
Doughty House* was printed in 1907 and designed for visitors to the
Galleries, but acquisitions of a limited number of very fine pictures by
Sir Francis's grandson, Herbert Cook made the abridged catalogue
incomplete.

Herbert Cook, a distinguished *amateur d'art* himself, edited the folio three volume catalogue of his family's collection[44] which was privately printed between 1913 and 1915. The first volume (1913) was written by Tancred Borenius and was devoted to the Italian pictures. The second (1914) by J. O. Kronig catalogued the Cooks' Dutch and Flemish pictures. The final volume (1915) by Maurice Brockwell covered the English, French, early Flemish, German and Spanish pictures. The titlepage of each volume, printed in red and black, was an impressive indicator of the quality of the catalogue, which was a model of its kind. The entry for each picture was scholarly and professional, with brief notes on the artist, a description of the picture, its dimensions, provenance and then location. All the pictures were illustrated. The book was finely printed with rubricated text and initial letters.

This catalogue was a monumental achievement as a private collection catalogue, which was printed in a generous edition of 500 numbered and signed copies. Tragically during the First World War, a zeppelin fell on the warehouse where the undistributed copies of the recently produced catalogue were stored: the inevitable firestorm destroyed everything inside. The catalogue remains of legendary rarity: no-one knows how many copies survived the fire.

The final residue of the Cook collection was sold as recently as 2005 at Christie's. The sale catalogue represented what we now think of as the standard for a single-owner sale. The sale catalogue itself was preceded by a ten-page essay on the Cook Collection, its founder and its inheritors, and the individual lots were provided with a full provenance, literature, exhibitions as well as a critical appraisal of each painting.

A number of collections formed in the nineteenth century were catalogued in the twentieth. The *Catalogue of the Petworth Collection of Pictures in the possession of Lord Leconfield* was written by C. H. Collins Baker in 1920. That the Petworth collection was (and is) so extensive may explain the relative brevity of the entries, but the essential information is all present. The author's copy of the catalogue formerly belonged to Francis Steer, the West Sussex archivist and historian, who annotated the volume, to show (*inter alia*) the thirteen pictures sold to Duveen in 1927, including portraits by Holbein of Derich Berck and by Frans Hals of Claes Duyst van Voorhout (both bequeathed by Jules Bache in 1944 to the Metropolitan Museum of Art, New York).

Another outstanding nineteenth century collection was made by Robert Stayner Holford (1808–93). At the age of only 30 he inherited a fortune of £1,000,000 from his bachelor uncle Robert Holford. His father died in the following year, 1839, leaving him another fortune.

THE HOLFORD COLLECTION
DORCHESTER HOUSE

WITH 200 ILLUSTRATIONS
FROM THE TWELFTH
TO THE END OF THE
NINETEENTH CENTURY

IN TWO VOLUMES
VOLUME I

OXFORD
AT THE UNIVERSITY PRESS
LONDON: HUMPHREY MILFORD
MCMXXVII

Fig. 12. Titlepage of the 1927 catalogue of the Holford Collection at Dorchester House, prepared to stimulate interest in the sales at Christie's in 1927 and 1928

His two houses, Dorchester House in Park Lane and Westonbirt in Gloucestershire and their magnificent contents, were the result. Holford's son-in-law Robin Benson, a collector in his own right, edited the catalogues of the collection at Westonbirt[45] and Dorchester House.[46] Both catalogues were beautifully printed by the Oxford University Press on hand-made paper with wide margins. The 1927 catalogues were circulated as a conscious first step before the sale of the collection at auction in 1927 and 1928. This catalogue was written in the spirit of the scholarly standard of the Cook catalogue, with a very adequate description of each picture with the dimensions and occasional details of references to the pictures in published works and the provenance, which included the collections of Queen Christina of Sweden, the Ducs d'Orléans and William Beckford.

In the twentieth century, the typescript catalogue made its appearance. It was akin to the manuscript catalogue of old, in that a typescript catalogue was prepared not for general circulation to other collectors and museums, but for the private use of the owner's family and their advisers. The undated *Catalogue of Pictures at Basildon Park*, which belonged to Captain Archibald Morrison, was as professionally prepared as any so far considered and contained all the scholarly information which a researcher might need.

What is the future of the private collection catalogue? The general change in ownership from private collections to public museums may have undermined their need. New collections continue to be made but concerns over security, which would have been considered unnecessary in the eighteenth century, lead some of today's collectors or inheritors to prefer not to advertise their collections.

Occasionally, a public-spirited collector will wish his collection to undergo the critical process stimulated by a catalogue. The late Sir Brinsley Ford (1908–99) who inherited his family's pictures by Richard Wilson and vastly enriched the collection, generously contributed £70,000 to help the Walpole Society to publish a double volume of his collection.[47] In a letter to the present writer dated 4 September 1998, he wrote: 'It was my intention to present the two volumes on my collection to the members of the Walpole Society . . . as a surprise, an exotic break, an unexpected novelty, as a reward to those who had supported us . . . over the years and above all to increase membership.'

The transition of a private collection into public hands is likely to stimulate the publication of a catalogue. In 1997 Sir Denis Mahon, scholar and collector, in effect promised his outstanding collection of Italian Baroque paintings partly to the National Gallery in London, in part to a small but fortunate group of museums in Britain and Ireland and partly to the Bologna gallery. An exhibition was held of the complete collection, for which a scholarly catalogue was prepared.[48] Likewise a loan exhibition can bring into existence a scholarly catalogue of a private collection, such as that of Andrew Lloyd Webber, which was shown at the Royal Academy, London in 2003, or a substantial gift to a museum, such as those to the Tate Gallery by Lord McAlpine and Janet Wolfson de Botton.[49] Some collectors collect primarily to exhibit art, such as Charles Saatchi and Frank Cohen, for whom the catalogue is perhaps the only record of past glories. Perhaps the most surprising, if not astonishing, of all recent published catalogues is that of Nasser Khalili's collection, mainly of the arts of Islam, which has reached 32 volumes and is still continuing.[50] Websites may play a bigger role in the future, as they have done for the collections of certain museums.[51]

For reasons of space, this article has not mentioned catalogues of houses such as Burghley, Corsham or Hatfield, or sale catalogues such as Fonthill, Wanstead, Ralph Bernal, Lord Northwick or Hamilton Palace. Inevitably this account has had to be selective, but I hope that it has conveyed a good idea of catalogues of private art collections from the 1620s to the early 2000s. The subject has been an absorbing passion for the author for some 40 years.

References

1. Frank Herrmann, author of *The English as Collectors* (London, 1972), in a private conversation with the author in January 2011.
2. All the printed books referred to throughout this article are in the author's library.
3. Oliver Millar, *The Queen's Pictures* (London, 1977), p. 46.
4. George Vertue and Horace Walpole (eds), *Catalogue and Description of King Charles the First's Capital Collection of Pictures, Limnings, Statues, Bronzes, Medals and Other Curiosities* (London, 1757).
5. Oliver Millar, *Abraham van der Doort's Catalogue of the Collections of Charles I* (Walpole Society, vol. 37, 1960).
6. Vertue and Walpole (eds), *op. cit.*, p. iii.
7. Printed by Randall Davies, *Burlington Magazine*, X (March 1907), pp. 376–82.
8. Brian Fairfax, *A Catalogue of the Curious Collection of Pictures of George Villiers, Duke of Buckingham . . .* (London, 1758), pp. 1–23.
9. See Arthur Macgregor (ed.), *The Late King's Goods: collections, possessions, and patronage of Charles I in the light of the Comonwealth sale inventories* (London, 1989).
10. No titlepage issued. The engraved dedication by Hamlet Winstanley begins 'Praenobili Iacobo Comiti Derby . . .'.
11. See Francis Russell, *The Derby Collection 1721–35* (Walpole Society, vol. 53, 1987), pp. 143–80.
12. Francis Russell, 'A Collection Transformed, The 8th Earl of Pembroke's Pictures', *Apollo*, July/August 2009, pp. 48–55.

13. *The Earl of Pembroke's Medals in V. Parts* is an undated quarto volume, with an engraved titlepage containing a brief index and introduction, signed 'N. Haym', and 304 engraved plates, each depicting between 4 and 42 images. It is not known whether the second copy of the first printing, referred to by Stukeley, survives or not. The book was reprinted posthumously in 1746 with a new title leaf reading *Numismata antiqua in tres partes divisa / collegit olim et æri incidi vivens curavit Thomas Pembrochiæ et Montis Gomerici Comes.*

14. *The Family Memoirs of the Rev. William Stukeley* (Surtees Society Publications, vol. 73, 1882), vol. I, p. 267.

15. The author's copy has a distinguished provenance, bearing the bookplates of Dr Charles Chauncey (an original subscriber), George Watson Taylor of Erlestoke Park, William Beckford and Lord Rosebery.

16. Horace Walpole to Lord Strafford, 13 September 1759: *Yale Edition of Horace Walpole's Correspondence*, vol. 35 (Oxford, 1973), p. 296.

17. Henry Rumsey Forster, *The Stowe Catalogue, Priced and Annotated* (London, 1848). Quarto, xliii and 310 pp.

18. Sale on 31 October 1676 of the library of Dr Lazarus Seaman, Master of Peterhouse, Cambridge. See *Under the Hammer: book auctions since the seventeenth century*, ed. Robin Myers, Michael Harris and Giles Mandelbrote (New Castle, DE and London, 2001).

19. Sale on 11 May 1686 of 186 paintings. The name(s) of the seller(s) are not given. Lugt number 8.

20. Author's collection: *A Catalogue of the Genuine and Capital Collection of Pictures, by the Most Celebrated Masters, of that Late Great and Learned Physician, Doctor Richard Mead* (London, 1754). See Ian Jenkins, 'Dr Richard Mead (1673–1754) and his circle' in *Enlightening the British: Knowledge, Discovery and the Museum in the Eighteenth Century*, ed. R. Anderson et al. (London, 2003).

21. Charles Fairfax Murray, *Catalogue of the Pictures belonging to His Grace the Duke of Portland at Welbeck Abbey and in London* (Chiswick Press, 1894) and Richard Goulding (finally revised for press by C. K. Adams), *Catalogue of the Pictures belonging to His Grace the Duke of Portland, K. G. at Welbeck Abbey, 17 Hill Street, London and Langwell House* (Cambridge University Press, 1936).

22. Horace Walpole to Sir Horace Mann on 10 May 1758: *Yale Edition of Horace Walpole's Correspondence*, vol. 21 (Oxford, 1960), pp. 199–200.

23. Horace Walpole, *Aedes Walpolianae: or, A Description of the collection of pictures at Houghton-Hall in Norfolk, the Seat of the Right Honorable Sir Robert Walpole . . .* First edition 1747, second edition 1752 and third edition 1767.

24. Wyndham Ketton-Cremer, *Horace Walpole, A Biography* (London, 1946), p. 276.

25. *Strawberry Hill, the Renowned Seat of Horace Walpole. Mr. George Robins is honoured by having been selected by the Earl of Waldegrave, to sell by public competition, the Valuable Contents of Strawberry Hill . . . on Monday the 25th day of April 1842 and twenty-three following days (Sundays excepted) . . .*

26. William Young Ottley and Peltro William Tomkins, *Engravings of the Most Noble, the Marquis of Stafford's collection of pictures, in London, arranged according to schools, and in chronological order, / with remarks on each picture by William Young Ottley, the executive part under the management of Peltro William Tomkins* (London, 1818).

27. John Young, *A Catalogue of the Pictures at Grosvenor House, London; with etchings from the whole collection . . . accompanied by historical notices of the principal works* (London, 1820) and later edition (1821).

28. John Young, *A Catalogue of the Celebrated Collection of Pictures of the late John*

Julius Angerstein Esq., containing a finished etching of every picture and accompanied with historical and biographical notices . . . (London, 1823). Text in English and French.

29. John Young, *A Catalogue of Pictures by British Artists in the possession of Sir John Fleming Leicester, Bart., with etchings from the whole collection including pictures in his gallery at Tabley House, Cheshire, executed by permission of the proprietor and accompanied with historical and biographical notices . . .* (London, 1825).

30. John Young, *A Catalogue of the Collection of Pictures of the Most Noble the Marquess of Stafford, with an etching of every picture and accompanied by historical and biographical notices . . .*, 2 vols (London, 1825).

31. William Carey, *The Descriptive Catalogue of a Collection of Paintings by British Artists in the possession of Sir John Fleming Leicester, Bart.* (London, 1819).

32. Anon., *Catalogue of the Pictures in the Possession of Lord Bagot at Blithfield*, R. Richards, (Uttoxeter, 1801). Large octavo, 10 pp., printed on rectos only.

33. Anon., *A Catalogue of Paintings, Statues, Busts, etc. at Marbury Hall, the Seat of John Smith Barry, Esq. in the County of Chester* (London, 1814).

34. Thomas Lister Parker, *Catalogue of the Paintings in the Gallery, at Browsholme, the Seat of Thomas Lister Parker, Esq.* Lancaster, 1807 and 1808. The 1807 edition has seven pages and lists the pictures unnumbered. The text was reset for the 1808 edition, which has eight pages and numbers the pictures consecutively 1 to 59.

35. A later account of Browsholme and its collections was printed in 1815: *Description of Browsholme Hall: in the West Riding of the County of York, and of the parish of Waddington, in the same county : also, a collection of letters, from original manuscripts, in the reigns of Charles I and II and James II / in the possession of Thomas Lister Parker, of Browsholme Hall, Esq.* (London, 1815).

36. George Scharf, *Catalogue Raisonné; or a List of the Pictures in Blenheim Palace* (London, 1860 (octavo); 1861 (octavo and as an expanded quarto) and 1862 (octavo and quarto)).

37. George Scharf, *A Descriptive and Historical Catalogue of the Collection of Pictures at Knowsley Hall . . .* (London, 1875). Edition limited to 300 copies.

38. George Scharf, *A Descriptive and Historical Catalogue of the Collection of Pictures at Woburn Abbey . . .* Part I – Portraits; Part II – Imaginary Subjects, Landscapes, Drawings and Tapestries (London, 1890) and *Third Portion of a catalogue of Pictures, Miniatures and Enamels, at the residence of His Grace the Duke of Bedford, 81 Eaton Square, London* (1877–90).

39. Thomas Brydges Barrett, *List of Pictures at the Seat of T. B. Brydges Barrett, Esq. at Lee Priory, in the County of Kent*, printed at the private press at Lee Priory by John Warwick, 1817. The edition was limited to 60 copies.

40. Author's collection.

41. J. C. Robinson, *Descriptive Catalogue of Drawings by the Old Masters, forming the Collection of John Malcolm of Poltalloch, Esq.* (Privately printed at the Chiswick Press, London, 1876). A first edition was printed in 1869.

42. J. C. Robinson, *Catalogue of the Works of Art forming the Collection of Robert Napier of West Shandon, Dumbartonshire, mainly compiled by J. C. Robinson, F.S.A.*, London, privately printed, 1865. This was printed by the Chiswick Press.

43. Henry Reveley, *The Reveley Collection of Drawings at Brynygwyn, North Wales. Photographed by Philip H. Delamotte, F.S.A., Professor of Drawing, and T. Frederick Hardwich, Lecturer in Photography in King's College, London* (London, 1858), folio. Reveley's *Notices illustrative of the drawings and sketches of some of the most distinguished masters in all the schools of design*, was published posthumously by his son Hugh Reveley in 1820.

44. Herbert Cook (ed.), *A Catalogue of the Paintings . . . in the Collection of Sir Frederick Cook Bt, Visconde de Monserrate* (3 vols, London, 1913–15). Folio.

45. Robert Benson (ed.), *The Holford Collection illustrated with 101 plates selected from twelve manuscripts at Dorchester House and 107 pictures at Westonbirt in Gloucestershire, privately printed for Sir George Holford and members of the Burlington Fine Arts Club . . .* (London, 1924).

46. Robert Benson (ed.), *The Holford Collection, Dorchester House, with 200 illustrations from the twelfth to the end of the nineteenth century* (2 vols, London, 1927).

47. *The Ford Collection* (2 vols, Walpole Society, vol. 60, 1998).

48. Gabrieli Finaldi and Michael Kitson, *Discovering the Italian Baroque: the Denis Mahon Collection* (National Gallery, London, 1997).

49. *Pre-Raphaelite and other Masters, the Andrew Lloyd Webber Collection* (Royal Academy, London, 2003); Monique Beudert, Sean Rainbird and Nicholas Serota (eds), *The Janet Wolfson de Botton Gift* (Tate Gallery, London, 1998).

50. *The Khalili Collection* (London, 1992–), multi-volume catalogues of the Islamic art, Japanese and other collections which are still continuing to appear.

51. For example www.khalili.org.

Index

References to illustrations in *italic*